POISON AT THE PUEBLO

A Simon Bognor Mystery

Tim Heald

CRÈME de la CRIME

This first world edition published 2011
in Great Britain and in the USA by
Crème de la Crime, an imprint of
SEVERN HOUSE PUBLISHERS LTD of
9–15 High Street, Sutton, Surrey, England, SM1 1DF.
Trade paperback edition first published
in Great Britain and the USA 2012 by
SEVERN HOUSE PUBLISHERS LTD.

British Library Cataloguing in Publication Data

Heald, Tim.
  Poison at the Pueblo. – (Simon Bognor mysteries)
  1. Bognor, Simon (Fictitious character) – Fiction.
  2. Government investigators – Fiction. 3. Poisoning –
  Fiction. 4. Salamanca (Spain) – Fiction. 5. Detective and
  mystery stories.
  I. Title II. Series
  823.9′14-dc22

ISBN-13: 978-1-78029-010-2 (cased)
ISBN-13: 978-1-78029-516-9 (trade paper)

All Severn House titles are printed on acid-free paper.

Severn House Publishers support The Forest Stewardship Council [FSC],
the leading international forest certification organisation. All our titles that
are printed on Greenpeace-approved FSC-certified paper carry the FSC logo.

MIX
Paper from
responsible sources
FSC   FSC® C018575
www.fsc.org

Typeset by Palimpsest Book Production Ltd.,
Falkirk, Stirlingshire, Scotland.
Printed and bound in Great Britain by
MPG Books Ltd., Bodmin, Cornwall.

As a virtual monoglot I would like to dedicate this to my multilingual family and friends with admiration, despair and envy.

ONE

Jimmy Trubshawe was into mushrooms.

Jimmy Trubshawe was not his real name, and the mushrooms he contemplated that evening in the mountains west of Salamanca were not mushrooms in the accepted sense.

'Bloody good-looking fungi,' he said, wrinkling his nose over the bowl of risotto. Risotto was the wrong word as they were in Spain not Italy. *Arroz* probably came into it somewhere or other. Despite the fact that he had been a more or less full-time resident in Spain for the best part of five years, he only had about half a dozen words of the lingo. 'Why faff around?' he asked anyone who was interested. He could watch Man U on Sky Sports, the credit card machine spoke English and so did the locals, especially if you talked at them loudly and not too fast.

The other three at his table also looked enthusiastically at their identical platefuls. The rice was moist and glistening; the mushrooms rich, brown and abundant; the whole sprinkled with emerald-green parsley. Simplicity itself, and none the worse for that. A stone jug of local red wine stood in the middle of the table. All four glasses of the stuff were full of it too.

Pablo raised his glass to his nostrils and sniffed absent-mindedly, 'The bouquet is, how you say, erm, h'unremarkable'. The 'h' he planted before the 'u' of 'unremarkable' came from the back of his throat.

'*Un*remarkable,' said Trubshawe. 'There's no "h" at the beginning.' He shovelled more rice and fungi into his mouth and slurped some red country wine in afterwards, fresh from the earthenware jug. All four ate in silence until they had finished, wiping their plates clean with the rough country bread that had been placed casually in the local peasant baskets, which were probably flown in from Harvey Nicks but still had an authentic, earthy appearance.

The man who claimed to be Trubshawe, but wasn't, burped

aggressively, almost daring the other three to be decorous. It was an English burp, he told himself. Rich, sonorous, un-Hispanic. The burp was a lesson in itself.

'Bloody good,' he said. 'Bloody good mushrooms. Bloody good rice. Bloody good sauce. Know what I mean? Bloody good.'

The other three said nothing, but looked. The looks spoke volumes; some louder than others.

The next course was plain. A grilled veal cutlet with a drizzle of oil and a splatter of garlic; chips chiselled from real local potatoes and deep fried in oil. That was all. Halfway through, the man who called himself Jimmy Trubshawe pushed his plate away from himself and took a slug of the earthy Tempranillo in his tumbler.

'Bloody good,' he said, mopping his mouth with a linen napkin, 'but I've had enough. Had enough.'

He smiled at the others, put the napkin on his side plate and dabbed his forehead with the palm of his right hand. He was sweating even though the room was cool. As he got to his feet he stumbled slightly and swore. By the door he stumbled again slightly and fumbled as he grasped the handle. Then he was gone, leaving silence behind him.

The other three at Trubshawe's table were Pablo Calderon, Felipe de los Angeles and Colin Smith, whose real name was almost certainly not Smith, and probably not Colin, but who seemed to be fluent in English and probably came from somewhere in the British Isles – though his accent might have seemed just a shade too cultured and his grammar and syntax too perfect, as if he had learned the language from the book or perhaps at a language school run by retired majors. Or possibly he had studied at an elocution school run by the same retired majors. It came to much the same thing, meaning that the voice, like the person, was too good to be true, too perfect to be entirely convincing. He and it came from some-where else.

Pablo and Felipe were probably as Spanish as Colin Smith was English. The former worked at the great oil refinery in La Coruna and the latter at a large sausage factory in the suburbs of Madrid. They spoke English because speaking only in English was the be-all and end-all of life in the Community. 'Community' was the English word for what was almost a community in the religious or monastic sense, and which combined a secluded, introverted, closed society with an exercise in English socio-cultural imperialism. The English spoken by the Spaniards who made up half the Community's members was not always fluent, or even coherent, but it was the only tongue tolerated. No Spanish in the Community. This was not an ex-pat community with Anglophile camp-followers but a sophisticated form of English teaching by immersion with natives. It worked and everyone seemed to enjoy it.

'He didn't look too hot.' The man calling himself Colin Smith took a considered mouthful of Tempranillo. 'Proper peaky.'

'Peaky?' repeated Felipe.

'Sorry,' said Colin. 'Slang. Not very well.'

'Heel,' said Pablo. 'Colin believes that our friend Trubshawe is heel.'

'Ill,' said Colin, 'Ill. No "h". And you pronounce it with a short sharp "i" not a long drawn-out "ee" – "ill". I thought Trubbers was looking peaky, seedy. Ill. Not "heel". Ill.'

The two Spaniards nodded. They were both far more sophisticated, intelligent and well-educated than either Trubshawe or Smith, and they much disliked being condescended to because they were not native English speakers. But needs must. English had become the *lingua franca de nos jours* and they had to learn to speak it fluently.

'Poor Himmy,' said Pablo, and Colin did not tell him that Jimmy began with a 'J' not an 'H'. Instead, he had more wine and silently wished he was back on his Costa having a pint of Doom in the Dead Duck.

'May I join you?' asked a suave olive-skinned man with a narrow matinee-idol moustache, slicked crinkly black hair, a blazer and espadrilles. He looked Spanish but talked English. He was Ernesto. Master of Ceremonies. Spanish father, English mother. Had spent much of his childhood in Eastbourne where he went to school.

'Trubshawe not well?' he enquired in well-modulated lounge-lizard of a mildly dated style.

'Quite unwell, I should say.' Colin pulled a face. 'Positively ill, in fact. Wouldn't you agree, chaps?'

The two Spaniards nodded, not risking their imperfect English in front of the MC.

'You and Mr Trubshawe are friends?' said Ernesto in a sentence which should have been a statement but carried an interrogatory intonation. It was too advanced a concept for Pablo and Felipe.

'I wouldn't say "friends",' said Colin. 'More like "acquaintances". We knew each other, yes, but I wouldn't say we were exactly "friends".'

Ernesto smiled at his compatriots. 'You understand the difference between a friend and an acquaintance. A friend is a friend, and if you are a friend you have affection for each other. But if you are just an acquaintance you may be an enemy. It is possible for an acquaintance to have bad feelings about his acquaintance. That is not possible for a friend. You understand?'

He smiled again. Pablo and Felipe bowed their hands and smiled a complicit smile. A waiter came and set down a saucer of wobbly yellow and brown flan in each place. Pudding in the Community was always flan, or a thinly disguised imitation. Puddings here were a 101 ways with egg and milk; custard with a hint of cinnamon or vanilla; occasionally a pastry crust or a sugary brown sauce, as in crème caramel or honey from local bees. Latin: *flado*; Old French: *flaon*; Middle English: flaton or flawn. There was a recipe for an ancient Roman version in Ilaria Gozzini Giacosa's book. Now, however, 'flan' was the national dish of Spain, and, even though English was the mandatory language, it was, in the Community, a case of flan yesterday, flan tomorrow and flan today, but not, this time, for Trubshawe, who was keen on the dish and had even been known to ask for a second helping.

Ernesto took a small spoonful and moved the helping around his mouth like an oenophile tasting wine. After he swallowed he exhaled lightly and smiled with satisfaction.

'You must listen to the way Jimmy speaks English,' he said. 'He speaks English like a native. Colin also. Listen to the words they use and do the same. Then you will be a credit to the Community.'

They all took spoonfuls of flan.

'You have flan in England, Colin?' enquired Ernesto.

'Um,' said Colin, who was not really into food, but ate primarily to stay alive. He was a meat and two veg man. Or frozen pizza. Maybe vindaloo. 'Jimmy's more of a gastro-bloke,' he said. 'Not really my scene.'

The Spaniards looked quizzical.

'Himmy a gastro-bloke.' said Pablo and laughed. Felipe joined him and they finished their flan without speaking any more. Afterwards they retreated to the lounge and drank short strong coffees before retreating for a siesta, followed by the usual walks through the woods. On each of these a Spaniard was supposed to walk and talk with an 'Anglo'. The language spoken was, as always, English. This was immersion. The participants talked about their partners, about sex, about politics, food, drink, motor cars, football. Two blokes together tended to have more blokeish conversations. Girls did girls' stuff – children, fashion, diets. Men and women together compromised uneasily.

Felipe was supposed to be enjoying an hour's conversation with Jimmy Trubshawe but Trubshawe failed to materialize.

'No Himmy,' he said to Ernesto, who was standing behind the bar counter ticking off names on a clipboard.

Ernesto told him to wait a minute. Trubshawe was not noted for his punctuality. He was nearly always late for conversation pieces, or charades, or simulated conference calls; seldom for meals. He was a trencherman, if not in reality a gastro-anything much. Ernesto went on ticking off names and dispatching couples into the woods. When he had done he glanced up at the clock.

'I'll call his room,' he said and pressed buttons. Felipe could hear the electronic ringing of a phone through the headset. There was no reply and eventually Ernesto replaced the receiver and stroked his chin.

'We must go look,' he said. 'You come too. Perhaps Mr Trubshawe is sick.'

'Heel,' said Felipe, and followed the Master of Ceremonies outdoors and down the tarmac path towards Mr Trubshawe's chalet. When Ernesto knocked loudly on the door there was no response from within. The little log cabin had an alpine feel to it, with a steep roof and shutters. The prevailing aura was one of snugness, of coolth in hot summer months and warmth in the winter cold. Technically there was no such word as 'coolth', but where there was warmth there ought to be 'coolth'; pace Oxford which Bognor invariably cited as the ultimate arbiter except when, as now, he disagreed. Logic and linguistics may not always go together but perhaps they should. Today, at the turn of the seasons, it was like the Lacedaemonians of the New Testament and neither hot nor cold. Nevertheless both men shivered slightly as Ernesto slipped a master key into the lock.

The drawing room was empty, but the door to the small bedroom immediately off it was open. The two men walked briskly towards it, neither saying a thing, but both experiencing the same premonitions.

At the entrance to the sleeping quarters they both paused for a moment, Ernesto in front and Felipe close behind.

On the bed the man who called himself Trubshawe lay flat on his back, clad only in a pair of floppy Hawaiian-style boxer shorts and a pair of white ankle socks. The sparse hair on his chest was white, the equally sparse hair on the top of his head was uncharacteristically awry, and his face seemed more than usually purple.

He was, of course, extremely dead.

TWO

The knighthood came as a shock.

The first Bognor knew about it was a letter from 10 Downing Street. It began in handwriting with 'My dear Simon' and signed off 'Yours ever, Gavin'.

Despite a lot of walking up and down and cogitating he had no recollection of ever having met the Prime Minister in this or any other life. Either Gavin had got the wrong Simon, or the wrong Bognor, or the wrong end of the stick. Or this was a fiendish Machiavellian stratagem of the kind for which politicians were notorious. Bognor was a committed cock-up man rather than conspiracy theorist, though life had taught him that it was full of surprises.

As so often at moments such as this he rang his wife.

'Monica, darling,' he said, 'I've had the oddest letter.' Despite the fact that he suspected he was being bugged on a regular basis due to his position as Head of Special Investigations at the Board of Trade he read it out to her.

There was a long pause.

'That's real,' she said, at last. 'Even a consummate parodist couldn't capture the cloying conspiratorial tone of the people's prime minister quite like that. Craig Brown could give it a whirl in the *Eye* but he would go over the top and be shot down in smoke. That's pure Gavin with just a twist of Gina. The real McCoy. Take it. Say "yes".'

'You reckon?' Bognor was unsure. 'You'd be Lady Bognor.'

'I can live with that. I won't be Lady Bognor to our friends. Just in shops. And at Number Ten, of course. "Lady Bognor always dines in her tiara. Lady Bognor this, Lady Bognor that." People will loathe it, I can't wait.'

Bognor thought for a moment. 'You'll always be Monica to me,' he said, eventually.

'*Au contraire* my *petit choux*,' she said. 'I shall expect to be

Lady Bognor to you, of all people. In public and private. Especially private.'

'Thus,' said Bognor, '"I'm turning in, Lady Bognor. Mine's a Horlicks."'

'Something like that,' she said, 'and I'll often call you Sir Simon. I shall enjoy it. Particularly the expression on the faces of certain third parties.'

At just that moment Bognor's aide, Harvey Contractor, shimmered into his presence in his inimitably Jeevesian way. Contractor was very young, very bright and was on secondment from elsewhere in Whitehall. He had a first in semiotics from the University of Wessex. Well, he would, wouldn't he, thought his boss morosely. He had only the barest notion of what semiotics were and knew nothing whatever about the University of Wessex. Bognor, ever paranoid, believed that Contractor had been sent to spy on him on account of his regularly long lunches and generally incorrect behaviour. It was his belief that there was a large government department devoted entirely to this sort of semi-secret monitoring, but he had been unable, hitherto, to prove it. On the other hand he was prepared to concede that the younger man had been put in place to keep him informed about a modern world with which he was increasingly unfamiliar. He liked Contractor, was impressed by him, but was gravely suspicious.

'I'd better go,' he said to his wife on the telephone, 'something's just come up.'

'Meaning Harvey Contractor,' said the about-to-be Lady Bognor, sounding mildly huffy. She wasn't stupid.

'Up to a point,' replied her husband, who, despite what some people thought and said, wasn't stupid either. He put the phone down.

'How does "Sir" Simon grab you?' he asked Contractor.

The aide looked sceptical.

'I'm not up for grabs,' he said, 'but I concede that "Sir" Simon has a certain resonance to it. Why do you ask?'

'Because,' said Bognor, trying to keep a note of truculent triumph out of his voice, 'I've just had a note from Number Ten telling me that they'd like to elevate me to the knighthood.'

'Funny,' Contractor said thoughtfully, 'I'd never have credited the PM with a sense of humour.'

'I beg your pardon?'

'Nothing,' said Contractor. 'Nothing at all. Except congratulations. It couldn't have happened to . . . well, let's just say "it couldn't have happened" and leave it at that shall we?'

Bognor regarded him beadily. He had a keen eye and ear for insubordination but he decided to put his immediate reaction on hold. He had Contractor's number and Contractor, he suspected, knew it.

'But you didn't come here to discuss my title?'

'No, sir,' said Contractor, not sounding at all as if he meant the second three-letter word. 'I've had a very interesting chat with my oppo at the Guardia Civil in Madrid. Carlos seems to think that they have an interesting British corpse on their hands. Died of a surfeit of mushrooms. Likely to be known to us as Trubshawe.'

'Trubshawe,' said Bognor ruminatively, 'not "Jimmy" Trubshawe?'

'That's the fellow,' said Contractor, 'Jimmy Trubshawe. He was found in some sort of chalet in the hills outside Salamanca. Food poisoning. Ate some dodgy fungus. No known antidote.'

'Your oppo being a *teniente*?'

'Carlos Azuela. A *teniente*. Very bright. He specializes in Brits. Particularly crims on the run in the Costas.'

'Like Jimmy Trubshawe, also known as Don Jones, Greg McDonald, Bert Simkiss and many other cognomens.'

'That's the guy,' said Contractor. 'Gang leader, drug dealer, super-pimp, all round bad hat. Escaped from the Scrubs five years ago and rumoured to have been in Spain ever since.'

'I'll deal with *my* oppo,' said Bognor with a hint of self-importance. 'The Admiral. Juan what's-his-name.'

'Picasso,' said Contractor. 'Quite an easy name to remember. From Barcelona. A political appointment. My spies say he's not particularly good.'

'No relation to the painter,' said Bognor, miffed at the criticism of his contact, 'but I wouldn't say your friends are correct. He comes across as a bit of a buffoon but there are no flies on Juan. Not many anyway. There's not much that the Admiral misses.'

'Well, *Teniente* Azuela says that Trubshawe's snuffed it,' said Contractor.

'Or whoever he is.'

'Was,' said Contractor. '"Was" not "is". Trubshawe is now past tense. But, yes, whoever he is, he's dead.'

'Murdered?' his boss wanted to know, and Contractor hesitated. He had a good enough university degree to be uncertain about certainty. A proper education sowed doubt. This was one of the many attributes he shared with Simon Bognor. To themselves, as well as the average outsider, they were poles apart, but actually they were quite alike. Contractor, however, was less adroit about concealing his intelligence and qualification. It made him seem more of a threat while actually making him less of one. The reverse of Bognor.

'The Guardia Civil are unhappy,' said Contractor. 'They don't seem to be saying that it's murder, but they *are* saying the death is suspicious. Trubshawe carried a lot of baggage; he seemed perfectly fit for a man of his age and taste. Death was . . . well . . . unexpected.'

'Bloody lucky he wasn't bumped off ages ago,' said Bognor with feeling. 'He almost makes me want to bring back the death penalty.'

He thought for a moment.

'I'll talk to the Admiral,' he said eventually. 'Maybe I'll even treat myself to a little Spanish trip. Lady Bognor, that is Monica, is very partial to Spain – a *tapa* or two, a chilled glass of Manzanilla, mosques, markets. And it's time the British criminal community on the Iberian peninsula got some sort of firework up their collective bottom. Wouldn't you agree?'

The younger man nodded and smiled. He had obviously noticed how much his boss savoured the words 'Lady Bognor.'

'Remind me though,' Bognor said, 'the man Trubshawe or whatever. He did a bunk after a road rage incident. That's him isn't it?'

'He was on remand in Wormwood Scrubs,' said Contractor, 'and was sprung by some mates with a ladder. Easy-peasy. Inside job. They had screws on their side.'

'Loose screws in the nick,' said Bognor, smiling thinly, 'dodgy proposition, very. But I am right, aren't I? The man Trubshawe was an old-fashioned mobster in the Kray style, operating south of the river in the Tooting–Colliers Wood area, enjoyed violence at a personal level, dealt in people-trafficking, drugs of every description, friends in high as well as low places, political party benefactor. All-in-all, the unacceptable face of the twenty-first century.'

'That's him,' agreed Contractor. 'Alive and well in sunny Spain and cocking a snook at the forces of law and order back home.'

'Not alive and well any longer,' said Bognor, sounding pleased.

'Doesn't sound like it,' agreed Contractor. 'Sounds dead to me.'

Bognor pushed back his chair, stood and walked to the large window overlooking the River Thames, which flowed sluggishly below his headquarters. 'Water under the bridge,' he thought morosely. He had been watching Old Father Thames ebb and flow ever since starting at the Board of Trade the best part of a lifetime earlier. Every morning on his way to work; every evening on his way home. For much of his life in that drab building his office had no window at all. Eventually he gradu-ated to a window, but only one looking out over the railway line which ran west from Waterloo. Since his elevation to the directorship he now had a sofa and a window overlooking the river. These were the symbols of authority. A room with a view and somewhere to sit with a visitor. By such tokens was a man's career measured out. Sofas and windows signified. And now he had a knighthood to go with them. How were the mighty risen! Almost without trace. Who would have predicted it? Not his teachers; not his contemporaries; not even Lady Bognor; least of all himself.

He sighed.

'Trubshawe must have made a lot of money,' he said, softly.

'Yes,' agreed Contractor.

'And done what he set out to do?'

'I suppose so.'

'Enjoyed the respect of his peers.'

'If you can call them that,' said his assistant. 'They're just a load of crooks.'

'That's not how they see themselves,' said Bognor, 'nor the

world at large. Not these days. Being a successful villain is rather desirable. Time was when you would have been despised and vilified, but not any longer. Courted by cabinet ministers, interviewed by personalities, invited on to reality game shows. What price honesty?'

'Isn't that unduly cynical?'

The boss gazed out at the grubby river and thought what a wasted opportunity it was. Once it had been a great artery, bearing the nation's commerce and the great and the good of the day, even while it was doing service as the national drain. Now it was nothing. The capital city had turned its back on it; men, women and goods went about on wheels. Excrement and other detritus disappeared down holes into sewers. The Thames no longer even had the guts to create a big stink. The river paralleled the nation: a gradual, turgid, unlamented decline.

'I'm feeling cynical,' said Bognor. 'It's age. It'll come to you one day. One moment you're bright-eyed and bushy tailed; the next minute you're unsound in wind and limb, and have but a short time to live.'

'Oh give over,' said Contractor. 'I mean, "with respect". "Sir".'

The Director continued to gaze out of the window, surveying the gun-metal-grey river and the city beyond. When he was young it had been 'Swinging London'. Whenever you expressed distaste for what it had become, ignorant critics parroted Dr Johnson's adage about a man who is tired of London being tired of life. But that was a quite different city in a quite different life. He, Bognor, had had enough of it. Maybe life as well. He was disillusioned by both. Only half-amused by his knighthood, and not at all amused by the elevation of men like Trubshawe to a sort of Pantheon for the undeserving. He didn't get it; was glad Trubshawe was dead, but sensed he would be obituarized in the national press. And for that he was more than irritated.

'Know Spain well?' he asked Contractor.

'Mmm,' said Contractor, 'so-so.'

'Well,' said Sir Simon, 'you're about to get to know it a great deal better. I'm taking you along as chief bag-carrier and bottle-washer. You can keep Lady B. company and do the dogsbody stuff. Keep an eye on me, too. As is your wont.'

He smiled.

'Serious crime investigation. Possibly murder. But fun as well. Which is the way I like it.'

Ain't that the truth, thought Contractor.

THREE

The Bognors were dieting as usual. It had been the same formula throughout their marriage, founded loosely on a popular regime of the 1960s or thereabouts, when it was known as 'the drinking man's diet'. It was right up there with the Royal Canadian Air Force Exercises which was designed to keep fit those, like the Bognors, not much given to exercise in conventional forms. The diet seemed to consist of very dry gin Martinis, as much dry white wine as you could manage – though not too much red – smoked salmon, steak, spinach and mouth-puckering fruit, preferably pineapple.

The evening meal therefore consisted of smoked salmon, a rare entrecôte with puréed spinach, and cubes of fresh pineapple. This was accompanied by Clare Valley Riesling with the fish and an amusing Wine Society Minervois with the steak, the whole preceded by stonkingly dry Martinis mixed by Sir Simon.

This was what he called healthy living. Both Bognors were appalled by supermarket-snackers who grazed on chocolate bars and crisps. Obese, them? Just a teensy bit overweight but nothing a serious sauna wouldn't sort.

'Fancy a few days in Spain?' enquired the new knight of his beloved.

'Why Spain?' Monica was in two minds about Spain. She was opposed to bullfighting and cheap package flights – being against blood sports on sound liberal grounds and drunken yobboes on grounds which she supposed were elitist and snobbish, but were a part of her upbringing and make-up that she was no longer going to pretend to deny. On the other hand she loved the climate, the long lazy lunches, Goya and El Greco.

'Why not?' asked her husband, pouring cocktails from the shaker. He favoured a twist, his wife an olive.

'Don't answer a question with a question,' she said.

He smiled. She had been saying this ever since they married more than forty years earlier. The refrain had all the persistence of a cracked gramophone record but had never irritated him. Despite continuing to pay little or no attention to the request he found it oddly reassuring. The older he became, the more comfort he obtained from its repetition. Habit, he supposed.

'I have to go to Spain on business. I thought you'd like to come too. It's somewhere in the hills near Salamanca. I thought you could spend time there and we could meet up for a long weekend. Longer maybe. A day or two in Madrid. Toledo. Train to Zaragoza or Barcelona. A break.'

'What's the business?' Monica accepted the proffered dry Martini and glared at her olive.

'Villains abroad,' said her husband. 'I'm getting rather fed up with it. The Costas have become a sort of retirement home for our undesirables. I think we should flush them out. One of the most significant of them has just been found dead in the mountains. I want to go and see for myself and try to round up some of his subordinates and bring them home to face music.'

'You mean the braying tones of hanging judges in sentencing mode?' Monica would have made an intimidating judge herself. She had a face which was more like a horse than a button, and a voice to match. No more musical than bagpipes or the braying of a hanging judge.

'That would be ideal,' Bognor sipped appreciatively at the ice-cold gin, 'though one of their leaders has had his comeuppance already. A man called Trubshawe. Sometimes, that is. Sometimes he was called Trubshawe. More often something else. He'd done a bunk to the Costa-something. Just been found dead. Very.'

'I remember him,' said Monica, who missed very few tricks. 'Sprung from the Scrubs and then stabbed someone to death in a road rage incident on the South Circular. Vanished, believed to be on a permanent package holiday with a new identity. Several identities in fact.' She took a ruminative taste of cocktail. 'Very nice, darling.' She smiled approvingly. 'One of your better ones. Plymouth?'

'Naturally,' said her husband. 'Funny, isn't it,' he went on, 'how crooks of one sort or another are all the rage. Honest indigence is passé. Ill-gotten gains are flavour of the month. Suddenly all the world loves a spiv. If you're still travelling on public transport when you're over twenty-five then you're a sad failure. Saints are saps.'

'I blame Thatcher,' said Monica crisply. This might or might not have been fair, but it was predictable. Monica blamed everything on Baroness Thatcher, from the weather to the war in Iraq.

'But is it true?' asked Bognor holding his cocktail glass up to the light and peering at the twist of lemon peel to see if there was any pith still attached to it. There was not. The potato peeler had done its stuff and his hand was obviously steadier than he thought. 'My father's generation thought it was bad form to discuss money and not really done to make much. Genteel poverty was the fashion. Nothing as extreme as bankruptcy or bad debt, though that was probably preferable to making a fortune on the black market. Know what I mean? But that's no longer true. We live in an age of "rich lists", peerages for cash, million pound bonuses, vast salaries for jobs ill-done. All apparently condoned or even welcomed by the powers that be.'

'That your sermon for the evening?' asked Monica.

'I don't see why telling the truth should be a sermon,' he said. 'I'm particularly offended by a whole load of crims poncing around in sunny Spain at the taxpayers' expense and apparently with the tacit approval of Her Majesty's Government, the Fourth Estate and received opinion almost everywhere. And I think I should sort it out before I finally retire.'

He swallowed gin and grimaced. It burned the back of his throat. Dry Martinis were, he thought, an oddly masochistic drink. No wonder it had been Bond's favourite drink. Or was that a vodkatini?

'I hope you're not suffering from delusions,' said his wife, trying not to pull a face as she also took too big a gulp, pretending that she had swallowed too much on purpose. 'Just because someone in silly little Gavin's office has got the wrong person for a knighthood. Don't take it too literally. Doesn't mean to say you've acquired shining armour and turned white overnight.' Bognor was, normally these days, a mild puce colour. Even *he* was prepared to admit to pink.

'I'd like to be remembered for something,' said Bognor

seriously. 'Cleaning up the Costas would be a good grabby theme for the obits. "Bognor will long be remembered for his successful campaign to prevent British criminals from success-fully seeking sanctuary in the Iberian peninsula. In a series of extensive investigations promoted by the sudden death of the south London villain, James 'Jimmy' Trubshawe, Bognor . . ."'

'Don't be so vainglorious,' said Monica, puckering her lip in acknowledgement of the cocktail's strength. 'You've done perfectly well just being you. Your achievements are positively Widmerpudlian. You have a knighthood. You run a government department. You have, more or less and in a manner of speaking, your health. You have an adoring wife. What more do you want?'

'I want to be remembered for something,' he said petulantly. 'I don't want to be just another Whitehall jobsworth with a flukey gong and an inflated pension.'

'You sound like Tony Blair,' said Monica, 'and look what happened to him. Just be content. Rest on your laurels like everyone else.'

They finished their drinks in silence and then adjourned to tackle the smoked salmon. They did themselves very well in a finicky way. The salmon was none of your supermarket rubbish, but came from a mail order company in West Cornwall who smoked it on the premises. The brown bread was organic and came from a Polish baker round the corner. Bognor liked to think that the Board of Trade had done more than its share for Polish bakers round the corner. Cornish fish smokeries too, come to that.

The Bognors had an old-fashioned separate dining room where they sometimes entertained quite formally, and where they tended to eat their evening meals when at home alone. One or two adequate but undistinguished family portraits hung on the walls and there were odds and ends of family silver salvaged from both sides of their ancestry. They took breakfast in the kitchen but seldom supper. They never ate in front of the television, and even though they would have thought it laugh-able to actually dress up for their evening meal they recognized that they were in this, and perhaps other respects, old-fashioned, even conceivably quaint.

Bognor remained in a retrospective frame of mind.

'It's different for women,' he said, tasting the white wine in a manner which he hoped was efficient without being pretentious. He hated the idea of being considered a pseud when it came to food and drink, but there were those who thought him overenthusiastic on both counts. In defensive mode he sometimes explained it away by the fact that he had never had children. This was not a deliberate decision on the part of either himself or his wife. It was just something that had happened. Or not. They both slightly regretted it, while acknowledging that they were both too selfish to have made much of a fist of parenthood. On the other hand it was difficult to know which came first; the lack of fecundity or the slight selfishness.

The Riesling was cool and flinty. The Bognors had visited the Clare Valley once and rather enjoyed it. Likewise Penryn where the fish had been smoked. They liked to source what they ate and drank.

'Why different for a woman?' Monica wanted to know.

'You're not subject to the same sort of pressures,' said Bognor in the lofty manner which so infuriated her. 'Males are constantly being judged and measured by their teachers and their peers. It's a sexual hazard. Women aren't judgemental in the same way.'

'Tripe,' said Monica, spearing a sliver of salmon. She flushed, which was always dangerous. 'If anything, women are even more judgemental than men. If you'd been to a convent school you wouldn't talk such bilge.'

'No, no,' said Bognor, vaguely sensing danger but not quite sure why or whence it originated. 'You misunderstand me. That's not at all what I meant. I certainly wasn't implying that women were less judgemental than . . .' He took refuge in Riesling and a slice of fish, which he chewed more than necessary.

'Men,' said Monica, through gritted teeth, 'men are, if anything, much *less* judgemental than women. Women are always eyeing each other up to see how well they're preserved; whether they've got their own teeth, their own hair, their own breasts. They're always judging each other.'

'But not,' he said, unwisely, 'in terms of achievements . . .
career . . . that sort of thing.'

'And why, Simon,' she said, 'do you imagine that should
be the case? Even supposing for one tiny moment that it *is*
the case. It's because for generation after generation women
have been denied the opportunities of achieving the kinds of
role on which your precious judgements are founded.'

More silence ensued, punctuated only by mastication. When
they had finished, Bognor rather ostentatiously stacked the two
plates and took them out to the kitchen, while Monica dished up
the main course. The Clare Valley Riesling was unfinished and
sat on the sideboard waiting for another opportunity. Bognor
opened the Wine Society Minervois with one of those cork-
screws that looked like the Croix de Lorraine. The steak was
very rare, the way they both liked it. It came from a third
generation family butcher round the same corner as the Polish
baker. The spinach was from one of the more farmer-friendly
supermarkets. Chiswick had almost everything.

'So are you definitely going to Spain?' asked Monica, when
they had sat down again and started on the meat.

'I think so, yes.'

'And if I preferred to stay at home?'

'I'd rather you didn't. I'd like your company.'

'I'm flattered. Except that you'll be working. What am I
supposed to do when you're chipping away at the coal face?'

'I can't work all the time,' he said. 'We can have siestas
together. Go on tapas crawls in the evening. And you can
spend your days in the Thyssen or the Prado. You'd like that.'

Bognor's museum and art-gallery attention span was severely
limited, unlike his wife's.

'I might do a course,' she said. 'Spanish for beginners.
Cookery. Art history.'

'Why not?' he wanted to know, though only rhetorically. 'It
would be much more improving than trying to flush out the
friends of Jimmy Trubshawe.'

And they finished their steak and spinach in a harmonious
discussion of the likely relative merits of Spanish courses in
Salamanca and Madrid, of whether Castilian cuisine was preferable to Catalan, and other non-controversial matters Iberian.

Monica had just gone to the kitchen to make coffee when the phone rang urgently. It was odd how one knew instinctively when a phone call was 'urgent' and when it was casual; when it was a 'cold' call from Bangalore on behalf of a double-glazing outfit and when it was from one's nearest and dearest. The ring was, Bognor knew, exactly the same in every instance. Yet this one had 'urgent' all over it.

He picked up the receiver on the table, placed there for just such an eventuality as this.

A voice which could have been from Bangalore but sounded closer, even though it carried an undefinable foreign inflection.

Could she, asked the caller, speak with Sir Simon Bognor.

'This is he,' said Bognor, self-importantly, even though the honour had not yet been officially announced.

'This is Pranvera,' she said, 'at Number Ten. I need a word. The Prime Minister insists.'

'Tomorrow morning,' said Bognor, a little wearily. 'You should phone my aide, Harvey Contractor. He'll do his best to fit you in.'

'I'm sorry, sir,' said Pranvera, 'but it's urgent. I have a car waiting. If you're at home I could be round in half an hour.'

'Can't it wait?' Bognor asked.

'I'm sorry, sir,' she said, not sounding in the least apologetic, 'but no. It can't. Half an hour, then.'

And the line went dead.

Bognor swore and poured another glass of Minervois.

FOUR

Pranvera was at the house in twenty-nine minutes, fifteen seconds. Bognor was counting. Her car was large, black, driven by a man in a suit and probably a Rover – a sad symbol of Britain's once-vaunted motor industry. Bognor's official car was a Rover too – British but obsolete. The girl was dark-skinned, wore a black trouser suit and a headscarf, spoke old-fashioned unaccented BBC English, but seemed, to Bognor's sceptical eye, indefinably foreign. He was absolutely not a racist, but he had been brought up in a different world and he was uneasy with the new one which contained so many Pranveras and Harvey Contractors.

He offered the girl a glass of wine, which she declined, preferring a glass of water and a cup of black coffee. Bognor had a coffee but no more wine. Later, perhaps.

They sat in his study which was snug, comfortable, masculine, cluttered.

'So,' he said, smiling, 'what's so urgent that it can't wait till morning?'

'It's about Spain,' she said.

He was no longer smiling.

'Spain?' he asked trying to keep the incredulity out of his voice. 'What about Spain?'

'Your plans,' she said. 'We understand you're planning a visit to Spain. We'd much rather you didn't go.'

'Who's *we*?'

'Alexandra in particular. But in this instance she's speaking for Gavin as well. For all of us at Number Ten actually. And Party HQ.'

Alexandra was Alexandra Thornton, the Prime Minister's éminence grise, dogsbody, enforcer. She was unelected, unrepresentative and far too close to the PM for anyone's comfort except her own. Bognor had only met her twice but disliked her instinctively. He sensed this was mutual.

'I'm sorry,' he said, 'I'm not with you.'

'We understand that you're planning a visit to Spain. We'd rather you didn't go.'

'Is that an order?'

Pranvera sighed as if the idea was ludicrous, which is more or less what she said.

'We're a team' were the words she actually uttered and which Bognor thought was one of the silliest and most untrue things he had ever heard, even from the Prime Minister's office. Which was saying something. If team games were being played he was on the opposite side to Gavin, Alexandra and Pranvera.

'As a civil servant I have a duty to offer my advice impartially and to the best of my ability. However, I do also have an absolute obligation to carry out the wishes of my immediate boss, namely the President of the Board of Trade. Or of *his* boss, the Prime Minister. If Gavin says I'm not to go to Spain I suppose I have to submit. On the other hand, I don't take orders from you or Alexandra. And in any case I think I'm due an explanation. Why don't you want me to go to Spain? And what on earth makes you think that's what I intend?'

As far as Bognor could judge the only two people who had any idea of his Spanish plans were Monica and Harvey Contractor. There was no way Monica would have told Number Ten, even if she had had the time and opportunity. Contractor was different, but even so Bognor somehow doubted that he would go running to Number Ten. The 'betrayal' seemed much more likely to be something electronic. He supposed he'd have to have his office swept again. It was bad enough to have to protect oneself from one's enemies, ludicrous to have to do the same to withstand those allegedly on your own side. This was the intelligence equivalent of friendly fire.

'Number Ten doesn't miss much,' said Pranvera with a poker-player's smile. Gioconda, thought Bognor. Not giving much away but implying omniscience, coupled with a dangerous, even sadistic, sense of humour. Dangerous. Very. Leonardo had a lot to answer for, and he didn't mean Dan Brown.

'Of course not,' said Bognor, reflecting inwardly that Number Ten was accomplished at seeing what it ought not to have seen but useless at seeing what it should have seen.

He decided to abandon the farcical pretence of abstinence and fetched his unfinished glass of Minervois.

When he came back into the room the girl was as she had been when he left, staring at her glass of water, immaculate and unmoved in every sense.

'So,' he resumed, 'let's accept that you don't miss much, and you thought I might be heading off for Spain and you didn't like it. Leaving aside why you came to this conclusion, I want to know what your worry is. Why do you want me not to go? And why is it so important that you have to come speeding round here after hours. Seems like an ill-informed overreaction to me. But then security is just my job. Not my obsession.'

It was the girl's turn to look embarrassed.

'I'm under orders,' she said.

'Quite,' said Bognor. 'I, on the other hand, am not.'

They looked at each other waiting for someone to blink.

The girl wavered first.

'We understand you're concerned about the Trubshawe death and that you are keen to use it as leverage to deal with the expat British community in the Costas.'

'And if I were,' said Bognor, 'I'd only be doing my job. Even the Prime Minister would understand that. And presumably approve. The taxpayer would simply be getting value for money.'

'The Prime Minister would prefer it if the Trubshawe death excited as little comment as possible.'

'Buried under the carpet?'

'Not unduly sensationalized. Just treated as a sad incident.'

'What if he were murdered?'

'Our information is that death was due to natural causes,' said Pranvera.

'My information is different,' said Bognor, lying but only in a white way. He was being economical with the truth but not completely disregarding it.

'We thought it would be,' said the girl, 'which is why we'd prefer you not to go.'

'I don't understand,' he said.

'I'd like to be able to tell you more,' she said, 'but, well, I can't.' She was almost convincing; almost made Bognor feel that she would like to have let him into her confidence had she been able. But she wasn't.

'It sounds to me –' Bognor took a minuscule sip of red wine – 'as if the man called Trubshawe had a connection with Number Ten which Number Ten is reluctant to reveal.'

'That's not rocket science,' she said. 'You don't have to be Einstein to work out that we don't want people sniffing around the remains of Trubshawe. It will be much better if he's given a decent burial as soon as possible, so that those of us who are lucky enough to survive can carry on with our lives.'

'Supposing I disagree?'

'We're hoping you won't.'

'You know something?' Bognor stood up, wandered over to the bookcase and pulled out a copy of his College Register. He opened it at random then put it back where it had come from. On the wall hung a photograph of his parents taken at their wedding. They looked serious but happy, virtuous, solid, old-fashioned. Bognor thought of them increasingly as he grew older and felt they were examples to be lived up to. The photograph was a tangible reminder of this. The picture had a talismanic quality.

'Trubshawe,' he continued, 'was a crook. A rich crook. So were his associates. Any prime minister of this country worth his salt would want people like him brought to justice.'

The girl studied her shoes and said nothing.

He sighed, gazed at the girl, then at the photograph of his parents, thought of Monica, considered life. It had all begun as a virtual joke. The man from the Foreign Office had, he remembered, rheumy yellowish eyes which suggested jaundice. He smoked. After what had seemed like a perfunctory interview in the rooms of his mediaeval history tutor, who had tactfully absented himself from the occasion, the man from the F.O. leant forward, winked a jaundiced eye, tapped the side of his nose and said in a melodramatic, black-and-white-movie sort of a way, 'There *is* another branch of the Foreign Office.' And Bognor being an innocent abroad, but consumed with a sense of curiosity and adventure which had never entirely left him, even though it was concealed by a natural indolence and a world-weary sense of nothing much mattering in the great scheme of things, had said in an encouragingly polite fashion, 'Oh really.'

Whereupon his interlocutor, who was, Bognor subsequently realized, almost certainly on some form of commission, had rubbed his hands, smiled oleaginously and said that he or someone else would be in touch. A week or so later Bognor was summoned to a country house in the wilds of Herefordshire, where he signed various papers, submitted to a medical examination and was thoroughly frightened and rather bemused. It had been much the same story ever since. He had been taken over by the state and most if not all independent powers of decision were removed. Until, perhaps, up to a point, now.

He turned back and faced the girl.

'Well,' he said, 'it's been extraordinarily nice meeting you. I hope you haven't got far to travel.'

'Crouch End actually,' she said, seeming confused. 'What shall I tell Alexandra?' she asked, suddenly seeming as young and naïve as she almost certainly was.

She had a car and a driver, he thought to himself, which was more than he had had at her age, and she was asking him to compromise, to fudge, to aid and abet. All his life he seemed to have been bailing out the Gavins of this world, helping fly-by-night bully-boy politicians to survive their incompetence and double-dealing. Some people became even more resigned to duplicity in high places as they neared retirement but Bognor was the reverse. The safer he became, the more inevitable his pension, the more cushioned his retirement, the more infuriated he became by the whims and deceits of his masters. After a lifetime of acquiescence, of cover-up and doing as he was told, he was the worm that had turned. Most people, by the time they reached his stage in life no longer cared. He, however, seemed to be caring greatly, possibly for the first time in his life. Funny, that.

The girl stood up and smoothed the imaginary untidiness of her immaculately ironed trousers.

'So you'll be travelling to Spain?'

'I haven't decided.'

'You're not going to let Mr Trubshawe rest in peace?'

'Trubshawe never allowed anyone rest or peace while he was

alive,' he said. 'I really don't see why I should extend those small mercies to him now that he's toppled off his grubby little perch.'

'Gavin won't like it.'

This was meant to be a threat but Bognor was suddenly tired and not interested.

'If you'll excuse my French,' he said, 'I don't give a flying whatsit whether Gavin likes it or not.'

'We all thought we could rely on you.' She was reproachful now, almost sulky. Bognor would have enjoyed being a fly on the wall when she reported back to Alexandra. Alexandra the notorious scourge of editors everywhere; Alexandra who, notoriously, swore like a trooper and scared the trousers off the most hard-boiled old Fleet Street hand left outside captivity. Alexandra wouldn't like it. Knowing her reputation she would probably pick up the phone and give Bognor an earful. Which, he thought wryly to himself, would be counter-productive. At times he could be quite mulish. This was one such moment.

'One can rely on me,' he said, falling into royal-speak without meaning to. Nevertheless it suited his sense of moral rectitude, lack of self-doubt and unaccustomed certainty. At last, he was not only right but seen to be right. If, at the same time, he could wrong-foot the Prime Minister, then so much the better.

He walked his visitor to the door and showed her out. Her car was waiting, parked ostentatiously on the double yellow line outside the house. It wasn't, as he had assumed a Rover, but a Mercedes. That followed, he thought sardonically, waving to her as the driver let her into the back seat. Bognor tended to sit in front with his driver, Sid. Sid was a Charlton supporter.

Bognor shut the door and hummed Mozart, slightly off-key, and wondered whether to make himself a mug of healthy soporific Horlicks, which was a habit he and Monica had recently developed.

He thought better of it, however, went to the sideboard and found a bottle of Calvados from which he poured himself a generous slug. Lady Bognor had gone to bed with a good book. Her husband settled down in a deep armchair to watch the highlights of the cricket from Hobart.

England were losing.

FIVE

'*Hasta la vista, Señora!*' exclaimed Sir Simon to his sleeping lady wife.

She was not amused.

'For Christ's sake, Simon,' she exclaimed irritably, 'put a sock in it. Some of us are trying to sleep.'

'You're no fun any longer,' he complained, sitting heavily on the end of the bed before removing his shoes and slowly peeling off his socks, wondering if Monica had spoken altogether metaphorically or whether she really would have liked him to roll the grey woollen sweaty objects into a ball and ingest them. Whether or not that was what she expected, he wasn't going to run the risk. It would be dangerous, a gesture too far. They exuded a definite whiff of mature Cheddar.

'Would you mind getting into bed and turning off the light,' she said, 'and don't snore. If you do then you're dead meat.'

Bognor stared at his feet. They were not bad for a man of his age. No more than marginally fallen arches, a suggestion of hardened calloused skin, which an enemy might have stigmatized as a corn or a bunion but was actually little more than the patina of age, a gentle acknowledgement of a long life riding Shanks's pony.

It wasn't just his feet that were good for his age, he reflected. He was in almost every respect a great advertisement for a certain sort of unfashionable British way of life. Critics might deride this as lethargic and self-indulgent, but as far as he was concerned it had to do with learning to pace yourself, knowing your limitations and, above all, getting your priorities right. And now look at him: own teeth, own hair – well most of both – own job, own house, own wife and now his very own knighthood. Well there was still some outstanding mortgage, so he supposed that, in a way, the house could be said to belong to the building society; and the job, well, as was the way with jobs, it was, he supposed, on loan. He had made it his own and it would take a big man to fill his shoes, because, frankly, they didn't make them like him any more. As for Monica. Well, yes, she was his original wife but at the same time there was no denying that she was her own woman as well. If she warned him about snoring then the warning should be heeded. Even as he thought this dangerous thought, his wife let out a restrained, almost sibilant, sound, which, while ladylike, was nonetheless a snore. He smiled. One day he would tell her that she too snored. For now, however, he did not dare.

He turned out the light and took off everything except his tartan boxer shorts bought for him by Monica, probably in an Oxfam charity shop – though she had hotly denied the imputation when he first made it. Other knights would have monogrammed knickers from a little place in Jermyn Street but that had never, he reflected, been the Bognor style.

He lay awake on his back for a few moments, reflecting. This was one of life's little luxuries. He liked to lie awake for a while with nothing to disturb him save the regular not-quite-snoring of his wife and the occasional gear-change from the road outside, often raspingly ill-executed. It provided him with a rare moment for contemplation and self-evaluation. Now that he was nearing retirement and had reached a certain age, he found himself increasingly worrying about whether or not he had achieved his aims; whether he had been a success or a failure.

On balance, he supposed, you would have to acknowledge a modest success, even though he was the first to acknowledge that judgements on these matters were subjective and relative. He had got off to a good start with the infamous business of the decadent monastics at Beaubridge Friary and their flagrant manipulation of the export trade in honey; then there had been the Stately Home Industry, and the blowing up in his steam pinnace of the nautical museum pioneer Viscount Abney. He had been involved with the dog-breeding business and the wretched stabbing of the Samuel Pepys diarist, St John Derby, in the old, unreformed, alcohol-fuelled manually typewritten world of hard-metal Fleet Street. Oxford, of course. The murder of the Master of Apocrypha, not to mention the demise of Escoffier Smith, chef-patron of the Dour Dragoon in East Sheen.

It was quite a litany and even included a railway murder in the UK and another in Canada, not to mention his crucial intervention in the archetypally Thatcherite world of provincial town politics at Scarpington and the ersatz English village with the real tennis-playing Maharishi and his followers. Oh, and that pornographic publisher, the boss of Big Books plc, crushed to death between the shelves of his blue basement library. He sighed reflectively. Life recently had gone rather quiet, but in those first two decades at the Board of Trade he had experienced enough excitement for several lives of special investigation.

His activities had tended towards the reactive rather than proactive, but that was in his nature. He was not the sort of investigator who went looking for trouble. Not like a few he could mention: self-important sleuths who were always sticking their noses into other people's business, where they were neither wanted nor needed. That was not his style. He did, on the whole, as he was told.

Now, however, there was no one to tell him what to do except for himself. He had become the man in charge. It was what happened in life. Buggins's turn. Someone had once told him who the original Buggins was supposed to be but he had forgotten, and now that he himself had become the latest in the line it really couldn't matter less who had originated the practice.

He smiled. Buggins the worm that turned. That was who he had become, and one or two people in and around Whitehall were in for a shock. He was fed up with keeping his nose clean and being a safe pair of hands who never went out on a limb of any kind. Now, in the twilight of his career, he was determined to become a loose cannon, a bull in a china shop. No longer good old Bognor who could be relied on to do the decent thing but dangerous Sir Simon, the unpredictable tilter at windmills. Don Quixote. And how apposite, therefore, that he should start this new quixotic period in his life with a trip to Spain to investigate the death of the man who was Trubshawe.

Bognor had first visited Spain when he was a student. He had hitch-hiked with a friend and found a country still shocked by civil war and governed by a fascist dictator. It was cheap but depressed. Most men over the age of thirty seemed to have a limb missing; most women wore shapeless black, as unflattering and unrevealing as the Moslem garb which caused such problems in later years. The Guardia Civil in their sinister black tricorne hats lingered on every street corner. Bognor and his friend ate flat bread, fruit and tortillas and drank rough red wine sometimes with *gaseosa*. Occasionally they drank brandy, which was even rougher than the wine. Food, drink and accommodation was cheap and basic. The country felt backward and insular and utterly foreign. Bognor spoke no Spanish.

Over the years he kept going back. At first he went with a variety of friends, latterly with Monica. He tried the bullfight, but was no Hemingway and proved more squeamish than his girlfriend, later wife. He found Goya and Velasquez more to his taste and enjoyed classical guitar. Flamenco was only a spectator sport if that. He had not yet made it to El Bulli, and although it was on his horizon it was a murky prospect and not one which he held out a serious hope of attaining.

Those middle years had been something of a disappointment. Since the Scarpington Case, which he had thought rather a triumph, he had been reduced largely to desk-driving around the corridors of power. He supposed that Scarpington had ruffled feathers in the sense that he had stepped marginally out of line, questioned conventions, set truth above morality and decency above expediency. These were not what was expected in the Civil Service.

He should not, of course, have entered the Board of Trade in the first place. It was the man in the mac who done it. Latterly, Bognor had come to think of the mac as dirty, as well as belted and broad-shouldered and wide-revered. In truth it was probably none of these things, just a middle-aged romanticism about Humphrey Bogart and Raymond Chandler. Maybe the man who had come down to Oxford on the recruiting drive had not worn a mac, but he certainly nodded and winked and told Bognor that there was, ahem, another branch of the Board of Trade, and, er, well, nudge, nudge, wink, wink, er . . . well, maybe Bognor might be interested in that. And Bognor being curious as well as indolent had said that, in that case, maybe he should have a think about it and the rest had been sort of, in a manner of speaking, up to a point, well . . . history.

He smiled again, pondered turning over, embracing his snoring wife, but thought better of all these things and remained flat on his back staring at the ceiling, looking back on life as he knew it. Such introspection was commonplace – at least among thinking people, and especially so when they had been educated at aspirational institutions. It had been dinned in to him at both school and university that one was expected to sew talent and instruction wisely, to work assiduously, take one's chances and to make at least the equivalent of brigadier. Bognor's background and upbringing were solidly middle class. They were not absolutely top drawer, so nobody ever expected Nobel Prizes or even a Booker or, God help him, a Crime Writers' Association Golden Dagger. However, he had at least lived up to expectations and, with the new knighthood, exceeded them. Very few from his school, and comparatively few from his college, could boast a handle to their name.

And now that he had come up to scratch, and even beyond, he was going to allow himself the luxury of risk and the indulgence of his conscience. He had left this late and it was typical of him that he should only put his head above the parapet when there was little or no danger of being shot at. He was all for safety first and a quiet life, or had been for much of it. Now, at last, he was going to surprise people – even, he turned to stare through the gloom at his sleeping wife . . . even Monica.

Playing safe. He rolled the words round his mouth and savoured them. He was not a natural risk taker. Never had been, except perhaps on that one fateful occasion all those years ago when he had opted for the Special Investigation Department of the Board of Trade. Everyone he knew advised against it. Teaching, banking, even accountancy would have been sound, respectable and dull. Any of those would have paid the mortgage and kept him off the streets. He could have written poetry on the side. Or painted watercolours. Anything approaching danger could have been ring-fenced as a hobby which carried little or no financial implication. Instead he chose uncharted territory and entered special investigation, which sounded edgy and interesting, even if it was conducted for the staid old Board of Trade.

He sighed. Time to sleep, perchance to dream. Now, in the

twilight of his career, he was going to surprise everyone, including himself. He was going to upset apple-carts and prime ministers, and having exceeded all expectations, most notably those of his former teachers and tutors, he was going to do all the things and take all the risks he would have liked to have done in the years of safety-first. At last he was taking the brakes off, changing gears and beginning to fire on all cylinders. Beginning with a visit to Spain.

He turned over, planted a kiss on the brow of his sleeping wife, and in a moment, had joined her in deep, noisy, but, alas, dreamless, sleep.

SIX

S ir Simon and Lady Bognor prepared for departure in a VIP lounge and travelled Club. Harvey Contractor took his chances in the terminal-at-large and flew at the back of the bus. This was, thought Bognor, only right. Time would come, and come faster than he would like, when he and his lady would be pensioners paying for themselves and relegated to below the salt, while Contractor took his turn at the high table and had legroom and sparkling wine. This was the way of the world.

Despite this discrimination they all had to pass through the same security checks and even Sir Simon had to remove his shoes and put them in a plastic box for inspection. Knowing something about security he recognized the rigmarole for the farce it actually was and accepted the fact that if a determined and professional bomber wished to destroy an aeroplane he would manage to do so no matter how many passengers removed their shoes. Nevertheless, it presumably made some people feel good and enabled various politicians to claim that they were doing their jobs. A life in Whitehall had made him intensely sceptical of politicians with their transitory ambitions and pretensions. He also believed that any old crook could make a nonsense of bureaucratic pretensions such as security and passport control. The man called Trubshawe was a case in point.

The flight was short and uneventful. Bognor read the *Spectator* which took a lot less time than it used to, but more or less, sort of, occupied his thoughts for the two or so hours in which they were airborne. Some of his thoughts, however, were on the job in hand. It was not difficult to think two thoughts at once, particularly when one line was provoked by a particular bevy of regular contributors for whom he had only the most perfunctory respect. Even so, he was mildly shocked to discover that he had seemingly managed to read through a page and a half of Rod Liddle while devoting his mind entirely to Trubshawe and his cohorts on the Costas.

It would be good to see Juan again. They had last met at an international conference on carcinogens in processed food which had been held in Helsinki two years earlier. Picasso and Bognor had enjoyed a substantial dinner of minced elk and herring lubricated with akvavit and Pilsner. They had talked about art and football and life. The old Admiral held political attitudes to the right of the former caudillo and made no secret of the fact that he would have liked Franco or a lookalike to continue in unchallenged office for ever and a day. Bognor, by contrast, regarded himself as a man of the enlightened centre-left. Despite this, the two men seemed to have much in common; being essentially civilized, cultivated men who enjoyed reading books, listening to classical music, eating good food and drinking good wine. The minced elk and herring and the raw spirits and icy beer didn't really come into that category, but they were both reasonably gastronomically adventurous, as well as having a relaxed and non-judgemental attitude to life and their fellow man.

'Live and let live,' Bognor had said, a touch woozily, as he raised his schnapps shot in the general direction of his friend, the retired Admiral. The 'Admiral' title which preceded Picasso's name was something of a mystery and he never mentioned the sea or ships. Bognor wondered vaguely if it was an honorific title which went with the job, so that the head of trade investigations at the Guardia Civil was always called 'Admiral' in the same way that the boss of Scotland Yard Social was always called 'ffiennes', or a certain sort of old-fashioned nanny was commonly designated 'Mrs' as a concession to her status, whether she was married or not.

Madrid airport had been 'improved' since Bognor was last in Spain. A modern architect of the Rogers-Grimshaw school had obviously been at work, so the place was now enormous, took a long time to walk through and had not a straight line in sight.

Harvey Contractor joined them at the carousel and Bognor noticed a striking blonde of a certain age and confident, mature allure wander off to the toilets. She was wearing a politically incorrect coat. Real fur, Lady Bognor declared. A few minutes later she was back, pouting a little obviously, at the emerging suitcases. She was wearing a figure-hugging black trouser

suit and jangly rocks. The fur coat had vanished. Bognor
frowned and pondered. It was definitely suspicious and the
woman had all the appearance of a high-class courtesan
involved in some sort of smuggling scam. At the end of the
day, however, it was none of his business. He decided to say
nothing, just waited for the luggage to appear, wheeled it away
with his wife, smiled at the customs officials and at the driver
sent to greet them by Admiral Picasso.

The car was a Mercedes; the chauffeur wore a dark-blue suit,
white shirt and striped tie. His English was unaccented and
fluent. Contractor sat in the front alongside him; the Bognors
lent back in the rear of the vehicle and inhaled the smell of
leather. Class distinctions were still applying. They would share
a hotel but Contractor would have a bog-standard single; the
Bognors a mini-suite.

Spain rolled past outside the tinted glass windows. She had
moved on amazingly in Bognor's lifetime, but remained the most
impenetrable of foreign neighbours. The Spanish capital had taken
on a sense of style. The women had become svelte and soignée
and the men well-groomed. When Bognor first encountered them
the Spanish were drab. He thought of the women in black shapeless smocks and the men in blue overalls. That can't have been
entirely true but it was how he remembered them. In those days
the British had looked down on them, regarding them as third-
world peasantry from a backward sad country, whereas they, the
British, were the victors of the world war and were taller and
more cultivated, richer and smarter. They were still, for the most
part, taller but that was about all.

Cranes and scaffolding dominated the cityscape making
Madrid feel almost Chinese. The prosperity was almost tangible.
In its wake came organized crime. Central and South America
spoke the same language and came with drugs. Eastern Europe
provided tens of thousands of illegal immigrants, many of them
subsisting on crime, mostly petty. Prostitution and pickpocketing
were rife. Lawlessness had become almost endemic. A natural
Hispanic disdain for such puritan ethics had been reined in
under the Generalissimo's regime, but, some argued, freedom
had bred licence. The old certainties had died; the church was
in decline; the country was in a state of flux.

It took about half an hour to reach the city centre, where they encountered a traffic jam engendered by what appeared to be a burst water main. It took them another half-hour to reach their hotel, which was old-fashioned and faded, with revolving doors, concierges in top hats and gold-braided topcoats, aspidistras and antimacassars, poodles and women with wigs as tightly-curled as their dogs' coats. The vestibule smelt of mint and mothball. Treatment from the receptionist seemed to be identical for Contractor and for his master and master's wife, but the similar warmth of greeting and width of smile didn't disguise the fact that Contractor had a standard room and the Bognors a suite. Back to class distinctions.

After they had checked in and acclimatized, Simon left Monica to unpack, took the elevator to the lobby, met Harvey, returned to the waiting Mercedes and drove on to Guardia Civil headquarters.

Carlos Azuela was waiting on the pavement outside. He smelt faintly of Serrano ham, manzanilla, untipped cigarette and aftershave. A very Spanish smell, thought Bognor. He had a dark five o'clock stubble which looked as if it had been cultivated with care and attention. He and Harvey embraced and kissed each other on both cheeks in a manner which Bognor found as mildly foreign as the *teniente*'s smell.

They took the lift to the top floor where *Teniente* Azuela escorted them to the Admiral's office which was large and enjoyed a view over the city rooftops. There was a boardroom next door, a terrace outside sliding glass doors, and a large photograph of King Juan Carlos over the Admiral's desk which was cluttered with papers and family photographs. The Admiral had several children and many grandchildren. Apart from this Bognor felt immediately and instinctively at home.

He and the Admiral embraced, a little more rigidly than Harvey and Carlos, then withdrew to inspect each other for signs of wear and tear, and to smile appreciatively. Both seemed quite reassured to find their counterpart still breathing.

'Long time, as you say in your great country,' said the Admiral, 'no see.'

Bognor nodded. 'That Helsinki conference about whatever it was supposed to be about.'

The Admiral laughed.

'Conferences are about corridors,' he said, 'about footnotes not agendas.' His English was disturbingly immaculate and idiomatic, a legacy of time spent on an exchange assignment with the British Home Fleet at Devonport dockyard. He had at the same time acquired an improbable affection for Cornish pasties and Plymouth Argyle Football Club. He was a Galician and therefore a Celt. His Spanishness was of a very particular and unusual variety, unlike Azuela who was from somewhere near Seville.

Coffee was produced: hot, strong, sticky-sweet, almost Graeco-Turk. The Spaniards smoked; the Brits, who had given up long before, feigned indifference and forbore.

Presently after a few minutes of ice-breaking catch-up conversation the Admiral drained his cup, smacked his hands together, and proposed a move to the boardroom next door. It contained a wide, state-of-the-art liquid screen. It was at this that they were invited to stare and presently, spurred on by Carlos, who was of an age, more or less, to understand and manipulate such things, the screen began to fill with images.

The first such image was a map of Spain. To begin with this was blank, but almost at once it began to fill with coloured images to illustrate the incidence of British expatriates domiciled on the Iberian peninsula. A high proportion of these, it appeared, were criminals, convicted or suspected, and most, if not all, were known to the Spanish authorities in general and to the Guardia Civil in particular.

The biggest concentrations, unsurprisingly, were around the Costas – Brava and del Sol. This was much more marked when the supposedly law-abiding segments of ex-pat society were removed from the screen. At the press of an Azuela button almost every evidence of inland exile vanished. Inland was where Hispanophiles, eccentrics and the poor hung out. Bloated British criminals centred their activity round a beamed country pub called the Bell and Balls or the Crooked Gasket, an eighteen-hole golf club with an English-speaking professional and an active branch of the Manchester United Supporters Club. That meant, very crudely, somewhere reasonably close to Malaga or Alicante. There were exceptions, but the beach was a prerequisite and these people were seldom, if ever, loners. They hung out together, took comfort in each other's company, liked to flaunt beer guts, tattoos and expletive-laden Scouse, cockney or similarly unreceived English. The man called Trubshawe had several villas mostly within a nine-iron of the prescribed un-Spanish amenities.

In due course they all came up on screen together with a mugshot of the deceased in the top left-hand corner, unsmiling, porcine and bald. The shots of the villas included detailed aerial ones taken, presumably, from a helicopter but possibly a satellite. Carlos was able to zoom in for closer shots of the naked girls lying by the pools, the driving range, or even through open windows. The villas all looked as if they had cost a lot of money.

'You seem to know a lot about our friend,' Bognor remarked, slightly sardonically.

His friend smiled.

'Naturally,' he said, 'we make it our business to know everything possible about people like him. It is our job.'

'But you didn't *do* anything about him?'

Admiral Picasso looked at his junior, *Teniente* Azuela as if to say, 'Honestly, these English!'

'We were unable to *do* anything, as you put it, my friend, because your Mr Trubshawe had committed no crime in Spain. We understood that he was a wanted criminal in the United Kingdom but our understanding was that your people were happy to be rid of him and did not want him back. So we watched, and we waited.'

He shrugged.

'Until,' said Bognor, 'he made a false move.'

His old friend smiled again and sighed like the thin wind that whipped across the strait from North Africa and assailed Algeciras.

'Until he went to the Pueblo,' said Picasso, 'and ate the wrong mushroom.'

'Wrong move,' said Bognor.

The Admiral shook his head.

'Very wrong move,' he said.

SEVEN

Admiral Picasso stared at his English counterpart quizzically.

'So,' he said, at last, 'you would like to visit the scene of the crime?'

'You sure it was a crime?' asked Bognor.

The Admiral smiled. 'Trubshawe was a convicted criminal. He ate poison fungi. He died.' The boss gave an expansive shrug. 'Maybe it was just, as you say, "one of those things", I myself have doubts. The coincidence is a little . . . how shall I put it? Coincidental.'

'I'd like to visit the Pueblo, yes,' said Bognor. 'Crime or no crime. That's why I want to go. Decide for myself.'

'Good,' said Picasso. 'It's been arranged.'

He winked at Carlos. 'Eh, *Teniente*? All fixed?'

'Yes, boss,' said his junior. 'Sir Simon is embedded as an Anglo and Lola Martinez has volunteered to be our Spaniard. Lola is very convincing. In fact, she will play the part so well that not even Sir Simon would know that she is one of us and not one of them. Lola and Sir Simon will make an interesting pair. She is so good at being submerged that she may be surprisingly little help. They are expected tomorrow morning.'

'Hang on, hang on,' said Sir Simon. 'I need more information.' He found the whole business of Lola oddly disconcerting, though unpleasantly familiar.

'Carlos is the case officer,' said Picasso. 'He can fill you in. I'd like to know more myself. So it's all yours, *Teniente*. Tell us the story.'

Azuela coughed. It was a strange expectoration – a mixture of diffidence and self-assurance. He knew he lacked seniority but what he lacked in that department he made up for in knowledge and intelligence. On this particular subject he knew more than anyone else in the room; he may not have been cleverer than Contractor, who was indubitably bright, but he certainly thought himself intellectually superior to Picasso and Bognor. In this, he was probably not as correct as he thought himself. Certainly he had a good degree, better than that of either of the two older men, but that did not necessarily give him a mental edge. Possibly even the reverse. It tended to make him smug.

Still, there was no denying that in this particular case he knew what he was talking about.

'The English Experience is a direct crib of *El Pueblo*,' he said. 'The idea is beautifully simple. It's designed to teach English to Spanish speakers, not by formal instruction but by exposing them to native English speakers and conducting everything, and I mean *everything*, in English. If you want someone to pass the salt or pepper, you have to ask in English; if you want to use the toilet, you have to do it in English; if you're making a pass at someone, you have to do it in English. Doesn't matter if it's two Spaniards together and there's no one to overhear them. They still have to use English.

'From a commercial point of view the Spaniards or their companies are charged an arm and a leg. The Anglos, on the other hand, don't pay anything. They have to get themselves to Madrid, but from then on everything is taken care of. You're bussed to and from your luxurious hotel and all your food and drink is paid for by the Experience.'

Sir Simon nodded. 'So the Anglos get a free Spanish holiday and the Spanish pay for them, plus a profit for the Experience. And provided everyone takes it reasonably seriously they're all happy.'

'Seems like it,' said Carlos. 'On the whole, as far as we can see, everyone does take it reasonably seriously and there are at least two Experience staffers to keep everyone in line.'

'How does it differ from the other outfit you mentioned? The one they nicked the idea from. *El Pueblo*?'

'They've gone way upmarket,' said Carlos. 'I'm fond of *El Pueblo*. It's very professional and on balance they work hard and play hard. The accommodation and food is perfectly good, but not – how would you say? – "gold tap and wall-to-wall caviar". The Experience is more in that class. They peel your eggs for you, pamper you. Much more expensive and more backsliding. The discipline is not as pronounced as elsewhere. Spanish is quite often spoken. Not like *El Pueblo*.'

'You're not a fan?' Bognor smiled.

The younger man shrugged. 'I'm not an inspector,' he said. 'It's not my business. But if you ask my personal opinion then I'd have to say the Experience is not exactly, as you would put it, "my cup of tea". For you, perhaps, it will suit you better. Is better, I think, for senior people.'

'Old people.'

The *teniente* smiled and contemplated his shoes. He said nothing.

'What do we think Trubshawe was doing there?' asked Bognor, shifting tack. Trubshawe was, in Bognor's view, trying it on, chancing his arm, flexing his muscles. He was proclaiming himself above the law, saying that he was impossible to catch.

The Admiral rubbed his hands together and seemed to think. Then he smiled gnomically.

'That is for you to say,' he said. 'Mr Trubshawe was one of yours. He was an Englishman and therefore, for us Spaniards, "a closed book". Why would he not visit the Experience like any other English speaker? Out of curiosity? Because he was in need of some sort of holiday and this was free? Perhaps he was escaping, running away from something? The Experience is an excellent hiding place. Like visiting a religious community for a "retreat".'

'Did Trubshawe need to run away from anything? Did he have to hide from anyone?' Bognor was genuinely curious. Trubshawe had seemed untouchable. The British seemed to have let him go and Spain had been a sanctuary for him. He appeared to be stuck between the Rock of Gibraltar and a not very hard place.

'You don't become Trubshawe without making enemies,' said the Admiral, 'There were many people who would have liked to see the end of Mr Trubshawe. Even if,' he added with an impish smile, 'that evidently did not include the British police or the British government. Which is peculiar, as they should have wanted to bring the man to justice more than anyone. But not apparently,' and he smiled again, 'so.'

'Nothing to do with me,' said Bognor almost involuntarily.

'I want to see villains brought to justice, and the man called Trubshawe was a villain or he was nothing. Unfortunately, in the real world which we inhabit being a villain is no sort of handicap. On the contrary – it can seem a positive advantage.'

'Quite so,' said Picasso. 'The villain should be punished. Exterminated, if possible.'

Bognor nodded. This didn't imply agreement, merely that he had taken on board what the Admiral thought.

The Bognors – Sir Simon and Her Ladyship – did a tapas crawl that evening. The highlight was hake's cheek in a vanilla froth. A Blumenthal-Bulli derivative. Actually, both Bognors preferred straightforward olives or chorizo. There was a lot of fish cheek and froth in modern Spanish cooking, a symbol of the Madrileño metamorphosis. Bognor would never have thought during his first visits to the peninsula, in the days of the caudillo, that Spain would ever be at the cutting edge of anything, let alone gastronomy. Now she was a world leader in Michelin stardom. Not to mention one of the world's leading havens for professional villains, especially British. Odd that. Not that the two were remotely connected. Far from it. Sir Simon chewed on a pinkly white tentacle of octopus and permitted himself a thin smirk.

'I'm getting cold,' said his wife, pulling her stole about her shoulders. 'I think we should find an indoors with acceptable scoff.'

He nodded. The atmosphere was suddenly chilly and darkness had fallen surprisingly fast. The city which minutes before had displayed an autumnal alfresco façade had gone wintery. The chairs in the plazas and on the pavements were being scooped and stacked; cigarettes were stubbed and blue smoke moved into crowded, panelled bars and cafés. Spaniards not only still smoked but their women wore fur. They still took long siestas and killed bulls. Despite its changes, the country was the most resolutely foreign in Europe. It was very deliberately and self-consciously its own place, resistant to outside influence, especially Anglo-American.

'I don't see Trubshawe enjoying this sort of Spain,' said Bognor. 'More of a Costa sort of person. Pubs with beams; chips with everything; HP sauce.'

'You're probably right,' said his wife. 'You and Trubshawe go back a long way. And you've always been close to his tribe.'

'Trubshawe's tribe,' said Bognor reflectively. 'Bit snobbish to think of the deceased's acolytes in quite that way. But inevitable all the same. I don't think of myself as snobbish but I would agree to "old-fashioned".'

'Same thing,' said Monica crisply and probably accurately. 'Old-fashioned people from your background and with your education are invariably snobbish. It goes with the territory, along with a plummy voice, striped ties and tweeds.'

'I don't do tweeds,' her husband protested.

'I speak figuratively not literally,' said Monica, 'you should know that by now. In a figurative sense you are tweedy man with a plummy voice and striped ties. You are also a snob. You can't help it. It's part of your conditioning. And it's why you're automatically suspicious of the world's Trubshawes – social condescension.'

'Whereas you . . .'

She did not allow him to finish the sentence, performing the task herself.

'Am inherently less prejudiced and more open-minded. Mainly because I'm a woman. We as a sex are like that. Men have closed minds, even though they are open books. A paradox but easy to understand – at least if you're a woman. Men don't read each other.'

'I think we should move,' he said, conscious of the chill and hoping to humour his truculent spouse.

She, on the other hand, was no longer feeling the cold but was warmed up by the combustible nature of her verbosity.

'I almost feel sorry for Trubshawe,' she said. 'He doesn't hold his knife and fork the way you do, so you pick on him and categorize him as a villain. You think he looks and behaves like a crook, ergo he is a crook. QED.'

'Don't be ridiculous,' he said. 'Some of my best friends don't know how to hold their knife and fork but they're not crooks. Trubshawe was a crook, end of story. He had a gang, hired killers, pimps, dealers. He was the ultimate bad hat. He had people killed, for God's sake, women raped. You name it, he did it.'

'His real crime in your eyes was that he came from below the salt,' she said. 'He wore brown shoes with a dark suit, dropped his aitches, wasn't one of "you".'

'I never subscribed to that tosh about brown shoes and grey trousers,' responded Bognor, 'and the one thing Trubshawe never dropped were his aitches. I didn't like him because he was an antisocial bastard and his subordinates and colleagues were the same sorts of shit. I'm in business to eliminate that sort of behaviour and the most effective way of doing that is to get rid of the perpetrators.'

'You just want to get rid of people with bad table manners and no dress sense. Or to be really accurate, people with different manners and a different sense of what to wear from the one you have. Wearing socks with sandals doesn't necessarily make a man a murderer.'

'I wouldn't be so sure of that,' Bognor sniffed, half-joking, half-conceding that perhaps his wife might have a point.

They both shivered involuntarily. Stars twinkled above them. In the shadows of a dark cobbled alley two dogs sniffed each other hopefully; a corrugated metal shutter rattled down to obscure a shop window. A Vespa farted. Sir Simon and Lady Bognor pushed back their plastic chairs which rasped on the ground. Man and wife stood ready for the next round.

'Becoming old makes a man seem reactionary,' he said, 'it doesn't mean that he *is* fuddy-duddy or old-fashioned. He just seems like it to those younger than himself.'

'And maybe to those who know him best.'

They thought about this in silence. Their marriage was a long one now, childless and sometimes compartmentalized, but by and large successful. It was true that she knew him better than anyone and the reverse was true, too, though her husband's knowledge of her was less obvious to those outside their long, close and, in its strange way, loving relationship. He knew that he was snobbish even though he tried not to let the fact rule his life. She knew even better than he did, but she also recognized that he tried to sublimate the feeling. After most of their adult life together they recognized each other's shortcomings, had even come to cherish them, much as, despite everything, they cherished each other.

EIGHT

Bognor ordered two glasses of cava from the Polish girl with the pink-streaked hair. The wine was a crisp, dry Summarocca from south-west of Barcelona. The girl was a crisp, dry PhD student from the University of Cracow. Sir Simon sampled the former languidly and smiled approvingly at the latter. He fancied himself as a connoisseur of wine and women, though he was circumspect about both. He did not wish to seem snobbish or pretentious about the booze. Let alone drunk. Nor too interested in sex. A studied indifference on both counts played well at home. Monica was both suspicious and censorious of anything else. He had learned to appear nonchalant.

'Changed, hasn't it?' she ventured, when the wine came.

'Madrid?' he countered, trying not to sound defensive. He suspected she meant something quite different.

She did.

'Life,' she said. 'I meant that life has changed. Madrid, too, but not as fundamentally. And Madrid has improved even while the basics are still there. She's sexier, more stylish, but deep down there's still something much more elemental than cold-blooded northern Europeans can do. At least in public. But I'm not so sure about life. Seems to me it's nastier and more brutish than it used to be.'

'Not shorter though,' said Bognor. 'A generation ago, we'd be dead.' He smiled but inwardly cringed. He wasn't convinced he was in the mood for a serious discussion about life. Jet lag, booze, age, excitement – all conspired to put him in the mood for more ephemeral natter.

Monica, however, had the bit between her teeth.

'Your job for instance,' she said. 'It's not the same as when you started.'

'Of course not,' he agreed. 'I'm in charge now. I write the script. In the old days I did as I was told. By Parkinson.'

'And everyone else.'

'That's a bit harsh.' He stared at the bead in his glass and watched the bubbles rise to the surface before vanishing as mysteriously as they had arrived. The bubbles suddenly seemed like a metaphor for life – coming from nowhere, departing to nowhere and dancing inconsequentially through elusive liquid in the interim. 'I like to think I called a few shots,' he protested, 'even when I was wet behind the ears.'

'In your dreams,' said his wife, smiling at her glass. 'You've always been a pushover. Especially when it comes to the crunch.'

'That's not fair either,' he said. 'I can be pretty bloody steely when the chips are down. I wouldn't mess with me. Especially when the cookie crumbles.'

Lady Bognor laughed and swallowed. 'Darling, I wouldn't have married you if you weren't you,' she said, 'and you've done frightfully well at whatever it is that you do. But don't let's kid ourselves about writing our own scripts. I don't think any of us deliver our own lines, as a matter of fact. And the worst self-delusion is believing that you do. Yet another of God's jokes.'

Bognor was irrationally irritated by this sally, not least because both he and Monica had always been determinedly agnostic. Both of them agreed that in the unlikely event that the Almighty did exist, he was a nasty piece of work with a warped sense of humour.

'Whoever's writing the stuff has given me a gong, a great salary, a fantastic index-linked pension and,' here he smiled at her not entirely convincingly, 'you, my little cauliflower.'

'Don't you "cauliflower" me,' she said. 'I'm being serious. When you started out on your journey through adult life the world was a more gentle, civilized place.'

Simon thought about this for a moment.

'I don't know,' he said. 'There was a veneer of civilization, a gloss of gentility, but it was skin-deep. There were a lot of knives around. Life was a pretty cut-throat business. It was just that chaps felt the need to apologize before placing the stiletto between your ribs. There was a premium on politeness.'

'When did you last sit in on an autopsy?'

Bognor bridled once more.

'I have never in my life attended an autopsy,' he said, 'you know that perfectly well.'

'You wouldn't know one end of a cadaver from another,' she said, 'whereas all the smart young things in your department spend hours in the morgue watching stiffs being dissected. Even Harvey Contractor.'

'Yes,' said Bognor, 'well.'

What his wife said was perfectly true. He would have to think about it. The girl with the pink-streaked hair came and asked them in perfect, though huskily accented, English if they were ready to order yet. Bognor asked for another five minutes and the girl dimpled at him. Monica looked mildly put out.

'You don't have to hang around dead bodies to find out what made them dead,' he said, sounding pompous and not entirely sure whether or not he believed what he was saying.

'You've built an entire career round death,' she said, 'but ultimately you're pathetically squeamish. You don't do blood and guts.'

'I should think bloody well not,' he said, 'blood and guts are for forensics. I'm about cause and effect, not body parts on slabs.'

'Your very first death,' she said, 'that poor colleague of yours who was garrotted with his crucifix in the potato patch at Beaubridge Friary. Did you ever check the body?'

'Of course not,' he said. 'Not my department. We employ people to do that sort of thing: boffins, scientists, doctors, pathologists. Chaps with white coats and rubber gloves. They present their reports and we decide what to do next. That's the way it is.'

'*Was*,' she said, loudly. '*Was*. It isn't like that any longer. Or hadn't you noticed?'

'I don't know what you're talking about.' He did, but he was not in the mood to admit it. Deep down, he acknowledged that everything had suddenly become different. Even Harvey Contractor did autopsies. He had become the last of a breed. A deskbound dinosaur without realizing it.

'You know perfectly well what I'm talking about. If that wretched colleague of yours had been strangled now, the equivalent of you would have been in the morgue or the dissecting room with a white coat, plastic gloves and a surgical mask making a first-hand note of every contusion and weal on the body.'

'Wouldn't have made a blind bit of difference,' he said. 'I'd have got in the way and I wouldn't have known what on earth was going on. Much better to wait for the pathologist's report and then apply one's particular skill to that. I have no skills when it comes to cadavers, as you so quaintly call them. That's a different area of expertise.'

'You're saying the old ways were better?'

He didn't care for his wife when she was in one of these moods. The Polish girl came with chorizo and calamari with crusty bread and olives. The Bognors eyed them thoughtfully.

'If you put it like that, then I suppose so, yes.'

'So,' she said, triumphantly spearing an olive with a toothpick. 'You admit it.'

'Admit what?'

'That there's an old way and a new way of doing things.'

'I didn't say that.'

'You did actually.'

Bognor was about to argue, but thought better of it and took his own olive instead. He used his fingers and not a toothpick.

'I simply don't see the point,' he said, very deliberately, 'of crashing in where angels fear to tread, if you follow my drift. Bones and hacksaws just aren't my thing. I do motivation, trade gaps, political intrigue, zeitgeists, grown-up stuff.'

'Meaning pathology is for other ranks?'

'I didn't say that. I wish you'd stop putting words into my mouth.' He put a ring of calamari into his mouth instead of Monica's words, chewed and took a sip of wine. 'I simply don't understand this modern obsession with gory detail. I don't need to examine the body to know that someone's dead. And if it's a question of "how", then I rely on the expert. I do "why". With the greatest respect to the Patricia Cornwells of this world, they can't do that.'

'That's not what most people think.'

'I don't give a flying whatsit for what most people think. I'm not interested in most people. I'm interested in right and wrong, the truth, eternal verities. "Most people", as you put it, aren't interested in concepts like that.'

'You don't like "most people", do you?'

'I'm indifferent to "most people",' he said, 'and, in a sense, I'm paid to be just that. I despise highly paid executives who hide behind majorities and committees. I'm not a great believer in popular opinion, best-sellers, fashion and all that garbage. Leaders are paid to lead and that means being decisive and, if necessary, unpopular. Only a fool fails to listen to advice, but only a fool always acts on it.'

'Max said to me the other day that the crime and thriller market is dominated by "serial killer novels, American forensics and the exceptionally gruesome".'

'You know my opinion of Max,' said Bognor. Max had been a contemporary of Monica's at the Courtauld but had decided there was no money in the history of art and its appurtenances. He had started his own publishing house specializing in British editions of American best-sellers. He drove a Porsche, had a mews house in Belgravia and was, as they put it, unmarried. Bognor did not think much of him on a number of accounts. 'In any case, Max deals in fiction. I do real life.'

She laughed. 'You call it real life but you never sit in on autopsies or get your hands dirty doing menial work. Home or away.'

He chewed chorizo. It was fatty and flavoursome. Bad for him. Which he approved of.

'I told you. I'm paid to think. I'm going to have hake with a green sauce and a red Ribiero. What about you? I'm not in the mood for white.'

She said she'd like the rabbit which came with a Portuguese sounding sauce involving clams and said she was feeling reddish too.

'Fiction mirrors life,' she said. 'If it's not realistic, it's no good.'

He snorted derisively. 'Fiction is fiction. If it just mirrors real life then it's pointless. It has to be a work of imagination. As such it's artificial. It can't possibly just echo reality. If it does that it ceases to be fiction. Otherwise why write novels or read them, come to that?'

'Max publishes a lot of true crime,' said Monica. She was on the defensive now. She always was when it came to Max.

'Oh God,' said Bognor, running a hand through his thinning hair, 'true crime books. Please spare me. I can think of nothing sadder. I suppose it pays for the Porsche but that's it.'

They ate in silence. The Polish girl removed plates and brought new ones. Then hake covered in green sauce. The rabbit had a plump, white, domesticated appearance. And a bottle. The red wine was dense and full of tannin.

'You're just an old cosy,' said Monica. 'An elderly dog with its hair falling out; a tartan rug for geriatrics to put over their knees; a Morris Minor estate with wooden beams like a Tudorbethan estate house. An old cosy.'

'I am *not* an old cosy,' he said irritably, discovering a bone in his fish and reflecting that if he were seriously rich he'd employ a man to remove such hazards. He could iron his morning paper while he was about it. '"Cosy" is a pejorative word invented by unimaginative writers of so-called "hard-boiled" fiction, mainly American, to denigrate their competitors, mainly British. To describe something or someone as "cosy" is evidence of an inferiority complex. It means you find thought difficult so you resort to violence and abuse.'

'No need to get overexcited,' she said, 'it's bad for your blood pressure.'

'I hate these silly oversimplified classifications,' he said. '"Cosy" doesn't mean what it's supposed to mean. It's just a term of abuse. Ageist as well. No one under about forty is ever described as "cosy". You have to be a pensioner to be cosy.'

Monica chewed thoughtfully on her rabbit.

'I'm not so sure,' she said, at last. 'I think "cosy" is a perfectly good word for you. You're warm, reliable, unthreatening. Everyone feels comfortable with you.'

'On the contrary,' said Bognor, 'I may seem "cosy". I might appear "cosy". But actually I'm where it's at. I'm state-of-the-art. I'm cutting edge.'

His wife continued to chew rabbit. At last she said, 'That may be the problem. Many experts, you included, confuse "cosiness" with "incompetence". That's the mistake. I know that you're both cosy *and* cutting edge. Very dangerous, rather sexy and possibly even unique.'

Bognor looked at his green-covered fish and mused on this intriguing and novel conceit.

'Cosy *and* cutting edge,' he said, at last. 'I rather like that. Cosy *and* cutting edge. Hmmm . . .'

NINE

Next morning, Bognor asked Harvey Contractor about Trubshawe's post-mortem examination. In view of the previous night's discussion this was always probable, as was the note of censoriousness in Sir Simon's voice. Nasty piece of work though he undoubtedly was, Trubshawe was still a British citizen and Bognor did not like the idea of a British body being dissected by foreigners, particularly without a single Brit to see fair play. He more or less believed in the European Union but there were limits. And perhaps Monica was right. Perhaps he was too hands-off. Too inclined to wash his hands of the nitty-gritty.

They were in a Guardia limo taking them to a rendezvous in Salamanca. The car was long, sleek, comfortable, bulletproof and only just the right side of stretched. Outside Spain passed by: cheerful, noisy, poorer than them, but not as ill-favoured as once upon a time. Monarchy had been good to its subjects. Today was a rebuke to yesterday's republicanism, though in fairness you could hardly call it democracy. It was a paradox that monarchy should set men free while dictatorship had enslaved them. Franco more monarchical than Juan Carlos? Discuss. The King less of a king than the caudillo? Mmmm.

'I take it that in a case such as this you'd normally sit in on the post-mortem.'

'Might,' said Contractor, who was drinking a very stiff black coffee and frowning over the main leader in *El Pais*. The limo had a minibar and a coffee machine. This was the new Spain. 'Might not,' he said. 'Depends.'

'On what?' Bognor was irritable. Last night's conversation still rankled, he was mildly hungover and, despite appearances which he attempted to maintain, his Spanish was not up to the morning paper. He could do menus but not leaders.

'Depends,' repeated Contractor, eyes furrowed, still engrossed. 'On what?' Bognor was at his most snappish. 'Decisions must depend on something concrete. Otherwise they're like hanging participles or, um, flying buttresses.'

'Circumstances,' said Contractor. 'Circumstances dictate dependence.'

'Meaning?'

With extreme reluctance Constructor raised his gaze from the *El Pais* editorial.

'Meaning that if I think my attendance at an autopsy is going to help me solve a case then I will attend. If not, not. On balance, I take the view that gratuitous butchery is a cheap thrill and better left to the specialists. That's not always the case but usually so. If I think I can bring an expert but essentially unqualified eye to the proceedings then, yes, reluctantly, I'll be an interested spectator. But most of the time I don't see the point. Some people are more ghoulish.'

'Quite,' said Bognor. '"Autopsy". "Ghoulish". Good words, both. I must remember them.'

Contractor made as if to return to *El Pais*, but his boss reckoned he had him on the run.

'I've heard it said that I'm old-fashioned,' said Bognor, trying not to sound peevish and, not to put too fine a point on it, old-fashioned, 'is that what you think?'

Contractor sighed.

'Of course,' he said, 'it's obvious.'

'And pejorative?'

'Not necessarily,' said Contractor. 'We're not ageists here. But age dictates behaviour and you act your age. We all do. Fact of life. Nothing wrong with it. Nothing particularly right. You're approaching retirement age and your attitudes and behaviour reflect it. I'm a tyro, just embarking on my career. I act the part too.'

The traffic was moving slowly, not quite gridlocked or jammed but moving at little above walking pace. There were roadworks. A man was drilling a hole in the road. There was noise and dust everywhere, and a small group of onlookers were watching the man at work. Bognor felt at home.

'Very enlightened,' he said drily.

'Just realistic,' said Contractor, turning a page. 'No point pretending to be something you aren't.'

'Quite.'

Bognor fell to contemplating mushrooms and toadstools. He had been doing some research before leaving London, had summoned up papers, checked the Internet, and was as up to speed as was reasonable for a layman. Fungi were not a speciality but then he was a generalist. That was what the fuss was about. It was why he was feeling threatened.

'Mushrooms,' he said to himself as he contemplated stalled Spanish traffic. 'Best on toast. Purchased from the supermarket. Preferably grilled. Risk therefore nil.'

Contractor had reached the sports pages and was reading about last night's match at the Noo Camp between Barca and Valencia. He did not appreciate being interrupted, especially when the question was a trivial query about mushrooms.

'I gather forensics think it was one of the *Amanita*,' said Bognor portentously, '*Phalloides, virosa* or *verna*.'

'Unlikely, I'd say,' offered Contractor. 'Death Cap, Destroying Angel and Spring *Amanita* produce vomiting and diarrhoea after about six hours and then there's a remission period of around forty-eight hours before the liver packs up. But our man Trubshawe felt ill almost immediately and seems to have died within the hour. That doesn't sound like an *Amanita* to me.' Valencia had won with a penalty in extra time. It sounded like a good game.

'So, oh wise one, what do you think?'

Contractor abandoned the paper with a sigh.

'I'm only guessing but I'd hazard *Coprinus atramentarius*. The common ink cap. Especially as Trubshawe was a bit of a boozer. I'd guess that the others ate *Coprinus comatus*. Common ink cap and shaggy ink cap to the layman.' Bognor felt patronized. 'Very difficult to tell apart but *comatus*, the shaggy one, is delicious whereas *atramentarius*, the common one is lethal. Especially with booze. Violent reactions within ten minutes.'

'Death?'

They had reached some sort of dual carriageway and picked up speed, passing blue-smoke-belching trucks on the inside lane.

'Not usually,' said Contractor. 'In fact, the *Amanitas* are generally deadlier. The ink cap produces unpleasant symptoms.

You go very red in the face, though from what I've learned about our friend Trubshawe he couldn't have gone more puce than usual – a combination of foul temper and high living. The heart rate increases dramatically, you get blisteringly unpleasant chest pains and headaches. It's all down to coprine which is a mixture of glutamine and cyclopropanine. Used to be confused with disulfiram which is the main ingredient in Antabuse, the anti-alcohism drug. We now know that nothing could be further from the truth and the two things have a completely different formulation. All the same, alcohol remains the key. If you take a drink on a cold day you should watch out for the common ink cap. Same goes for the club-footed funnel cap or *Clitocybe clavipes*, which is sometimes said to be edible but makes you sick and brings you out in spots if you have a tincture at the same time. But I think club-foot is an innocent party in this case.'

'But death?' insisted his boss, reluctantly impressed by this all too typical display of knowledge unlightly worn. 'Isn't that a bit extreme?'

Contractor appeared to think, frowning at yet another belching juggernaut exceeding the speed limit on the inside lane.

'Not with sufficient booze. Particularly if the victim had a dicky heart and/or high blood pressure. Which Trubshawe did. He was on all sorts of medication. Beta-blockers mainly.'

'How do you know that?'

'I make it my business.' Contractor stared longingly at the sports report on his lap. He yearned to return to it but judged such a tactic premature.

'I see,' said Bognor. 'I didn't realize that mycology was part of the semiotics course at the University of Wessex.'

Contractor's degree, like so many new qualifications, meant something and nothing at one and the same time. What exactly it meant was another matter. Different things to different people, reckoned Bognor. It was like *Alice's Adventures in Wonderland*: it meant whatever you wanted it to mean. That was the meaning of meaning nowadays. Being a degree-holder in semiotics, he seldom said quite what he meant and if his message was difficult to understand that suited him. It might have encompassed mycology but then again it might not. It was immaterial anyway.

Contractor was irritatingly well read, to the point of almost being a genuine post-Renaissance man. A latter-day polymath, certainly. Sir Simon liked to think of himself as more of a tortoise than a hare. He might have known comparatively little but, by God, he knew a lot about it.

This time Contractor did pick the newspaper off his lap. He made a meal of studying it thoughtfully and ignoring Sir Simon's cheap jibe. Bognor had been at Oxford and read Modern History, which he seemed to think was an indication of higher intelligence and greater learning. As far as Contractor was concerned both Oxford and so-called 'modern' history went out with the Ark. Semiotics at Wessex was where it was at. And if mycology came under the general umbrella of semiotics, then so be it.

The only sound in the limo was the ticking of the clock. Contractor read football; Bognor thought mushrooms. He supposed the mushrooms didn't really matter. They were the instrument of death. Of that there seemed no doubt, but it was a bit like attaching undue importance to the dagger in the library or the lead-piping in the conservatory. It was the why, rather than the how, which lay at the root of the problem. That was essentially Bognor's line of thought. On the other hand, he was aware that there could be clues in the contents of Trubshawe's stomach, what had been cooked for lunch and who prepared the dishes. Even if the murderer was not a top-whack mycologist they would have needed a good working knowledge of fungi, and Bognor knew enough about mushrooms, toadstools and their ilk to understand that it was a subject shot through with ambiguities and nuances. The difference between lethal and innocent was not even skin-deep. Even an expert could easily be fooled by the wrong sort of gills or an apparently innocuous fruit body.

They were skirting the walled city of Avila whence came, Bognor recalled albeit dimly, Saint Teresa. He had never been there and all he knew about the place was that it had a famous wall and a famous saint. Something told him that Harvey Contractor would be able to provide chapter and verse on the walls and the saint, as well as providing much extra information. This might or might not derive from the semiotics course at the University of Wessex but he was not going to tempt

although that would have been misleading. On the other hand, it was certainly full of apprehension and mutual worry, if not actual distrust.

'Forget the staff for a moment,' said Bognor, feeling, rightly or wrongly that he was in the driving seat. 'Talk me through the volunteers. Spanish first.'

The young policeman smiled sadly as if to say that the funny foreigner was barking up completely the wrong tree, while accepting that it was only polite for him to do as he was asked since Bognor was not only his senior but also a guest in his own country. Such courtesies would not necessarily have applied had the circumstances been reversed and Harvey Contractor was having to deal with Admiral Picasso.

'Leonel, Belen, Eduardo and Lola,' said the *teniente*. 'We have their second names but they are, in a sense, immaterial. The late Trubshawe would have known them only by their first, given, Christian names.'

'Aha,' said Bognor, knowing as he said it that it was the sort of verbal tic that meant nothing while, he hoped, signifying all. The throat-clearing noise sounded portentous and omniscient, but it didn't fool him and it almost certainly didn't fool anyone else either. 'And the Anglos,' he continued, following vacuity with substance. Or intending to.

'The deceased,' said Azuela, 'plus Tracey, George and Camilla. From our point of view these are more interesting, but we can offer you provisional profiles of the whole lot if you'd like.'

'I would,' said Bognor. He accepted a thick black coffee which he would have called a double espresso back home, regarded it bleakly, found a seat and settled back. 'Shoot,' he said.

There was a large flat screen along the wall controlled by a keyboard linked to a laptop. The *teniente* frowned at it, stabbed at a button or two and produced a close-up, head and shoulders shot of a dark, bearded bloke in a New York Yankees baseball cap and open-necked denim shirt.

'Leonel,' he said, 'sales and marketing director of a big pet food company with head office on the outskirts of Seville. Thirty-five years old. MBA from the Opus Dei University in

Oviedo. Keen on football. Married. Two sons. Plays bass guitar. Fan of Johnny Cash. Moderately good English but low on colloquialism and conversational skills. Model pupil. Inclined to be over-orthodox and dull. Reasonably devout Christian of Roman Catholic persuasion.' He paused. 'Enough?'

Bognor nodded. 'Enough,' he said. 'Next please.'

'Belen,' said Azuela as a picture of a svelte thirty-something with big brown eyes, high cheekbones and a go-yonder expression appeared on screen.

'Strange name,' said Bognor. 'Common?'

'Not especially. It means Bethlehem in Spanish. Birthplace of Christ. Spain is no longer as religious as she once was but old habits die, as you would say, hard.'

Bognor said he was familiar with the Gospels but that it was not British to call people after place names from the bible. The Spaniards glanced at one and another but said nothing. Contractor shifted uneasily in his chair, wondering, as he did, whether anyone ever shifted easily or if it was only ever something one did with difficulty. Clichés were strange birds. Why did errors, for example, always glare? Who ever heard of a woman with low cheekbones?

'Belen is the export manager of a small boutique hotel chain with its headquarters in Madrid. She is thirty-eight, lives with a long-term partner in an apartment on the outskirts of the city; works out twice a week at her neighbourhood gym, eats very carefully and barely drinks. English is serviceable but needs to become more colloquial and chatty, as a lot of her business is with the UK and Scandinavian countries where English is the preferred language of communication.'

Bognor looked thoughtfully at the tips of his fingers. They were quite clean.

'Eduardo,' continued the *teniente*, conjuring up a picture of a clean-shaven, square-jawed, blue-eyed, mildly Opus Dei-looking character with piercing blue eyes and an uncompromising expression.

Bognor always thought of shiny black suits and a sprinkling of dandruff when referring to Opus Dei. It was difficult, pace Brown, Dan, to say for sure what an 'Opus Dei character' looked like, since the famous instrument of self-flagellation lay beneath the shirt (hair or otherwise) and well out of sight. He thought of smug suffering, conscientious condescension and a sallow complexion – an indefinable air of 'this is going to hurt me more than you'. He did not much care for Opus Dei. The *teniente* continued, 'Started his own shipping company a few years ago and specializes in dates from North Africa, and other exotic fruits. He is opening up deals with the new European countries such as Romania, Bulgaria and the Baltic states. Married, two children. Great fan of Paco Peña; plays classical and flamenco guitar. Paying for himself which is unusual. Most people on these courses are paid for by the bigger companies who employ them. Eduardo employs himself.'

Bognor nodded once more.

'And Lola,' he said, the words hovering between a question and a command.

Azuela tapped away at his keyboard and a woman's head and shoulders appeared. She looked predictably Lola-ish. Brunette, bee-sting lips, high cheekbones, almond eyes. She had all the attributes of the archetypal movie star, except that she was dressed as a nun.

'Nun?' asked Bognor fatuously. It seemed an unlikely cover.

'Yes,' said Azuela. 'What I believe you would call a Poor Clare – a female Franciscan.'

'Why?' he asked, surprised.

'She is –' said Azuela, frowning, 'how you would say? – an "upwardly mobile nun". Tipped for the top. She is likely to be sent to North America or Britain as boss of a big convent. They would like her to be a media personality; make Catholicism popular.'

'I'm sure she'd be brilliant,' said Bognor, 'but at the moment she doesn't have enough command of the vernacular to do battle with the likes of Jeremy Paxman.'

'*Que?*' said the policeman, not understanding.

Bognor did not feel up to explaining and let the remark pass.

'Do you have a lot of media-nuns in Spain?' he asked, fatuously.

Azuela shrugged. 'Until recently the church was very powerful in our country,' he said. 'Now it is less so, but the Church, she is fighting back. The best priests of both sexes are having media training. They attend media courses at the university, here and abroad. They are becoming, as you would say, "sassy". Sister Lola is just that. She is already one sassy nun. She dances the Charleston; she cooks *huevos revoltas*; she is a fan of Wayne Rooney. She says she is "a child of the times". One day she will be Mother Teresa, only Mother Lola will have sex appeal.' Azuela gazed at the nun's image. He was obviously smitten.

Bognor wondered if he might follow suit. He knew that fantasizing about sex with women in uniforms was a stereotypical male chauvinist dream. It implied a dislike of the opposite sex – a degree of rape. Thinking of himself as a decently liberated feminist he rejected that sort of image-making, but he still had to acknowledge that he possessed some unpleasantly blokeish testosterone-fuelled desires. Bedding a sexy nun came into that category. Bit of a worry.

'Pet food executive; boutique hotelier; self-employed greengrocer; Poor Clare. Sounds like an interesting job lot. Typical would you say?' He raised an eyebrow towards the room in general and got nothing back. 'Maybe there's never such a thing as "typical",' he said. He took a small black notebook out of his briefcase and jotted down some words, considered them for a moment and then, rather ostentatiously, returned his fountain pen to his inside jacket pocket.

'Let's look at the others,' he said. 'The Anglos. Principal suspects; discuss, compare, contrast . . .'

ELEVEN

Everyone seemed to be smoking. The blue, acrid atmosphere reminded Bognor of the days of his youth when even the London Underground in the early morning was a mist of exhaled cigarette fumes and the floors were deep in butts. Part of him felt almost wistfully nostalgic, and he found himself craving one of the cheroots that a bossy superannuated doctor from an insurance company had ordered him to cut out on pain of massive financial recriminations. He resented having his habits determined by invisible spivs in faraway office blocks of which he knew nothing, and had half a mind to beg a flaky foul-smelling fag from one of the local policemen. He thought better of it, scared, though he would never admit it, of played-out sawbones from insurance companies, but – much more – of Lady Bognor, who would be bound to find out even though he never quite knew how.

'The late and unlamented Trubshawe,' said Bognor. 'We'll come to him later, when we've dealt with the quick as opposed to the dead. That means Tracey, George and Camilla. Take it away, *Teniente*.'

And he leaned back in his chair and waited.

'Face value,' said Azuela slowly. 'Face value is how you say it in English and that is what these people have been taken at. The village accept what they are told by the Anglos. No checks. No investigation. Tracey says she is called Tracey and gives details, and she is believed.' He shrugged and spread his hands as if washing himself of any responsibility for Tracey's true identity.

'Essex girl,' said Azuela. His command of vernacular English and its underlying assumptions and conventions was remarkable. When he said that Tracey was an Essex girl he spoke a truth at which most of his fellow countrymen could only guess. Her picture came up on the screen and provoked an instant frisson of recognition in the head of SIDBOT. She absolutely had to be called Tracey; she absolutely had to be an Essex girl; you saw her on a regular basis at the supermarket checkout or at the bar of any nightclub from Southend to Walthamstow. She was straight from central casting, and although Bognor felt guilty as he voiced the thought to himself, she was one of a kind, a type not a character.

Yet, even as he formed this disobliging opinion, he heard little birds whispering. They quickly formed a dawn chorus of dissent. He shouldn't jump to conclusions, they warned, shouldn't be so swayed by appearances, let alone by a name. It was not her fault that she was called Tracey and looked like it.

Bognor had been in the game long enough to know that thinking things were what they seemed was the surest path to copper's ruin. There was always pressure to deliver an instant result. Public opinion preferred speedy resolutions and public opinion was more concerned with haste than with truth. That, at least, was the perception. And it was easy to go for the obvious.

'What do you think?' he asked, sweeping the room with a stare that encompassed the whole Spanish team, though since Azuela was their spokesman he was really asking the question of just the one person. It was, indeed, he who answered, though he was delivering a majority, if not a unanimous, verdict.

'We,' he said, 'do not believe that Tracey killed Trubshawe. Our reasons for thinking she is innocent are basically because she is relatively young. She herself says she is thirty-one years old and we have no reason to believe that she is not telling the truth. She lives with her parents in Colchester in the south-east of England. They are called Percy and Edna. Tracey is unmarried and has a five-year-old son called David and a three-year-old daughter called Tiger-Lily. She is not in touch with the father or fathers. She has trained as a hairdresser and as a florist, and works occasionally at both, usually in the Colchester area, although she has been to London and has worked there. She has not been to Spain before.'

'Trubshawe was originally an Essex boy,' said Bognor.

'This is true,' said Azuela. 'We believe that he owned garages around the Southend and Westcliff-on-Sea areas. Specializing in Jaguar motor cars. We do not believe there is any connection between him and Tracey or her parents.'

'Do we know anything about the parents?' Bognor wanted to know, and the *teniente* made a studied performance of consulting his notes before answering. 'The father, Percy,' he said, at length, 'he is a heavy smoker and suffers from emphysema. Both he and his wife, whose name is Edna, were in what you call "service". He was a butler and chauffeur while she cooked and performed housework. They are now retired or unemployed.'

'Hmmm.' Bognor glanced at Harvey Contractor who was making notes in an officious, not to say flamboyant manner that was clearly designed to impress, though it did not fool Bognor himself. His assistant gave him what could only be described as a subliminal wink. No one else noticed and the gesture was so understated that it would have been easily deniable. But it was there nonetheless – the product of an almost osmotic understanding – the sort of tacit relationship that characterizes a long marriage. Like it or not, thought Bognor, he and Contractor were in bed together.

'Are we saying . . .' Bognor felt the need to spell out Spanish beliefs, 'Is it your contention that Tracey is not a prime suspect?'

Azuela shook his head.

'We are not in a position to rule anyone out,' he said, 'but it is our belief that Tracey is too, how would you say, "obvious". Capable of all sorts of small deceptions and deceits, but not, we believe, of killing someone.' He shrugged and splayed his fingers. 'We are not ruling her out. We just do not believe she is a natural born killer.'

'OK,' said Bognor. 'So you're putting Tracey on hold for now. What about the other Anglos?'

'George,' said Azuela, 'is a more likely suspect. He also came from Essex. A town called Braintree. He played cricket for a club there and was involved with used cars. He does not give the impression of being an honest person.'

'But crooked?'

Once again the *teniente* shrugged. 'We know nothing to prove that, but he gives the impression of not telling the truth. Or, as you have it, of being economical with it.'

Once again Bognor was impressed with his grasp of idiom. 'We don't believe that George is his real name. Perhaps this is not important. He seems to have several identities; several passports – nationalities, even. When his room was searched our people found an Irish document in the name of Oliver O'Flaherty. The photograph was of George but the person was not him. Oliver is described as a butcher. The address is in County Limerick. We checked with colleagues in the Irish Republic. There is no such place.'

'You think this is important?'

Azuela did buck-passing incomprehension with an aplomb that impressed even Bognor, who was exposed to the practice on a regular daily business in his dealings with government ministers. Nobody passed buck quite like a top-line British politician. In Bognor's experience they yielded to no one when it came to blaming other people for their mistakes. Even so, they could get some useful tips from at least one Spanish policeman.

'There were some other unexpected items in George's room. A copy of *Mein Kampf* by Adolf Hitler. We found one also in Mr Trubshawe's room. Also bottles of *Heil Hitler Rotwein*.'

'Of what?!' Bognor was scandalized, both morally and oenologically.

'*Heil Hitler Rotwein*,' repeated Azuela.

'Good grief,' exclaimed Bognor. '*Appellation contrôlée*? Or does it come from Algeria in a tanker?'

He was becoming perplexed by this peculiar cosmopolitanism. He wondered if Jimmy Trubshawe had an Irish alias like George. He couldn't imagine Trubshawe in an Irish persona, but these days, he supposed, Irishmen were no longer Irish in the accepted sense, but had become homogenized so that they might as well be English or even, well, Spanish.

'Whatever else,' said the *teniente*, '*Hitler Rotwein* is not German.'

'Any more than George was English.'

Silence fell like a cliché on tin ears. Nothing was what it seemed. *Appellations* were simply not *contrôlée*. The English were Irish. A man was dead because he liked mushrooms. Nothing made sense any more.

'So,' said Bognor after a slightly desperate silence, 'two Anglo's down and one to go. Tracey, who seems to have been a Tracey in every conceivable respect, and George, who appears not to have been George with any consistency. One who was as consistent as a stick of rock and another who was as elusive as a, er, blast of dry ice in a pantomime. Not wishing,' he smiled, 'to fall into such cliché traps as "will o'the wisp" or,' and he glanced meaningfully at the massed smokers, '"the exhalation of a half-spent cigarette".' The remark seemed to go over the collective head, as transitory in its way as the pantomimic dry ice.

Another pause, as dodgy as the last, ensued, before Sir Simon appeared to snap a chapter shut and open a new one. 'So,' he said, 'Camilla. Is she a Camilla or is she not? Does she conform to the example of Tracey or of George? Is she a Duchess of Cornwall? Is she an Essex girl? Discuss. Compare and contrast. Enlighten us Señor Azuela.'

The *teniente* shuffled his papers again, refocused, turned knobs, pressed buttons and produced an almost in focus head and shoulders shot of a forty-something blonde with bling. She had a slightly peeling bleached complexion, a gash of scarlet lipstick and a 'been there, done that' expression.

'Australian,' said Azuela. 'Claims to run a boutique bed-and-breakfast in a resort called Byron Bay somewhere in New South Wales, north of Sydney.'

'I know it,' said Bognor. 'Used to be a marginally hippy sort of a place. Beads and sandals and Bob Dylan. Alternative. Or as alternative as you're ever likely to get in the Antipodes. Which is to say pretty mainstream by British standards. My sense is that Australians don't do alternative.'

Azuela looked puzzled.

'"Alternative"?' he repeated. '"Antipodes"?'

Bognor realized he had struck blank.

'Australians,' he explained, 'have a reputation in Britain for being, how shall I put it, a little uncouth. Behind the times. Not up to speed. Camilla might have seemed bohemian in Australia but in Britain she probably wouldn't have been thought unusual. We have a different sense of what is conventional and what is not. What is your view?'

'Camilla has a tattoo of a butterfly above her right shoulder-blade.'

'Tattoos . . .' said Bognor, without much first-hand knowledge since Monica, Lady Bognor, was resolutely un-tattooed – it was true that she came from a pre-tattoo generation, but even if she had been born twenty or thirty years later she would, Bognor felt sure, have remained unmarked by needles of any kind – 'Tattoos,' he continued ruminatively, 'are commonplace among young to youngish women in the UK. Any female of under, say, thirty is likely to be quite extensively marked in this way. It carries no stigma. In the old days tattooing used to be a hallmark of a certain sort of British male. Usually naval and military. The Sergeants' mess was full of heavily tattooed hairy forearms. Any naval petty officer worth his salt would have tattoos all over himself. Nowadays most young women have a tattoo or two. Usually small and discreet and invisible, save in a state of undress.' He paused and seemed to think for a while. 'Or so I'm told,' he said.

At length he asked, 'How old would you say Camilla was?'

The *teniente* smiled. 'She and her passport both say thirty-five,' he said, 'but we feel they are both, as you would say in your country, being economical with the truth.'

'That's a very sophisticated use of idiom,' said Bognor, 'particularly for one who has problems with "Antipodes" and "alternative". But never mind. You're suggesting that Camilla is older than she claimed?'

'We believe that the woman claiming to be Camilla is approximately forty-five years old. She does seem to be based in the resort area of Byron Bay, Australia, to which she emigrated from the United Kingdom some years previously.'

Bognor inspected his fingertips, which were mildly chipped and grubby in the fashion of privately educated Englishmen of his generation. It was not, he reflected, a crime to lie about your age. And, if female, was easily explained as the product of vanity.

'And she is supposed to have emigrated from the United Kingdom,' he repeated, playing for time. 'Can we be more precise?'

'She claims,' said the *teniente*, pausing for effect, 'to have come from Essex.'

TWELVE

'One middle-aged gent who has a number of aliases, most of them dodgy,' said Bognor. 'One archetypal Essex girl and one Essex girl transplanted to Oz. That's your Anglos.'

He and Contractor were conducting a 'sitrep' in a small room next to the larger smoke-filled incident room. They had this all to themselves and spoke in fast-moving English with relative indiscretion. If they were bugged they didn't care. Everyone else was foreign, which meant that they were basically un-English and didn't therefore count. Some of Bognor's best friends were foreign but that didn't stop them being foreign. He would never have been caught using a phrase such as 'lesser breeds without the law', but that didn't prevent him from feeling basic contempt for people who were not as he was. Some people didn't like this side of him, but he maintained that it was better to be honest and that it never interfered with his sense of fair play.

He sighed.

'The most obvious common denominator seems to be an element of secrecy or deception,' he said. 'If you want to take part in this exercise you either maintain relative silence or you're economical with the truth. I shall say as little as possible and what I do say will almost certainly not be the truth, the whole truth, let alone nothing but the truth. What do you think?'

Contractor sighed back. The sound was infectious as was the accompanying and undeniably Iberian gesture of frustration that accompanied it.

Neither of them thought anything much.

'Time to stop theorizing,' said Contractor. 'Time to get to the coalface.'

'Yes,' Bognor agreed. It would be quite like old times. He enjoyed the coalface, even though it was years since he had actually been there. He remembered the friary at Beaubridge;

sundry dog breeders in and around Crufts; the Stately Home Industry; a freezing Toronto and the mysterious business with Gentlemen's Relish; the publishing industry and death involving Big Books plc; Fleet Street and death on the Samuel Pepys Column; a foray to middle England at the height of Mrs Thatcher's rule. It all added up to a formidable list of battle honours and he was proud of his regimental colours; yet even he was forced to concede that these front-line exploits belonged to the dim and distant when he had been, relatively speaking, a fresh-faced boy. Now he was long in tooth and short in wind.

'Part of the problem,' he said, musing, 'is that I feel absolutely nothing in the way of regret about Jimmy Trubshawe. He was a thoroughly nasty piece of work and, as far as I'm concerned, if he choked to death on a nasty mushroom then it serves him right.'

'Hmmm,' said his sidekick. This was code for dissent. Contractor, being a naturally cold fish, seldom if ever allowed any personal feelings to interfere with his work. He didn't have much in the way of personal feelings anyway. He did, however, have a highly developed sense of justice, of what was right and wrong, and, above all, of what his job involved and how to do it properly. He was a professional. Cold, but professional. Bognor was the opposite. Prone to amateurism, but warm with a heart of gold. As they said. Which they did. Frequently.

'It'll be quite like the old days,' he said, rubbing his hands together.

'Not really,' said Contractor, applying cold water as he did so frequently, and thinking, evidently, that it was part of his job. 'You'll have me rather than your tiresome sounding old boss Parkinson as your only link with the outside world. You'll have a state-of-the-art Nokia phone to connect you with me and anyone else you choose to call. There'll be no need to ferret around looking for the nearest public phone box and pressing button "A" and button "B". We're in the twenty-first century now.'

'How did you know about button "A" and button "B" in public phone boxes?' asked Bognor. 'They were before you were born.'

'Read about them in books,' said Contractor. 'Crime novels mostly. Lots of interesting period detail in crime novels. Drivel otherwise. Oliver James says so.'

'Who is he?'

'Media-savvy shrink.' Contractor smiled with a smug-bastard, condescending 'I've forgotten more than you'll ever know' sort of expression. 'Not that he writes any sense except when it comes to crime fiction.'

Bognor wasn't going to argue the toss when it came to whodunnits, even though he disagreed quite profoundly.

'You'll be here on the other end of my mobile,' he said. 'Lady Bognor likewise. And you'll liaise with our friends here and with HQ in London.'

'Yup,' said Contractor.

'The common denominator among the Anglos seems to be Essex,' said Bognor. 'Do you think that's significant?'

'I'm not convinced the murderer is one of the three Anglos,' said Contractor, 'and my sense of Essex is that it's a state of mind not a geographical entity. Thatcher was the personification of Essex, but she was a Lincolnshire lass with a constituency in North London and a home in Chelsea. Like I said "state of mind", not a place in the accepted sense. And you could argue that England as we knew it has been engulfed by Essex as we knew it. Thus Trubshawe, whoever he may have been. Doesn't matter whether he was living in Leytonstone, Southend or the Costa d'Essex, he possessed a sort of spiv, *garagiste* mentality which has become endemic.'

Bognor had a strong sense of what was taught at Contractor's old university.

'My real contact is going to be with the Hispanics,' said Bognor.

'That is correct,' said Contractor, sounding like a daytime TV game show host. Probably from Essex in a manner of speaking, if not a strictly factual fashion.

'And it could perfectly well have been one of them,' continued Bognor, musing. 'Lola, for instance. Anyone with a name like that has to be a suspect, wouldn't you agree?'

Not really,' said Contractor. 'I don't think you should judge people by their names. Besides I very much doubt whether Lola is her real name. Most people in the Pueblo seem to be operating under some form of alias.'

Bognor sighed. He seemed to be doing a lot of sighing these days.

'There are certain unassailable facts,' he said. 'The man calling himself Trubshawe was a professional criminal of British origin and specifically from Essex, which in his case was a physical place as well as a state of mind. So he was doubly false, maybe trebly so, if you face the fact that he absconded to the Costa d'Essex, which while technically in Spain had become a sort of Iberian East Anglia with pubs, Man U supporters' clubs, chips with everything, bling, peroxide blondes and the whole paraphernalia of a certain sort of nouveau riche existence.'

'Sounds a rather snobbish perception . . . sir . . . if I may say so.'

'You may not,' said Bognor. 'Old-fashioned possibly, but snobbish very definitely not.'

Contractor smirked. He regarded his boss as old-fashioned *and* snobbish; didn't necessarily think the worse of him for it, but was genuinely perplexed by his inability to admit it.

Bognor, for his part, was not really thinking about such matters but was suffering from an unexpected attack of nerves. He was not essentially a shy person, but he felt as if he were a nervous wallflower at the door of a swinging party at which he would know neither the hosts nor any of the other guests. He had not been at the cutting edge or the coalface or whatever you called it for as long as he could remember. He had worn out many dark pinstripe suit trouser bottoms and eaten a lot of lunch since then; had become a Whitehall mandarin, a long way from the lean machine which, in truth, he had never really been, though he liked to believe that once he approximated to such a condition. He had been a front-line troop once, the sort of second lieutenant who went unthinkingly over the top and perished on the Somme. Not for a long time though, and being thrown back in at the deep end, even of his own volition, and under his own orders, was giving him cold feet.

'I don't have a handgun,' he said, fatuously.

'That would be rather a melodramatic gesture with respect,

sir,' said Contractor. 'Apart from the fact that our Spanish friends would have picked it up first thing. On the other hand, if you were to ask the Admiral or the *Teniente* with your customary tact then I'm quite certain they'd be happy to lend you one. If it made you feel better.'

Bognor felt his subordinate bordered on the insolent but he said nothing. He had vaguely hoped that age and seniority would bring respect, but this appeared not to be the case. Contractor's attitude towards him was not the same as his towards Parkinson. Where once there had been deference now there was familiarity, if not quite contempt. Such was life. *Sic transit*, but not for the better.

He was, he realized, being taken out of his comfort zone. In the most obvious sense he was being removed from the panelled, personally assisted office and the back seat of the chauffeur driven Rover – a discontinued line, now acquired, over his not-quite-dead body, by some Chinese consortium in a deal he and the department had fought tooth and nail to subvert. He would be exposed sans chauffeur, sans secretary, sans everything. Not only that, he was going to behave in a gregarious, life and soul of the party manner, which was emphatically not his style. He was not, God knew, aloof or chilly. He stood his round, played his part, mucked in, enjoyed a joke, was even up to a point, and in a manner of speaking, one of the lads. But at the Pueblo he suspected everyone was required to be the life and soul of the office party. He hated forced jollity and he suspected that this kind of immersion language course relied all too heavily on a jollity that was less than spontaneous. He was not looking forward to it as much as he had been. What had seemed a good idea in London seemed much less so now that he was approaching the front line.

'This is a murder,' he said unnecessarily.

Contractor nodded. 'And the killer or killers is or are still at large,' he said. 'I'd steer clear of mushrooms on toast, if I were you, sir.'

'I think that's a joke in remarkably poor taste,' said Bognor.

Contractor was about to make a further feeble punning gastronomic joke involving toast and taste, but then saw the look on his boss's face and thought better of it. This was serious. So was the boss. And despite the intrinsic absurdity of the situation, the central fact remained true and as stated. They had a corpse on their hands. You may not have liked Trubshawe but he was dead. Murdered. It was a crime and, as yet, a crime unsolved.

'I'm sure it will all work out in the end,' he said, instead of trying further levity. 'And if there's one consolation the murderer, single or plural, can't have escaped. It's a classic closed-room mystery. The killer is still in situ.'

He realized as he said it that the remark would have been better left unspoken. The boss was at risk and recognized the fact. He was reminded of a line in a Sherlock Holmes story by Conan Doyle to the effect that you could forget your dark Satanic Mills, it wasn't the dark narrow alleyways of the big smoke which harboured vice, depravity and sudden death, it was your smiling, bucolic, verdant countryside. That was where crime flourished. It was, perhaps, a clunking truth, but none the less so for being obvious.

There was a sharp tap on the door to which Bognor said, in familiar almost self-confident, English.

'Come!' just as his schoolmasters used to say.

The door opened and the Spanish policeman stood framed in the opening, all stubble, leather jacket and cigarette smoke.

'Your chariot awaits,' he said, with the triumphant air of a foreign language student who has done his prep. 'I will run you down to the plaza so that you may make your rendezvous.'

THIRTEEN

Dolores Calderon was draped around the cab of a state-of-the-art khaki Range Rover. She was talking on a mobile phone and was dressed entirely in black, with tight shiny black leather trousers and a bum-freezer jacket which looked as if it was made from real fur. She wore a black Stetson-style hat on top of her blonde hair, which might have been helped with dye from a bottle; her lips were scarlet and so were her long fingernails, some of which were on the hand she extended to Bognor as he smiled at her diffidently and yet ingratiatingly. On second thoughts he decided, stomach lurching in a disquieting and half-forgotten manner, 'coiled' might have been a better word than 'draped'. There was something snake-like about her and it wasn't just the long leather legs. Even the words 'Dolores Calderon,' which she breathed at him between more raucous instructions into her mobile, were sibilant, almost hissy.

Bognor swore. Silently. It may have been years since he had been out in the field but his experience was that whenever he was away from the security of his own office there was always, sooner or later, a Dolores Calderon. And she always meant trouble.

The phone conversation was obviously more important than him, for it continued despite his presence. La Calderon was shouting, something that, in Bognor's experience, almost all mobile users did without seeming to realize it. She also seemed to be angry, a fact which added to the decibels. Bognor had ample opportunity to examine her charms, which were, he realized to his dismay, definite and considerable. He was not going to be immune from them and despite his age and condition, well, maybe because of his age and condition, he was perfectly capable of making a fool of himself. If that was what she wanted.

The car park was virtually empty. He reckoned it would be

busy in the tourist season, which this wasn't. Dolores Calderon's nostrils flared and her breasts heaved. It was incorrect, he knew, but he always found real fur on a woman disturbingly sexy. Anger too. His stomach lurched in a way that he had almost forgotten. He was old enough to be the woman's father; he had no children and to concede lust for her should have made him feel like a paedophile. He didn't and even more alarmingly felt no guilt. It was all to do with parts of himself ageing at different speeds. Many aspects of the essential Bognor felt way past retirement; others, of which the libido was the most obvious, seemed not to have moved on from the late teens. It was all very disconcerting.

Suddenly she spat out a final phrase which sounded to Bognor like a command wrapped in an expletive and then snapped the mobile shut, tossed it on to the driver's seat, removed her dark glasses and gave Bognor a dazzling smile. She had Cambridge-blue eyes and high cheekbones. Bognor thought she was stunning.

'I'm sorry,' she said, 'the phone call was necessary. Not pleasant but essential. You must be Simon, Mr Trubshawe's replacement. It is good of you to come at such short notice. We are very grateful. The village is a half-hour's drive from here. May I assist with your bags?' And without waiting for a reply she hefted Bognor's ancient leather overnight case and his much newer computer-container and deposited in them in the back of the vehicle. 'Jump in,' she said, 'or should I say "hop"?' Her English was self-conscious and heavily accented.

The car smelt of leather and disinfectant, though his chauffeuse was wearing a strong and expensive-smelling scent.

'We were very sad about the accident to Mr Trubshawe,' she said, changing gear crisply.

'Accident?!' Bognor was unable to suppress the note of surprise in his voice. Then he remembered who he was supposed to be – or more accurately who he was not supposed to be, and said, 'Sad! Yes, very.'

She looked at him sharply. Not, he thought to himself, just a pretty face.

She braked to avoid a man in a beret, on a bicycle, making heavy weather of a hill.

'You believe that Mr Trubshawe's death was not accidental?' she asked.

He was not supposed to know anything about Trubshawe, least of all the circumstances of his death and even less the cause of it. There suddenly flashed before him some words from as pompous internal briefing document he had recently received from a government department, of which he had previously known nothing. It opined, pompously in Bognor's view, that crime was no longer resolved by such outmoded things as 'clues, red herrings and least likely suspects'. It was no longer a question of puzzles but of serendipitous confession. Madness not method, in his own opinion, but the document seemed to believe, as was the way with such pieces of paper, that this in some way represented progress. Dolores Calderon, however, made his antennae bristle. In forensic terms, she seemed to represent all the old-fashioned enigmas: clues, red herrings and least likely suspects. None of which, naturally, had anything to do with sex.

'Absolutely,' he said, nervously, as they swerved past a horse and cart. He thought horses and carts had passed away with the Generalissimo, were not part of the new Spain, with its glorious pan-European aspirations and Gehry-inspired architecture.

'As I already said it is good of you to come,' said Dolores, turning to face him, eyes not making the least concession to looking at the road in front of her.

'No worries,' he said. 'Glad to be able to help out.'

'How did you hear about us?'

'Oh, friends,' he said, as vaguely as he could and tried to change the subject, 'I have to admit I'm a bit apprehensive about stepping into a dead man's shoes. In such a literal manner, if you see what I mean. I have to confess I know very little about the circumstances of poor Mr Trubshawe's death. Something to do with mushrooms, I believe.'

If he been Dan Brown, grappling with the *Da Vinci Code*, he would have said that Dolores now 'gunned' the Land Rover past a smoke-belching articulated lorry, narrowly avoiding a similar monster coming in the opposite direction. He was, however, not entirely sure what the verb 'to gun' meant in this or any other context, so he preferred the word 'accelerate'.

This was what the girl did, jamming her foot hard on the appropriate pedal. He inferred the gesture to be as much a response
to him as to the lorries.

'Your friends,' she said, not to be deflected, 'had they been
guests at the village? Participated in one of our programmes?
Perhaps they were known to me.'

She was driving fast but not unnervingly so. Bognor almost
relaxed.

'Um . . . er . . . I'm really not sure,' he coughed and held
on to the door handle as they swung hard round a corner. Dolores
glanced across and grinned. 'Mushrooms,' he said fatuously,
'You said "mushrooms".'

'No, Mr Bognor,' she said, 'I didn't mention mushrooms. It
was you who said something about mushrooms. However, I am
not here to beat about bushes. Mushrooms it was. Which did
for Mister Trubshawe. A mushroom disagreed with him.'

'Violently,' said Bognor. 'In fact, terminally.'

She smiled and changed down with a gratuitous double-
declutch. Showing off, he thought. Not that there was any
need.

'Do we know where the mushrooms came from? Who cooked
them? Whether everyone else ate the same mushrooms?' He
paused.

'You sound like the Guardia Civil,' she said.

'*Oreja del gato,*' he said, '*Oreja de judas, hongo comtesino,
ninja, tricolonia, rodellon, canterolo cabrito, colmanilla, armi-
laria, rebellon.*'

He paused and smiled with self-satisfaction.

'*Rebellon,*' he repeated, 'I'm particularly keen on "*rebellon*".'

'I'm impressed,' she said, flashing him a smile which disappeared as rapidly as it had emerged.

So was he. He had no idea there were so many different
kinds of mushroom. Even in Spanish.

A rabbit ran across the road and she served and swore. They
were still climbing and the woods were thicker. Conifers.
Occasionally they passed a dwelling. These were looking
progressively more alpine, with more shutters, a propensity
towards timber. Thin blue smoke eddied up from chimneys. It
felt like ski-country and not what he associated with Spain,

which he realized guiltily was all Costas and Hemingway: an Englishman's cliché. Not the real Spain at all.

She braked hard and swung a sharp left between the stone pillars of an ancient gateway. The drive was rough and bumpy, but she made no effort to slow down, instead attacking the potholes and ruts with a panache that was obviously intended to unsettle her passenger. She glanced sideways to see what effect this rough passage was having. Bognor, recognizing that this was a form of initiation rite was resolutely relaxed.

'So this is it,' he said, through teeth which were more gritted than he hoped they seemed.

'*Sí*,' she said. 'This is the Pueblo. We take it for about twenty weeks of the year. The proprietors have promised to have the drive fixed. Until then we do have four-wheel drives, SUVs, whatever you prefer to call them in English.'

'Land Rover will do,' said Bognor, patriotically. At home he drove a Mini, which was, he believed, still made in Oxford, though only under licence from some foreigner. Some of his best friends were foreign, of course, but you knew what he meant.

The drive was long as well as rudimentary. It curved and swirled through more woods until, without warning, it emerged into a clearing of half a dozen or so chalets grouped around a larger and more substantial house with a large, planked deck outside the front door. Two enormous mountain dogs came barking towards the vehicle.

'That's Marks and Spencer,' said Dolores. 'The village dogs. Actually they're father and son but they behave like twin brothers, which is how we treat them. They are very friendly unless, of course . . .'

Bognor cocked an eyebrow at her as she braked hard, sending a spume of mud and gravel in the general direction of the dogs, who were now on their hind legs, snuffling their muzzles against the cab window.

'Unless – how shall we say? – you get on the wrong side of them.'

'Shouldn't be any worries,' said Bognor, faux-nonchalant. 'I like dogs. They like me too. As a rule.'

He opened the door, leaped down and was almost knocked

flying by Marks or Spencer, who jumped up on him, a paw on each shoulder, and gave him a preposterous lick. Bognor responded with a rough rub of the hand behind one ear.

'You and I are going to be friends, old shopkeeper,' he said.

Dolores was watching appraisingly. Bognor knew she was and responded accordingly.

'You're in Cervantes,' she said. 'The chalets are named after great Spaniards. I'll show you, then you can have a quick wash and brush-up before your first assignment at noon. A walk with Lola in the woods.'

'A walk with Lola in the woods.'

'Yes.' She patted the dogs. Bognor didn't think she had a sense of humour. 'Follow me.' She took his overnight bag and computer case from the Land Rover and set off towards one of the chalets, sashaying like an Irish Guardsman on parade. Bognor reckoned it was deliberate. He fell in beside her, carrying his briefcase with its self-important files and papers.

'Mushrooms,' he said. 'You were telling me about mushrooms.'

'On the contrary, Mr Bognor,' she said. 'It was *you* who was telling *me* about mushrooms. You seem to know so many Spanish words to describe them. But, of course, you won't be needing them here. It is English all the time. There are penalties for anyone caught speaking Spanish. Even when describing the mushrooms.'

She smiled coquettishly but unconvincingly.

'But there are mushrooms growing around here? In the woods and fields?'

'Of course, I'm sure Lola will tell you. But only in English please.'

'Not even Latin?'

'Not even Latin,' she said, and took a key from the pocket of her fur jacket. They had arrived at Cervantes.

'Home.' she said. '"Home sweet home," as you English say. Or to be a little more accurate: "Home sweet home from home."' She laughed and opened the door on to a dark panelled room with a sofa, chairs, kitchenette, smouldering wood-burner and stairs leading up.

'The convention is that an Anglo has the downstairs while

one of the Spaniards lives above,' she said. 'I am not sure. It will naturally be a man.' She smiled meaningfully and mirthlessly. 'And now I will leave you for the wash-up. Please come to the main house just before noon in order to meet with Lola.'

It was on the tip of his tongue to say that actually he was no longer Mr Bognor but Sir Simon, actually. Instead, however, he smiled feebly and said, 'Please don't call me Bognor. I much prefer, er, just Simon. And, if you don't mind, I shall call you Dolores, Dolores.'

She looked at him rather blankly, then smiled again, in automatic response.

'Of course,' she said. 'I will see you in a little while. And welcome to the Pueblo . . . Simon.'

FOURTEEN

A walk in the woods with Lola was exactly that – no more, no less, and certainly didn't resemble the innuendo laden art film from an obscure Baltic or Balkan state which that description might have implied, at least to the imaginative, of whom Bognor was one.

Lola herself was wholesome, eager, attractive and even pictur-esque in an understated thirty-something way. She made Bognor feel tweedy and avuncular which was, he conceded, probably no bad thing. He tried to remember the briefing from the *teniente* earlier in the morning, but failed to recall more than the fact that she was a nun who danced the Charleston. And one of us. The figure in the blue jeans, tan boots, Barcelona anorak and silk headscarf did not seem remotely nunnish nor Charleston dancing. It seemed more than likely that the Spanish police had muddled the files and botched the identities. Bognor decided that it would be better if he began with the metaphorical blank sheet and made his own portrait up as they went along.

'Hi,' he said, identifying her by the nametag they all sported in their lapels, 'I'm Simon.'

'Hi,' she said, 'I'm Lola. You like to walk?'

There was no sign of Dolores Calderon or of anyone else official. There were just the eight of them in the large beamed entrance hall which had a well-stocked but unmanned bar running along one wall and an open fire smouldering with huge logs at another. Marks and Spencer lay in front of the hot logs, half asleep and unbarking.

'You're taking the place of Billy?' said Lola managing the correct inflection to turn an apparent statement of fact into an actual question.

'You could say that.' There was a brisk wind. All four couples – each one a Spanish speaker and an English speaking partner – headed along the same forest track that led eventually to the bare, treeless hills at the edge of the woods. The path

was holed and rutted, pebbled and stoned, so that you negoti-
ated it rather than walked it; hopping, skipping and jumping,
rather than proceeding in the placid stroll that Bognor had
anticipated, and which would lead, he believed, to a mutually
rewarding conversation. As it was, one had to devote most of
one's attention to staying upright. He shivered and noticed
that his breath was steamy. In the distance a dog barked and
was answered by another some way off. Or were they wolves
howling? His imagination was becoming fevered and he imag-
ined killer mushrooms in every forest clearing, clinging to
every trunk. This was Dracula country: Transylvanian in all
but . . . well, not Transylvanian at all, but, nevertheless, having
a threatening menace redolent of savage wilderness, nature
red in tooth and claw, evil monks, man-eating wolves . . . Dan
Brown would have had a field day.

Lola, he saw, was wearing a crucifix which swung blingishly
every time she hopped from one rock or boulder to another.
She was, he remembered, some sort of nun. He said so, sounding
diffident and disbelieving, and she laughed at him.

'How you would say in your country?: "There are nuns and
there are nuns".' She smiled. 'It is not so usual in *España* for
a woman to be a nun.'

'*Un*usual,' said Bognor, 'I think you mean *un*usual.'

She clapped her hands and missed a rock by inches, a high-
heeled boot sinking into deep brown mud.

'Unusual. You are right. I mean "unusual". It is not unusual
for a woman to be a nun. Not usual is the same as unusual. I
remember now. It is in the books. *Un*likely. *Un*interested.
*Un*usual. *Un*-nun. What, please, is the difference between "dis"
and "in"?'

'Too complicated,' he said. 'It's too complicated and it doesn't
really matter.'

'We come here to be complicated,' she said, rubbing the mud
from her boot on a tussock of wiry grass. 'The difference
between "dis" and "un" is something that matters very much.
It is what we pay for. It is what we ask you to teach us.'

'I can't teach you anything,' said Bognor, 'since I'm told
we are on the same side.' He felt he should tap the side of his
nose or wink, but instead did his best to look complicit and

conspiratorial. Lola simply looked blank. Well trained, presumably. Disconcerting, though. They could not be overheard and this was quite possibly their only chance of a secret conference. For a second, he allowed himself ugly doubts. Suppose that, after all, she was not one of 'us'. Suppose she was even one of 'them'. It hardly bore thinking about, but Bognor recognized that he had to tread carefully.

It felt like rain. Black cloud was thickening above the treetops. Over by the mountains there was a low rumble of thunder.

'Do you think we should turn round?' asked Bognor, nervously, 'We don't want to get wet.'

'I thought the British were accustomed to being wet,' she said, skipping between boulders again. 'You sound like Trubshawe. He said he came to Spain to get away from the rain. He said there were some famous words in a musical play saying that "The rain in Spain falls mainly in the plain".'

'*My Fair Lady*,' he said.

'*Que?*' she asked, obviously not having a clue what he, or Trubshawe were talking about.

He laughed.

'It's a famous musical,' he said, 'adapted from the play *Pygmalion* by George Bernard Shaw, the famous playwright. Lerner and Loewe. Rex Harrison created the part of Professor Higgins and teaches this Cockney flowergirl how to speak proper. Things like sounding her "aitches", which seems to elude you Spanish. Thus, "In Hertford, Hereford and Hampshire hurricanes hardly happen." See what I mean? The musical is by Lerner and Loewe. Julie Andrews was in the stage musical. Audrey Hepburn starred in the movie, but she didn't sing because she couldn't. So she's dubbed.'

He realized that the Charleston-dancing nun was looking at him incredulously, that none of this meant anything to her because she was not English (or conceivably American) and was too young to have gone through the experiences enjoyed by Bognor, who vaguely remembered sitting in a box at the Theatre Royal in Drury Lane, courtesy of his godmother, and drinking ginger beer in the interval.

'Sorry!' he said. 'I forgot.'

He felt a definite drop of rain on what he persisted in calling his 'bald patch', but which was actually larger than the remaining hair on his head. He had in late-middle age, become seriously follicly challenged, and there was no getting away from the fact that, if there was a patch, it was the hairy one. Welcome baldness, my old friend.

'You weren't even born,' he continued. '*My Fair Lady* was 1956. I was hardly born myself.'

'Doesn't matter,' she said, looking up towards the livid clouds and the impending storm. 'Maybe we should return. The rain will come.'

'Looks like it,' he confirmed. He did not much want to get wet, but was anxious not to appear a wimp. He could try 'gallant' but he had a nasty feeling that Lola was a lot feistier than he was. She could cope with cold and wet in a way that he couldn't. Nor Trubshawe. He risked asking.

'Trubshawe,' he asked, 'would he have minded getting wet?'

'Wet?' she asked. 'Trubshawe liked what you seem to call "the creature comforts". He preferred always to stay indoors beside the fire with the slippers and the pipe and the glass of whisky, and his feet on the dogs.'

'Ah,' said Bognor, 'I get the picture. So Trubshawe was something of a couch potato.'

They were standing opposite each other, not apparently sure whether to go forward or back. A large puddle lay between them.

'Couch potato?' she asked, perplexed again. 'I am not familiar with "couch potato".'

'No,' said Bognor. 'Do you think Trubshawe's death was an accident? Or did someone kill him?'

'An accident, I think,' she said. 'Why would anyone want to kill Jimmy? He ate the wrong mushrooms. He was not very well anyway. Very sad.'

Thunder rolled again. Closer this time. There was no mistaking the rain now. It was falling in heavy regular plops. It was like an overture – more of a signal than the real thing. Once it came, Bognor, guessed, it would be a downpour. How much grace they had was anyone's guess. In the distance he could see another couple, presumably an Anglo and a Hispanic, scampering for home.

'I think we should head home,' he said. 'Discretion being the better part of valour.' He wondered why, when he really should be keeping his language simple, he was lapsing into archaic Brewerisms, metaphors, similes and figures of speech. It was not like him and it was inappropriate.

She smiled. 'As you wish,' she said. 'You know, incidentally, that I am really called "Sister Lola" and that I am what I believe in your language you refer to as a "Poor Clare".'

'A little bird whispered something of the sort,' he said. Kicking himself yet again for a confusing descent into metaphor. It was banal too. Unforgivable.

'Also known as "poor ladies of Assisi",' she said. 'We are linked to the Franciscan brotherhood which is many hundreds of years old.'

'The eight-hundredth anniversary of the founding of the Franciscan order was in 2009,' he said, unexpectedly, and before she could question the source of this improbable knowledge, he added, 'I was involved in, er, something to do with honey at a Franciscan Friary at Beaubridge in Oxfordshire.'

This was the truth but an economical one. He had been sent down to Beaubridge on his very first case many years ago after one of SIDBOT's agents, passing himself off as a friar named Brother Luke, had been garrotted with his own crucifix chain, in the potato patch. It was a baptism of beeswax, being a murky affair centred on the friary's unique premium grade honey.

'Beaubridge,' said Lola, glancing at the clouds and shivering slightly, 'I have heard about it. But you are right. It is going to rain very, um, very hard. Cats and dogs, indeed.' She looked pleased with herself, almost purring with self-satisfaction at this mastery of metaphor. '"Cats and dogs",' she repeated. 'That is what you say when it rains very wet. But why? Why cats and dogs?'

'Trubshawe would have known the answer,' said Bognor, without conviction, 'We can discuss the business of cats and dogs when we get back to the ranch. Come on, let's hurry or we'll get wet.'

She laughed. 'You English!' she said. 'You say it is wet to be afraid of wet weather. But that is wrong surely? To be wet you must stay in the rain, not run away from it.' She was skipping lightly between the puddles and the rain was beginning in earnest. The heavens were sending a succession of liquid grenades to earth. They splattered on impact, sending water and mud back up again. Her agility was much greater than the Englishman's and in a few moments she was well ahead of him. Bognor, struggling with slippery stones and clinging mud, felt like a retreating baggage train being sniped at from the shadows.

She stopped and waited for him to catch up, disregarding the grenades of rain exploding all round her.

'I enjoy it,' she said turning her face to the sky and catching a raindrop on an outstretched tongue. 'How did you say? "The rain in Spain falls mainly in the plain" and "Hurricanes hardly happen". This is not usual for me, so I enjoy it. It is a novelty.'

'Trubshawe was used to rain,' said Bognor, 'being English. Perhaps that's why he came to Spain. For the climate. Hotter in Spain. More sun.'

She shrugged.

'Perhaps,' she said, and started to walk again, deliberately slowing her pace to make it possible for the older person to keep up.

The rain was still almost holding off and they were just being peppered with slingshot. Bognor had brought little in the way of a change of clothing. Getting wet would have been more than usually inconvenient. They only had about a hundred yards to go before the safety of the main building. He was relieved.

Suddenly she stopped and grabbed hold of his hands, looking almost beseechingly into his eyes.

'I come here to learn English,' she said, 'not to experience death. It is very sad, I know, but we have a saying in Spain that life must go on, no matter what . . .' Her voice trailed away but she went on looking at him knowingly.

'We have a similar saying in English,' said Bognor, sounding pompous even to himself. She was some nun.

Out of the corner of his eye, just over one of her almost heaving shoulders, he spotted in a clearing among the ubiquitous conifers a cluster of mushrooms poking priapically up from the green, green grass.

'Aha!' he said, out loud. 'Mushrooms. So you wouldn't have to come very far to find lunch? Or the murder weapon.'

She spun round on the muddy heels of her boots and followed his gaze, then smiled.

'*Boletus pinophilus*,' she said. 'They are everywhere at this time of year. I like very much.'

FIFTEEN

Lunch, ordered in advance by a system of coloured tags attached to hooks by the menu board outside the dining room, had a Spanish and an English option. The Spanish option that day consisted of a garlic-impregnated cold soup along gazpacho lines, some sort of grilled meat, with what looked like a whole head of more or less raw garlic, plus chips, and flan. The English alternative consisted of the same first and second courses, but without garlic and with the soup heated. The dessert was described as 'custard' but was indistinguishable from 'flan'. A carafe of wine and a carafe of water were placed on the table. Everyone got crusty bread with an airy middle. Bognor reflected on gastronomy as a weapon of cultural diplomacy, but came to no conclusions.

His companions were Lola and Leonel, the pet food executive from Seville, who made up the Hispanic half of the table, and George who, with himself, was batting for the Anglos. Bognor and the two Spaniards went for the garlic and flan option; George opted for no fancy foreign muck and custard.

'I admire your sense of adventure,' he said to Bognor, as he eyed his warm tomato soup and compared and contrasted it with the three gazpachos, 'but I always say that when it comes to food you can't be too careful. Back home in Essex we have the most wonderful raw materials in God's own acre and we never seek to adulterate any of them with noxious foreign elements. I appreciate that in other worlds, where the raw materials aren't exactly *comme il faut*, God may need a bit of a helping hand. But when in Rome I never do as the Romans do. I always bring my own lunch box. As it were.'

'Quite,' said Bognor, not wishing to appear rude.

'If poor old Trubshawe had stuck to good straightforward English grub he'd still be with us. But he insisted on fooling around with foreign muck and, hey presto, he's gone.'

George leaned back and burped.

'Me,' he said, 'I had the prawn cocktail.'

He smiled. 'Morecambe Bay prawns, dollop of Hellmans and a bit of Heinz tomato. The whole thing bunged on a glassful of shredded cos lettuce. Bloody wonderful. Bloody British!'

Lola, the unlikely nun, and Leonel, the pet food chappie, both looked expectantly at Bognor. They were obviously waiting for a lead.

'I always thought of prawn cocktail as being an American invention,' he said gently. 'By Craig Claiborne out of *Ladies Home Journal*. That sort of thing. Back of an early colour supplement with a ditzy photograph.'

'No,' said George with the self-assurance of the truly ignorant. 'British as bangers and mash or proper bitter. Americans don't do prawn cocktail.'

This time Bognor did not demur. Instead, he took another sip of the gazpacho, slurping inadvertently, which annoyed him, and thinking the soup tasted really rather surprisingly good.

'Lola and I went for a walk this morning,' he said. 'So I feel we know each other a little already. George and Leonel, though, not yet. I'm sure we'll become great friends over the next few days.'

George didn't look at all sure about this; Leonel said, '*Sí*', but rapidly corrected himself to 'yes'. Lola came close to simpering. Bognor tried desperately to think of something coherent to say about pet food but failed. Instead, he fell back on the weather, the way the British so often did.

'Bit brisk out,' he said. 'And wet too. Lola and I got caught in the rain, didn't we, Lola?'

She nodded.

'Yes,' she said, 'it rained cats and bitches.'

'Dogs,' he corrected her, 'it rained cats and dogs.'

'Why,' asked Leonel, breaking off some crust and dipping it in his soup, 'do you use the same word for male and female cats but you use a different word for the dog and the bitch?'

It was a perfectly fair question but Bognor didn't have a clue. Nor, apparently, did George. This time he didn't attempt to bluster.

'You're the pet food man,' said Bognor, seeing an opportunity to lighten the mood and to lead Leonel on to home turf. 'What

do you think? How does it work in Spanish? Do you have
hermaphrodite cats but heterosexual dogs?'

Leonel looked blank. 'Please?' he ventured.

'Our friend was making a joke,' said George, unhelpfully.
'It's a failing in a certain sort of Brit. Can't take anything
seriously.'

Bognor didn't think he was going to like George, whoever
he might be.

'I was only trying to see if the English and Spanish languages
took a different line on cats and dogs,' he said. 'I wasn't trying
to be funny. Not my cup of tea.'

'Why,' asked Lola, 'is it that the English spend so much time
talking of cups of tea, storms in teacups and so on and so forth?
Also dogs?'

Bognor closed his eyes and reminded himself that the
Spaniards were here to learn English and the Anglos to teach
it, if only by osmosis. He also remembered that George almost
certainly wasn't George, though he was unlikely to be Oliver
O'Flaherty from Limerick either. Also that Leonel was as dull
as he seemed, but played bass guitar and was keen on Johnny
Cash and football. There was no accounting for taste. He also
claimed an Opus Dei fabricated MBA from some university in
Oviedo. Shades, he thought, of the da Vinci file, though Opus
Dei was more interesting than that. You could also say the
same about a pet food company executive with that sort of
background, but exotic backgrounds did not always translate
into an interesting, let alone exciting, reality. Leonel was dull
despite his CV.

'Tea is an important part of British culture,' he found himself
saying in response to the nun's question. And we like dogs. He
was wracking his brains, trying to think of something coherent
to say to Leonel about either Johnny Cash or football. He
supposed Leonel was a Seville supporter but he knew nothing
whatever about the team and precious little about popular music.
Mozart was about as low or middlebrow as he got, though he
had once been rather keen on Manfred Mann. Something to do
with an unattainable girl some time before Monica arrived on
the scene.

'Not in Spanish,' said George, making an uncouth noise

sucking soup from his spoon. 'They don't do tea the way we do. Just bags and hot water. It's a coffee culture. Precious little in the way of biscuits. I could die for a chocolate digestive. Give me Australia any day. They understand tea and biscuits down there. Bloody good show. They still do elevenses and proper tea breaks. Civilized.'

'Is different,' said Lola, rather pointedly finishing her gazpacho with a fastidious flourish, 'in *España* one drinks the coffee, not the tea. Also we take the long siesta in the middle of the day. Otherwise, we work. Not like England.'

'The English work bloody hard these days,' said George, with feeling. 'One of the reasons I live abroad. All work and no play. You know the saying. Many a true word spoken in whatever they say, if you know what I mean. Same went for poor old Jimmy Trubshawe. Sense of perspective. That's what the modern generation of Brits don't have. Sense of bloody perspective.'

A waiter cleared their plates. Bognor sensed George spoiling for a fight. Preferably with him. He could think of no proper reason for this and the feeling was uncomfortable. Part of him wanted to plunge into a sort of soft interrogation of George, who had, tacitly and perhaps unintentionally, admitted to knowing more about the late Trubshawe than he might have intended. Part of him wanted to ingratiate himself with Leonel by saying something affable and knowledgeable about pet food, Johnny Cash or football, and part of him wanted to follow up on the alluring nun because . . . oh well . . . he thought to himself, irritably. Just because.

'I never actually got to a Cash concert,' he said, knowing that he sounded feeble, 'but I had some of the LPs. They've gone now, of course. Out of date technology.'

'No such thing as out of date technology,' said George. 'Built-in obsolescence. That's the name of the game. These Johnnies couldn't make money if their gizmos lasted for ever. The whole basis of making money these days is to build in the need to replace whatever it is you've got with the latest fashion. Take razors.'

'Razors?' asked Leonel, seemingly incredulous, though Bognor wasn't so sure.

The waiter reappeared bearing meat on plates stacked impressively up one of his arms. Skills such as this impressed Bognor no end, particularly as he was singularly inept in matters such as this. Manual dexterity, hand-to-eye coordination, DIY and other traditionally attributes of the British male were not his bag. He had a nasty feeling that George would be a dab hand at DIY, even if he were not adept at stacking plates up his arm. He would probably regard such a feat as homosexual and foreign: 'pansy, woofter, Johnny foreigner'. Bognor could already hear the bizarre combination of truculence and defeat which was, he believed, characteristic of men like George.

'You know Jimmy Trubshawe?' he asked, surprising even himself. It was much too obvious a question. He should have been oblique, playing his cards close to the proverbial, not laying them out for all to see. At the same time there was an instinctive trait in his approach, which led sometimes to a breaking of the rules, a statement of the obvious when something more obscure would have seemed appropriate. There was a considerable part of Bognor which defied the textbook.

George didn't seem unduly fazed by the question, direct though it was.

'Maybe,' he said. 'Maybe not.'

And stuffed unseasoned meat into his mouth.

Bognor retaliated with a garlicky mouthful of his own.

'Well,' he said, with an aggression which surprised even himself, 'maybe or maybe not?'

A mutual glower ensued. The two Spaniards recognized a shared hostility but were unable to be precise about it. It was clear that their Anglo friends and instructors were not getting on, but it was not clear to them precisely why. It was not clear to the protagonists either, which made the whole impasse more difficult to explain or even to understand. The mutual dislike was visceral. It was echoed in the mind but it stemmed from the gut.

'Why,' asked Lola attempting, perhaps to pour oil on troubled waters, 'is the storm in the teacup?'

This was not an easy question to answer.

'It is a way of saying,' he tried, 'that the disagreement may seem to be very significant and upsetting, but it's actually not as important as it seems.'

'But,' she persisted, 'why teacup?'

Bognor chewed on his meat and smiled at George.

'Good question, eh?' he tried, round grisly meat that might just have been horse but was probably just goat.

Lola was determined to add milk to the stormy brew.

'In *España* we have the Twining bag,' she said brightly, 'which is unusual, no? In *España* it is not common to use the convenience food. It is more usual to cook with the fresh ingredients. Like the mushrooms, for instance.'

Mention of mushrooms reminded them all of death.

'Yes. Well,' said Bognor, 'the meat is very tasty. Tell me, Leonel, is Lola right? Is it more common in your country to use fresh ingredients. For instance, do pet owners give their animals fresh meat?'

Leonel seemed eager.

'Is a problem for us, yes,' he said. 'We are anxious to sell the cans of processed food for the dogs and the cats because we add the vitamins and the good things that improve the diet for the pets. But most people are not understanding that it is better to have the food from the tin.'

'I see,' said Bognor.

George chewed and looked daggers.

Lola smiled sunnily.

'Jimmy and I went to the same school,' said George unexpectedly. 'He was a year above me. Good at football. You wouldn't say we knew each other. Not then. But he was a bit of a hero in those days. Always was, if you want to know.'

Bognor wondered if this was halfway to a confession of guilt, but he said nothing, just cut another mouthful of tough but tasty meat and chewed thoughtfully.

SIXTEEN

The rest of lunch was sticky. Bognor floundered. Lola and Leonel smiled and trotted out phrases from text books. George glowered. The flan and the custard were acceptable and identical. The wine evaporated; the water likewise. And coffee arrived. It was as thick as glue and very sweet. Sticky as the conversation.

Housekeeping followed on the agenda as an add-on to the coffee. Housekeeping meant Arizona Brown and Felipe Lee, who were staff. They were glib, suave, professional, good at their jobs and Bognor took a more or less instant dislike to both of them. They, for their part, spoke well of him, or at least bade him welcome, thanked him for joining the team at such short notice and called him Simon throughout. Neither of them gave the slightest hint of an identity other than his simple given name. It made him feel like a Latter Day Saint or an Anonymous Alcoholic.

The Brown girl had the willowy figure and unspotted complexion of someone who ate sensibly, worked out regularly, drank no alcohol but might conceivably have a dangerous drugs habit. Bognor had heard that her sexuality was ambiguous, which he could well believe, and he suspected that she had some native American blood. Navajo possibly. She also had perfect teeth, a characteristic Bognor had long associated with a certain sort of American nubility and Heath Robinson-esque wire mouth devices worn throughout adolescence.

'OK guys and dolls,' she said winsomely, after Bognor had been introduced and had stood diffidently to acknowledge that he was indeed he, 'following walkies and the five o'clock tea break we will be splitting in to two teams for a not so simple game of charades. I will mentor one team and Felipe will do the same for the other.'

She smiled a great deal and phrased everything as if it were a genuine request, whereas it was a command.

'What we would like – though ultimately, of course, it's for you to decide – channelling everything through your team leaders – who will, naturally, be Spaniards – and, so as not to prolong the suspense, let's tell you that the team leaders for this exercise will be Lola and Leonel – so, what we would like is for the two teams to devise advertising and marketing strategies for two very characteristic products which is to say . . . *sausages*. One team will present the case for the British banger and the other will do the same for the Spanish chorizo. You can add in any typical ingredients like mashed potato or jalapeño peppers, but essentially we want to hear it for the banger on the one hand and the chorizo on the other. You'll have the whole time up to and including supper to work on your scheme, and then we'll do the presentation out in the bar after we've all had supper together. Any questions?'

George had a question. He would, thought Bognor. He would.

'What if we don't like our product?' said George. 'May we change teams?'

'No, George,' said Arizona, smiling brightly through her pearly teeth, which were almost but not quite gritted for the gesture. 'You can't change sides. You just have to pretend. It's what we do all through life: we pretend to be advocating one particular strategy while privately preferring another. It's a necessary compromise.'

If George were a dog he would have growled.

Arizona sat down, crossing her leggy jeans and smilingly dared anyone else to attempt a challenge. No one dared. No one even got near.

Once it was clear that Arizona was unchallenged, Felipe Lee rose to do serious housekeeping. He seemed something of a fusspot but this was, Bognor recognized, almost certainly a ploy. He was wearing a dark suit which seemed more Anglo than Spanish and a collar and tie. He seemed more like a merchant banker than an executive of a language school.

'The bar,' he said, 'doesn't take credit cards and they won't let you run a tab. You have to pay as you drink. Old Spanish custom.' He flickered a smile which was gone almost as soon as it was signalled. 'Please make sure that any laundry is left in the bag outside your room by nine a.m. If any of you have problems understanding the code system for ordering meals, please contact me before supper this evening. If any of you are having trouble with your mobile phones, I have to advise you that the signal is weak and variable so you may have trouble. If so, I advise you to make use of the landlines provided for guests' use in reception.' He paused and stared round unblinking at his audience.

'Any questions?' he wanted to know.

There were no questions. Felipe was not the sort of factotum who genuinely invited them. Like Arizona, he told. It occurred to Bognor that the Pueblo was an extraordinarily regulated and orchestrated place for one which people paid good money to attend. Both Felipe and Arizona were treating their guests like new boys in a boarding school. Bognor had endured such indignities many years ago and the experience was not lightly forgotten.

Strange, thought Bognor, that sudden death, maliciously contrived, should so often take place in such well-ordered surroundings. In this, as in so much, appearances deceived. This expensive, exclusive language school was one of the last places on earth that he would have expected to be associated with murder. But then his entire career had been built on the premise that nothing was ever quite what it seemed.

Arizona was back on her feet. She and Felipe were a well-synchronized, polished act.

'You have fifteen minutes to finish your coffee, take a quick comfort break and generally do whatever it is that you want to do, then it's onward and upwards. The weather forecast is fine so there should be no problem having a gentle stroll through the woods. Talk about anything you like but please, just remember, *no Spanish*. Everything you say must be said in English.'

Bognor grinned. House rule. The other three got up and left. He was finishing his coffee and musing quietly, when Felipe and Arizona came and sat down either side of him.

'Dolores has told us about you,' said Arizona.

'Dolores doesn't know enough about me to be able to tell you,' said Bognor, confidently.

'Dolores is one of the richest women in the whole of Spain,'

said Felipe. He pronounced Spain with a slight lisp where the
's' should have been, so that it came out sounding like a 'th'.
He also prefixed it with the slightest hint of an extra 'e'.
'Ethpain'. It was OK but not the way an Englishman would
have said Spain. Just different enough to be Spanish. Like calling
Mozart, M'sah. Bognor guessed that it was important for Felipe
to be fluent but not bilingual. Subtle difference.

'I didn't know that,' said Bognor, 'but you don't entirely
surprise me.'

'She owns half the company,' said Arizona, whose English
was immaculate, though American, which bothered Bognor a
smidgeon.

'And what did she tell you?' he asked.

'That you like mushrooms,' said Arizona. She wasn't smiling.
'Dolores doesn't seem a hundred per cent happy about you. She
wants us to keep an eye on you. We thought you ought to know.'

'Thanks,' said Bognor, 'good to know. I'm grateful.'

'Don't be,' said Felipe. 'We think you have a nice face.
Trustworthy eyes. And there is a "quid" that we would like to
request in return for our "quo".'

'Try me,' he said.

They looked at each other, exchanging complicit glances.

'The conceit,' said Arizona, 'is that you came to us out of
the blue. Just happened to be passing.'

'So,' he said, 'how considerate of me. You're a man short; I
happen to be passing, hey presto, I'm helping you out. And
you're duly grateful. Good news all round.'

'Life doesn't work like that,' said Arizona. 'People don't just
appear out of the blue. They don't just happen to be passing.
Things don't just happen. They occur because people make
them happen. There is a purpose. You were passing on purpose.
You were in the blue because you meant to be; you came out
it for a reason. You're not a coincidence.'

He drank coffee, thought and shrugged.

'So I emerged on purpose,' he said. 'So what?'

'Not possible,' said Arizona. 'People like you don't just arrive.
Particularly not after the strange death of James Trubshawe.'
She smiled. 'Don't worry. We're not going to blow the whistle.
The reverse. We're just letting you know we know.'

'Know what?'

'That you're not what you seem,' said Felipe. He seemed nervous, glancing over his shoulder at the door into the bar and reception area, where the group were due to gather before the next round of walks. 'We want you to know that we have become wise to your deception, but that we won't blow the whistle. In return, we just ask that you level with us, at least to an extent. Otherwise the two of us are in the dark, which is not a place we like to be.'

Bognor could imagine. It was important for the way in which Brown and Lee functioned that they knew more than their charges. It was quite clear, however, that all they knew about him was that they didn't know enough. Their suspicions had been aroused but not allayed.

'We're not going to shop you,' said Arizona. 'We just want you to tell us something about what's happening. We don't think Trubshawe's death was an accident. We believe your sudden arrival has something to do with explaining it, with solving the mystery, if you like. All we ask in return for remaining silent on your behalf is that you tell us at least a little of what is happening.' She paused, then smiled at him. 'Please,' she said.

He wasn't expecting it and felt duly melted. Despite this, his cover was blown. Well . . . He frowned and tried getting his head round the idea. In a sense, he had no cover. He had neither heard nor told lies. Not consciously at least. None of the Anglos in the operation said more than they wished, and whether or not they told the truth was up to them. Vide Trubshawe and, as far as he could see, George. Both were extremely economical with the truth. By contrast he was virginal. He had said practically nothing. His silence wasn't an admission of guilt or wrong doing. It was, after a fundamental right, under proper law. One did not have to give evidence which might condemn you. Thus he.

'What do you want?' he asked, hoping that this did not of itself constitute an admission. He didn't feel he was revealing anything other than a simple and laudatory desire to please. But he wasn't at all sure. It sometimes seemed as if everything he said was open to contrary interpretation. Better to keep your trap shut – the minute you opened it your listeners put their own spin on whatever you said, no matter what. Saying absolutely nothing was the first rule of being interviewed. Hence 'No comment'. But he wasn't in a 'no comment' situation; he was in a situation for which there was no precedent and no training. He had to wing it; which meant flying by the seat of his pants. Not a comfortable cliché.

'To be friends,' said Arizona, sounding disconcertingly as if she meant it, 'we don't need to know all your secrets; we just need to have you admitting that secrets are what you are dealing in; that you are not what you may seem or what you are pretending to be. We have to agree that the death of Jimmy Trubshawe was not an accident. You know. We know. And we behave accordingly.'

'I don't think I have a huge problem with that,' he said thoughtfully. 'Except that you have absolutely no proof and you're denying the possibility of coincidence in a way that is statistically unsound. Trust me, I know. When I say that I just happened to be passing by and that my presence is entirely fortuitous, you have absolutely no grounds for not believing me.'

'You're saying you really just tick the boxes and it's all a happy chance,' said Arizona, looking as near-outraged as her demure self-controlled façade allowed.

'Well,' said Bognor, 'I could. And I'm saying that you completely lack the ammunition to contradict me. You can't conceivably prove I'm wrong.'

'Intuition,' said Felipe Lee, 'is a vital part of the game. There is always an element of magic that defies explanation. If we could explain everything then everything would be explained and life would lose its mystery.'

'This is all very metaphysical,' protested Bognor, wishing that life were simpler. He didn't believe that Felipe or Arizona had killed Trubshawe, though, he conceded ruefully, he had no proof of their innocence and was simply acting from the same sort of intuition that they were professing themselves. His intuition was more professional and better attuned, as was only to be expected of one in his position. But it was still, when all was said and done, just intuition. Nor did he think that they were acting on any outside authority. They were simply taking what was laughably described as their own 'initiative'. But they could be a nuisance. And/or possibly a help.

'Maybe,' agreed Arizona, 'but there's a concrete side too. We're straight with you; you're straight with us. We tell you what's up and you do the same for us. Deal?'

Bognor considered. He did not understand too clearly the nature of the proposed deal. Neither did the other two. It would make them allies in a loose, ill-defined sense, and he was feeling exposed and knew that he could use allies. In return, he would communicate in a relatively unspecified way that would acknowledge some, but not all, of his true identity. He couldn't see that it presented any great problem and it would make sense to have Arizona and Felipe at least marginally on side.

He studied his fingernails, appeared to think deeply and genuinely about the offer, looked up, smiled at both, and in a manner that would have won plaudits on popular daytime television, said, simply:

'Deal.'

SEVENTEEN

The first walk of the afternoon was much like the last walk of the morning.

Walks were like that and like each other. That was part of the point. The infinite variety of each individual encounter was coated in a veneer of predictability. Within a strictly controlled routine, eccentricity and experiment could flower. That was the theory.

That afternoon Bognor had Eduardo. Eduardo was the shipping magnate who liked to strum along to Paco Peña. At least that was what Bognor recollected from the briefing. The photograph in the smoke-filled room in Salamanca had shown a raw-boned, intensely blue-eyed, square-jawed, clean-shaven blokey bloke. In real life, he seemed to have shrunk a couple of sizes, gone saggy at the jaw and lost much of the intense lustre of the eyes. They still had something marginally fanatical about them, but it was shiftier, less piercing and self-confident.

There was something of Opus Dei about him when he introduced himself. Not in any dramatic hair-shirt or concealed scourge sort of a way; more shiny black suit, dandruff on the lapels and an aura of pasty-faced slug-under-stoneware. Bognor associated Opus Dei with Mormons, Seventh Day Adventists and others who came unbidden to his front door when he and Monica were having one of their self-indulgent weekend lie-ins. He did not subscribe to da Vinci code fantasy theories, but was not keen on organized religion, especially in its more regimented and extreme forms.

Despite Eduardo's mildly disturbing dark suit; shiny at knees and elbows; drizzled with dandruff around the neck and lapels; polished shoes and pasty complexion; Bognor felt strangely at peace. The sun shone, birds sang; some sort of vulture or other bird of prey was effortlessly ascending a spiral of miraculously hot air; the trees were still green; a vulpine animal howled in the distance, and all seemed pretty right with the world. For a man staring at almost imminent retirement and the prospect of a not too distant death, Bognor felt happy and relaxed.

Eduardo was not just a fly in the ointment.

He struck about five minutes in to the walk, when they were out of sight and earshot of the other marching couples.

'SIDBOT,' he said, lisping the 's'. 'You are the man from SIDBOT?'

It took Bognor a moment to register the danger of the phrase which hovered between a statement and a question but had a horrid certainty about it. Eduardo was clearly not expecting the answer 'no'.

'You what?' he asked, obviously flustered but trying to retain a composure that was eluding him.

'SIDBOT,' repeated Eduardo. 'You are the man from SIDBOT. Camilla told me to say that we had been informed and we were to tell you.'

The vulture was still twisting upwards, a small black speck in the distant sky.

'I'm sorry,' said Bognor, 'but I don't understand. You are in shipping. You are here to practise English. I understand you like Paco Peña.'

'That is correct,' said Eduardo. 'Classical guitar. Very good. But you are from SIDBOT because you believe that Jimmy Trubshawe has been the victim of foul play. Camilla has asked me to tell you that it does not matter, that the world is better off without Mr Trubshawe. He is gone and that is good. You should go home quickly. Or, if you must stay, you must keep what in English you call the low profile.' The forest was as idyllic as it had been a few moments earlier, but it did not seem like it to Bognor. He shivered. Eduardo seemed such an insignificant slug of a person. How come he knew that Bognor was the man from SIDBOT? How come he even knew that the Board of Trade had a Special Investigations Department? Let alone that it boasted such an ignoble acronym? And what did it all have to do with Camilla? Bognor remembered that she seemed faded, save for the gash of scarlet lipstick; that she had a butterfly tattooed near a shoulder-blade; that she was probably older than she claimed and that she said she ran a B. & B. in Byron Bay.

'Fruit,' said Bognor, 'I understand you're in fruit.'

'I ship exotic fruits around the new Europe,' confirmed Eduardo. 'My company would naturally be of interest to your Board of Trade.'

Bognor shrugged. 'Maybe so,' he said, 'I wouldn't know. What sort of fruit?'

A twig snapped under Eduardo's foot. A dog barked in the distance.

'What sort of fruit?' he repeated, parrot-like.

'Yes. Oranges? Bananas? Mangosteens? Papayas?' Bognor tried to keep the irritation out of his voice.

Eduardo frowned. 'Yes,' he said, 'oranges, bananas, mangosteens, papayas. All sorts of fruit.'

'And vegetables too?' Bognor was floundering and wondered if it showed, 'Mushrooms for instance.'

If Eduardo knew what the Englishman was talking about he made a convincing pretence of incomprehension. It had never occurred to Bognor that Eduardo would have had any inside or expert view on mushrooms, but then it had never occurred to him that there was any connection between Eduardo and Camilla. Much less that either of them would have known about SIDBOT. Much less his position at its head. *Who's Who* included an entry under his name because of his new knighthood. It did not however identify him as the head of the Special Investigations Department at the Board. His status was supposed to be a secret – an open one in the corridors of power, but closed to those not ensconced in the upper echelons of the establishment.

'Principally fruit,' said Eduardo, 'and most of the fruit is what you . . . or we . . . would call exotic. That is strange, expensive, out of the ordinary, unusual.'

Bognor was not good on fruit. Nor classical guitar. He was floundering.

'Why fruit?' he asked, helplessly.

'It is a commodity.' said Eduardo. 'In Spanglish we say "there is money in movement". If fruit stays where she is grown there is no profit to be made. If you move the fruit there is profit. The further the move, the more the money.' He smiled.

'What about the carbon footprint?' Bognor wanted to know. He had read the papers, watched TV, been briefed. The world mania for shuffling commodities around the globe for the financial benefit of the few, threatened the very existence of the many. Every schoolboy knew that.

Eduardo shrugged. He was obviously not a man who subscribed to green ideas on the dangers of global warming. He also came with a warning.

'SIDBOT,' he said, returning to his opening gambit. 'Camilla says that you are the man from SIDBOT and she has instructions from London to make sure that you do not interfere.'

Bognor's reaction to this information was unprintable and he said nothing, pretending instead to digest it. His reaction, naturally, was to tell Eduardo and Camilla, whoever they might be, to eff off and mind their own business. It was intolerable for someone of his standing and importance to deign to take charge of a case such as this, and then to find that some foreign squirt had got hold of his identity and was presuming to tell him how to behave. He was outraged. Heads would roll. Had they no idea who he was?

They walked on, outwardly happy and engrossed in improving talk; inwardly they seethed. At least, that was what Bognor was doing internally, even though he appeared imperturbable and phlegmatic as ever. He swallowed hard. He was being ridiculous. He, the least pompous, the least self-satisfied, the least puffed-up person he knew. He was the absolute acme of modesty; positively supine with self-doubt. Nevertheless, at his age, with a knighthood, a pension, and his own civil service department, he surely deserved to be treated with a modicum of respect. It was intolerable to be fingered as 'the man from SIDBOT' by some fruit salesman and an Australian boarding-house proprietor.

'I'm afraid I don't know what you're talking about,' he said, primly.

Eduardo trod on a twig. It snapped.

'So,' he said, 'you must talk with Camilla.'

'I don't want to talk to Camilla,' he said. 'I came here to talk to Spanish people and help with their English. I didn't come here to talk to an Australian landlady of a certain age.'

He realized as he said thus that it sounded ungallant.

'I didn't come here to speak to native English speakers. *Any* native English speaker. I have no interest in them. I have quite

enough English-speaking friends and acquaintances already. I
don't need more.'

It was on the tip of his tongue to add disparaging remarks
about Sheilas, colonials, Byron Bay, landladies and women of
a certain age but he thought it might seem misleading. Besides,
he wasn't that sort of person. Really. There wasn't a sliver of
snobbery, sexism or racism in him. He was a new male. Well.
Sort of. Up to a point. Anyway, he was here to do a job. He
did not wish to be deflected. Least of all under circumstances
such as this. He was, above all, a pro. Never let it be forgotten.

'You should listen to what I say,' said Eduardo, who seemed
to be doing some bristling of his own. 'I just want to help. You
are an old man. You should enjoy retirement. In Spain it is a
moment for a glass of Pedro Ximénez and some bowling. You
should smoke a pipe and wear the slip-over shoes.'

'For Christ's sake!' Bognor spoke with feeling. 'I didn't
expect to find ageism in Spain of all places. I'm an old man in
a hurry. Barely begun. Just watch this space.'

A rook cawed. Or was it a raven? He had never managed to
distinguish satisfactorily between the two and suspected that
the Spanish had a different bird altogether. Rooks were relatively
commonplace and could be turned into pies. Ravens were altogether more baleful and unusual, harbingers of death. They
were evil and strange, and when they left the Tower of London
it would be as if the apes had left the Rock of Gibraltar, which,
of course, was claimed by the Spanish, much as the Chinese
had claimed a similarly inhospitable piece of rock known to
the rest of the world as Hong Kong.

Musing thus and thinking of himself, Trubshawe and the
concomitant of an unlikely and unexpected death, he said, 'Paco
Peña. I understand you are something of an aficionado?'

'That is a Spanish word. There is a fine for using such things,'
said Eduardo. 'But, yes. I like Peña very much. He is from
Cordoba. Is very nice. Very special.'

'So I'm told,' said Bognor, lengthening his gait to traverse
a puddle without getting wet. 'Never been there. But I like
Peña's music. Very . . . er . . . Spanish.'

'*Sí*,' said Eduardo, snapping another twig underfoot. 'Yes.
La Musa Gitana.'

'Julio Romero de Torres,' replied Bognor, who prided himself on not being just a pretty face.

Eduardo had the grace to look startled. He obviously hadn't expected this sort of erudition from the apparently bland and, in a nutshell, typically English Englishman. It was Bognor's most effective disguise. He himself liked to think of it as a thick-edged carapace round a razor-sharp mind, though at three o'clock in the morning he acknowledged that this was an exaggeration. He might not have been as clever as he thought, but he wasn't as stupid as he looked.

'You know the *Musa Gitana*,' asked Eduardo suspiciously.

'Know is a bit of an exaggeration,' said Bognor. 'But one is aware of it. Naturally. I admire flamenco a great deal. That doesn't make me a professional, but even so . . .'

They passed another couple who had turned for home. Bognor knew from what he had learned in the earlier briefing, and from the look of negative complicity that passed between them, that the Anglo woman walking in the opposite direction was Camilla, the one time Essex girl, now translated to Northern New South Wales.

'So how do you come to know Camilla?' asked Bognor. It seemed an obvious question.

'Bananas,' replied Eduardo. 'She lives in banana-growing country. We import from her neighbours.'

Bognor smiled. Silly him.

'And I suppose she plays flamenco?' he said.

Eduardo frowned again.

'Yes,' he said.

'Forbidden fruit,' said Bognor. And they turned back, following the others towards HQ.

EIGHTEEN

Camilla was faded.

Had she been a flower, thought Bognor, she would have been dried and pressed between the leaves of a collector's volume, preserved for posterity as an example of what had once been alive and beautiful and was now merely an item of academic interest.

She was leftover, but then maybe that's what most women were once they had passed their notional sell-by date. Bognor himself felt as much like a front-line foot-soldier as he had ever done, yet part of him knew that he was a rusty old desk-bound bore who was out of practice and ill at ease at the sharp end. If you were making a direct comparison, you would have to say that he was, on any strictly rational basis, well past the age for active service. On the same computer-style analysis, she wasn't. If either of them were faded, then it was Bognor.

He, on the other hand, was an alpha male, even if grizzled.

'You shouldn't be here,' she said. This was called 'cutting to the chase', though Bognor, who knew a thing or two about the phrase's provenance considered it a misuse of language. It didn't mean what the user thought it did.

'I don't know what you mean,' he replied. The conversation was, he sensed, going to be like chess, full of feints and false initiatives until suddenly one of them embarked on something that carried risk but also the prospect of success. There was a break in the schedule before the next walk. They were encouraged to lie down, take it easy, possibly sleep. Bognor suggested coffee in a quiet corner of the bar. She acquiesced and led the way to a spot by the open fire, where they would not be overheard and barely overlooked. Presently the bar man brought two Americanos, black for him, white and sugared for her.

'So you're from Byron Bay by way of Essex?' he tried, judging this almost as non-committal as a judgement on the

weather, or a question about the frequency of her visits to the
Pueblo.

'I was on the permanent staff at SIS,' she said. 'Both Six
and Five since you ask, but they decided it would be in everyone's interests if I went to ground after the Diana and Dodi
business. I was on Diana's staff at the time.'

This was a serious gambit, the sort of move that would make
a controversial column in one of the smart London weeklies.
Bognor was inclined not to believe a word of it. In his experience anyone who had worked for the secret services was, well,
secretive about it. Those who blabbed and showed off almost
certainly hadn't gone near either Five or Six, or even, come to
that, SIDBOT. Not many people knew about SIDBOT, which
was part of its charm, and also made him even more suspicious,
though not entirely sceptical, about Camilla or whoever she
really was.

'"Ground" being New South Wales?'

She nodded. 'Almost as far as one can get,' she agreed.

'And what exactly were you doing with Diana?'

She sighed.

'Let's just say I was on her staff,' she said. 'Old-fashioned
usage would probably have described me as her "dresser", but
that would have been hopelessly old-fashioned. "Companion"
would be nearer the truth, but that's misleading too. You'll
see me in a lot of the photographs, sort of hovering.' She
smiled, and Bognor was almost inclined to believe her. 'Most
people fell for the cover-up,' she continued. 'That ludicrous
inquest and poor old Fayed. If ever a man played into establishment hands. Not that "the establishment" had much more
of a clue than the jury. No one understands the reality of
power. You could blame the press, though I think that's too
easy. One way or another, the world fell for the cover-up.
Only fruitcakes believe that Diana was murdered, but the
fruitcakes are right. Actually fruitcakes are right more often
than not. If you were to write the fruitcake version of history,
you'd have a truer and more accurate version of events than
the one that's peddled as the truth. Strange.' He stared hard
at her coffee. 'None of which detracts from the fact,' she said,
'that people like you have a marginal nuisance value. You can

get in the way, and it would be boring to have to eliminate
you if it could be avoided.'

Bognor had not got where he had by listening to this garbage.
On this occasion, however, he judged it inappropriate to say so.

'Whoa,' he interrupted, 'you're going too fast. Start at the
beginning and talk me through everything stage by stage. It's
a lot for an old bloke to get his head round.'

It was too. The trouble in dealing with the secret services
was, obviously, secrecy. It was difficult to establish truth when
the very definition of their organization was its obfuscation. It
was patently ludicrous to ask one's allegedly secret services to
tell the truth. They are in business to tell lies.

'I was reading sociology at Keele. Then I spent a summer
inter-railing and pitched up at the British Embassy in Bucharest.
They recruited me for their local intelligence operation hanging
out with Securitate and the friends of Nicolae Ceausescu, and
then I was approached by London when I got home.'

'Simple as that?'

'Simple as that.'

'Life is never as simple as that.'

He disguised the platitude with a slurp of Americano. On
consideration, the sentiment may have been obvious but that
didn't prevent it being true. Most analysis and description
was concerned with reducing complex issues to black and
white simplicity, but life, in his experience, was seldom quite
like that. Life was complicated, blurred, muddy grey. It was
only journalism and history which rendered clear in outline,
simple in cause and predictable in effect. Novelists, too. They
imposed patterns and structure on stuff which didn't have any
of either.

'Oh,' said Camilla, 'life is unbearably simple. You're born;
you live; you die. Beginning; middle; end. How do you compli-
cate that? I was born; I live. Sooner or later, I'll die. No one
much will notice at the time. A while later and no one will
notice anything at all. We bring nothing in; we take nothing
out. That's true for all of us. Simple.'

Long pause. They both stared into their coffee.

'I wouldn't say that,' said Bognor. 'But be that as it may,
you seem to have got the wrong end of the wrong stick. You

obviously want to tell me about it, so crack on. Don't let me interrupt. I'm all ears.'

He wasn't. He was playing chess and he was responding to her ambitious opening by playing the equivalent of a dead bat. Life, he reflected, was one sporting metaphor after another. Maybe life was just a game after all. Now that games had become a highly financed industrial part of economic life, rather than an extra-curricular activity, the notion had become quite different from Henry Newbolt's Corinthian-Victorian notion of warfare being a deadlier form of cricket or rugby football, with a Gatling gun instead of a Gunn and Moore cricket bat, and bloodthirsty fuzzy-wuzzies on the other side instead of fifteen brutes from school house. Bognor, like so many of his contemporaries, had been brought up in an old-fashioned tradition where boys – he had, naturally, been to an all male school – were prepared for a world which had long since vanished. It was not always easy to adapt, even though he considered himself the most adaptable, liberal person he knew. Nevertheless, he had to acknowledge that the conditioning of people such as Harvey Contractor was significantly different.

Or even Camilla.

'I was recruited on my gap year,' she said. 'When I was inter-railing I ended up in Bucharest. My passport was nicked and I met the local head of station at the Embassy. He liked the idea of controlling a girl studying sociology at Keele.' She spelled out the name of her *alma mater* and Bognor found it irritating.

'I do know about Keele,' he said, tetchily. 'It's good. Not so sure about sociology, but there's nothing wrong with Keele.' He knew she thought he was being snobbish. Too bad. It was her fault not his. Conditioning. Prejudice. The class system might have shifted in the last half century, but it was still alive and kicking. And not just in the UK either.

The trouble was that out here in the Spanish sticks it was going to be much more difficult to run the sort of routine checks on Camilla that he would have run off at home. There he had only to pick up the telephone, or thumb through one of his many reference books. Here he was under virtually constant surveillance of one sort or another and he was far removed from his usual sources. He would have to call Harvey Contractor on his mobile; or Monica; or both. But it would all take too long, was too complicated and essentially unreliable. He had long ago recognized that when it came to research you had to do your own, and you couldn't even trust your nearest and dearest.

Basically, he would have to trust his instincts and decide for himself, by himself, whether or not this woman was telling the truth . . . He was not disposed to give her the benefit of the doubt, except for the fact that she appeared to know about him and SIDBOT. That was inside, privileged information and not the sort of thing you would expect to be known by the average boarding house landlady from Byron Bay.

'I've only got your word for this,' he said. 'And even though I can believe that our Intelligence Services are run in a thoroughly ramshackle way, I find it hard to believe that even they would just go round recruiting any old student who comes crashing into their vision during an inter-rail gap year.'

She smiled. 'Intelligence is about intuition; about breaking the rules; about snap judgements. A good intelligence operator should be able to fly by the seat of their pants, not be governed by rules and regulations, not have to refer everything back to some sort of committee.'

'Even so,' he said.

'You have to believe me. Or not.'

She said, 'There's nothing and nobody to hide behind. You're on your own.'

This was true. And both knew it.

'Go on,' he said, 'I'm still listening.'

'I went straight from university to the training course for Secret Intelligence; then I had two years in London before being sent off to the High Commission in Gambia to run the Intelligence side of things there; then Ecuador. Then home, and after a while I was placed on Diana's staff. On secondment.'

'You're not serious.'

'Perfectly,' she said.

'And did she suspect?'

'What?'

'That you were not what you seemed.'

'She knew that I was on secondment from the Foreign Office.

There was no subterfuge involved with that. No one knew that I was in Intelligence. At least, I don't think they did.'

'Not even Mr Al Fayed?'

'He came later.' She smiled. 'And it was absurdly easy to make him look ridiculous. Still, safer to have me out of the way for a while. Clever, too, because when the time came to be reactivated I'd have been dormant long enough to allay suspicion.'

This was perfectly true.

'But why Trubshawe?'

'Why indeed?' she said, drinking coffee. 'I've long since learned not to ask too many questions. It doesn't pay in this line of work. As you ought to know by now. Let's just say that I'm acting on the very highest authority. I'm kosher; sanctioned; and everything so far has gone according to plan. All we have to do is hold out till the end of the course and then make our separate ways home.'

'Except for Jimmy Trubshawe,' he said.

'Except for Trubshawe,' she said. 'He wouldn't have anticipated leaving feet first in a wooden box, but these things happen. Someone should have told him he had a lethal mushroom allergy. Regrettable, but not completely out of the ordinary.'

'So you're telling me that you're responsible for Trubshawe's death and that you're carrying out orders which would rule out anything directed by SIDBOT –supposing that SIDBOT even exists.'

She nodded. 'Just about sums it up,' she said.

'So what do you want me to do?' he asked. 'Assuming for just a moment that I am who you say I am, which I'm not. But if I were, what would you ask?'

'Nothing,' she said. 'Absolutely nothing. Think nothing; say nothing; but, above all, *do* nothing.'

NINETEEN

t would have been easy to do nothing. Doing nothing came naturally to him, and there were those who considered that inactivity had got him where he was. If so, the inactivity was masterly, for knighthood and pension were not the usual rewards for inertia. Not that he considered that he had done nothing. It was just the way it looked to others, and most of them, he reckoned, were jealous. They couldn't see the feet paddling frantically beneath the waterline in order to preserve the swanlike serenity of his visible presence.

Monica, that is Lady Bognor, would have chortled at the idea of 'swanlike serenity' being applied to himself. But in her particular way, she was, Bognor reckoned, as myopic and undiscerning as everyone else.

He dialled her all the same.

'Had a fabulous day!' she trilled before he could say anything. 'Manuel is divine and I had him all to myself doing basic grammar and conversation. Salamanca is fabulous and Manuel and I had horse for lunch. Not bad. In fact, scrummy.'

Then, almost as an afterthought, she managed, 'How was your day?'

'Mixed,' he replied, truthfully, if economically. 'That is to say good and bad. I'd like you to do something for me.'

It didn't particularly occur to him to be jealous of or about Manuel; nor to reflect on his wife's apparently naïve enthusiasm for the man's charms, as well as for those of the city and the rigours of grammar and conversation. He had known her too long and he was too preoccupied with the job in hand. Had he had the time or the inclination to reflect, he would have said that he found her girlishness endearing rather than past its sell-by date. When all was said and done, he still loved the old bat.

'I'm being stitched up,' he said, 'Here, of all places. Just when I assumed I'd have the field to myself. Long arms are even longer than I'd realized.'

'How so?' she wanted to know, Salamanca, Manuel and Spanish conversation, apparently forgotten.

He told her.

'So you've solved the murder?' she asked when he'd finished.

'I have someone who has, in so many words, admitted to the crime. And I have a named accomplice. No more details. And I'm sceptical. The story doesn't stack up!' He was calling from the mobile, a hundred or so yards from the main building, just short of the woods. He couldn't be too careful. Walls had ears. It was getting dark and chilly.

'But this woman knew who you were. And why you were at the Pueblo. Bit of a coincidence. I mean, she can't have been that intuitive. Besides not many people know about you know what.'

She meant SIDBOT but she too was being careful. If Camilla was as resourceful and high-powered as she claimed, then she could be listening in, even on their mobiles.

'Can you do the usual?'

Monica was brilliant at other men's wives. Not bad when it came to other men, but completely brilliant when it came to their wives. He sometimes wished the same could be said of him for he occasionally fancied other men's wives, though a combination of fear, Monica and a public school education meant that he invariably kept his hands to himself. He missed Monica, he realized ruefully. This was particularly so at moments such as this, when he needed her physical reassurance. It was one thing to have her musky, lavenderish, familiar smile and a large, dominating hand clasping his; quite another to have her marginally braying bossy wife coming at him down his mobile phone. Better than nothing though, and she was a good player to have on your team.

'Not a problem,' she said. 'Though I'd rather be able to do it face to face. There's something dispiritingly depersonalizing about distance, even when telephony is so plausible and uncrackling. Are you all right?'

'Fine,' he replied, not quite meaning it. 'Feeling a bit exposed and vulnerable, but I suppose it does one good to be taken out of one's comfort zone.'

'Not at our age.' She laughed, sounding almost as if she

meant it. 'Bit of a worry though,' she continued. 'To be honest, I'd rather thought your friend Trubshawe had died of mushroom-assisted food poisoning. I envisaged a risk-free freebie in España, not a real-life murder. Takes a bit of the shine off Manuel and the language course.'

'Not to worry,' said Bognor, again not really meaning it. 'Rum do, though. I'd dismiss both of them as particular slices of fruitcake, except that they seemed to know precisely who I was and whence I came. And without some kind of privileged information, I'd say that was impossible.'

'SIDBOT isn't exactly something to be conjured with,' she agreed, and then realizing that she might have said something not entirely complimentary, added, 'Outside official circles of course.'

'If it's true,' he said, 'it's frankly outrageous. It means that HMG has been carrying out assassinations in the territory of a supposedly friendly country, and then concealed the fact from the head of one of the said government's leading intelligence agencies, even when he has ventured into the murder zone in order to clear up the whole bloody mess single-handed and at considerable risk to himself.'

'Quite,' said his wife.

'You sound as if you don't agree.'

'I do, darling. I think the whole thing is perfectly outrageous. Particularly at a time when our so-called government is blathering on about an ethical foreign policy and having secret services which are open and accountable. If what you say is true, then it's lamentable and heads should roll. Having said that, however, I have an unpleasant feeling in my water that it's par for the course and heads are going to remain resolutely attached to the shoulders. There's a lot to be said for the Middle Ages and the executioner's axe. But we live in a more enlightened age, as you well know.'

'The absence of sanctions leads to a dissolution of morality,' said Bognor, playing a familiar but favourite tune.

Lady Bognor had heard it before. Many times.

'Yes, darling,' she said. She knew the dictum really applied most of all to her husband: without sanctions he would run amok; without control he was uncontrollable. Or so he liked to think.

'I don't want to know how you gain your information,' he said, 'provided you obtain same. How you do it is your business. I won't even ask you to reveal your sources.'

'No dear,' she said, with barely a trace of sarcasm or irony. This too she had heard many times before. She never did reveal her sources; nor her methods, but this was not because he failed to ask. Practising what he preached was not one of her husband's virtues. The service she performed really was secret – as befitted the senior.

'Would you like me to come out?' she asked. 'I could get a cab. It wouldn't take long.'

'Then my cover really would be blown,' he protested.

'Sounds as if it is already,' she said. 'I can't see how I can make things much worse. And I might conceivably make them better.'

Bognor was floundering. Part of him would actually much have preferred to see his wife, then packed his bags, taken the first plane home, and gone for the early retirement and the congenial pottering about which usually followed a knighthood. A combination of morning crosswords and evening snifters, presaging a gentle slide into senility. Another part, however, rebelled and told him what he had always believed: that he had always had it in him and that it was still there, if only for one more time.

'I'll call at about the same time tomorrow, unless there's some unforeseen disaster,' he said. 'But I'd better call Harvey Contractor. Better do things officially, as well as our way.'

'OK,' she said. 'If you say so. Love you.' The last phrase was something she had picked up from some North American soap. Bognor thought the expression and the sentiment affected and fey, but he reckoned it was more than his life was worth to say so.

'Absolutely,' he said, sounding stiff upper-lippish and not in the least like a character in a soap, North American or not.

He pressed the button with the red telephone on it and then dialled Contractor. It took the younger man a while to answer but he eventually did so. He sounded frazzled.

'Hi, boss,' he said, injecting some enthusiasm which sounded contrived. 'How's business?'

Bognor told him, keeping his report brief and to the point. Apart from anything else he was getting cold. A crescent moon, lemon-yellow, was rising theatrically over the blackening hillside. He smelled woodsmoke which had a whiff of pine about it. He wondered if he was right to be worried. In the normal course of events he would have regarded Camilla as ineffectually mousey and Eduardo as a banana freak with a flamenco subtext. He wouldn't have regarded either as a particular threat, but then one never did. Everyone was unthreatening until proved otherwise.

'You want to me to check them out, boss?'

'If you wouldn't mind.'

It was a very old-fashioned way of giving an order. He doubted whether Harvey would employ velvet gloves if and when he assumed command. On the other hand, Bognor regarded good manners as preferable to bad, even when dealing with the enemy. Particularly when dealing with the enemy.

'If the locals are right,' he said, 'we're being stabbed in the back. Despite all the evidence to the contrary, I'm not disposed to believe that there is quite such dishonesty elsewhere in the corridors of power.'

'We have real nuisance value,' said Contractor. 'It's what I like about you. You know that. I've said it often enough.'

This was true, and Bognor would have been flattered if the implication was that this was the only thing about him which Contractor admired. Bognor may have seemed conventional and not given to the rocking of boats. In fact, these appearances were deceptive, but Contractor, who was good at what he did, had no trouble in recognizing where angels should fear to tread. Angels who got too close had their wings singed and tended to beat a confused retreat. Most people judged Bognor to be one of life's middle order batsmen, a sort of retired major forever banging his head on an impenetrable khaki-serge ceiling. This wasn't strictly speaking true. Deep down, Bognor was by way of being an iconoclast. Monica recognized this; Contractor likewise. They regarded it as a redeeming quality. Not many shared their insights or their perception.

'Normal channels, boss?'

'Up to a point,' said Bognor. Contractor knew about Monica;

would have been locked away in a maximum security joint on the Isle of Wight for the term of his natural life.

He had been put away, that was true, but only in Wandsworth, which was the most insecure prison outside holiday camps for white collar crims, best-selling authors and outed Conservative politicians. Open prisons, indeed. Bognor prided himself on his liberalism and enlightenment but 'Open Prison' was an oxymoron if ever there was one. The only good prison was a clink so closed that they threw away the key after they'd locked the door. With Trubshawe inside for preference.

The death of Trubshawe was the one given. Other than that, 'facts' were elusive. There seemed to be no doubt that the mushrooms had, at the very least, precipitated Trubshawe's demise. However, had he been a normal healthy person of perhaps thirty years younger he would have survived, possibly without even realizing that he had been the victim of even the mildest form of food poisoning. To have been murder, therefore, the person responsible for making sure that he ate a relatively peculiar form of fungus would have needed to know that Trubshawe was not as fit as a fiddle or flea, and was particularly prone to the sort of attack likely to be triggered by this particular mushroom.

That meant the killer either knew Trubshawe well – and that pointed towards George – or had access to the Trubshawe file, a possibility which pointed towards Camilla, if she were to be believed. The question of believing Camilla was obviously paramount. If she were to be believed, then she was the killer. Indeed, she was more or less boasting of it. Even though she was only obeying orders.

If Camilla was telling the truth, she had been activated by SIS, who saw this as a perfect way of getting rid of an awkward enemy in the least obtrusive way possible. Camilla would be flown in to do the deed and flown out again. If she carried out the murder successfully it was highly unlikely that anyone would have suspected foul play, even privately. This all made perfectly good sense.

The most convincing argument in favour of Camilla was that she seemed to know all about Bognor and his provenance. This would have been possible without any form of inside knowledge, but it was unlikely. Bognor was a shadowy figure whose *Who's Who* entry was ambiguous and elusive unless you counted his chosen recreations of 'eating, drinking and holding forth'. This implied a convivial gregariousness that was entirely in character, but a garrulity which, on balance, was not. He could maintain a conversation and could occasionally, when required, manage 'life and soul of the party', but he was also good at keeping his counsel and staying shtum when required. He would not have stayed in his job if this were not the case.

He was sceptical about her claim to have worked for Diana, Princess of Wales. Along with most Establishment figures he was sceptical about almost everything to do with the late Princess, and contemptuous in a decidedly unamused way about the buffoonish but tenacious Mohamed Al-Fayed. It would be too tiresome if Camilla turned out to be telling the truth, and the odious Egyptian shopkeeper turned out to be telling the truth, despite the inquest. It was not that Bognor questioned the motivation of the Security Services, merely their competence. They could have murdered the Princess if it were simply a question of wish-fulfilment. On the other hand, Bognor doubted very much whether they would have been able to do so without botching the job, and certainly without being detected. It was the fact that his assailant had missed an easy potshot a few minutes earlier that led him to believe in the involvement of the British Security Services. Not many, under those circumstances, could have fired and missed. Britain's chaps could have done it, though. Bognor was as disdainful about them as he was about Al Fayed. One reason why he had gone into SIDBOT, just as he never shopped in Harrods.

He picked up one of the Archers, read a couple of lines and replaced it, frowning. He had a confession on a plate; a warning shot by way of corroboration. He would have been entirely within his rights to accept Camilla's word, scuttle home and have a blazing row with Fergus or one of his colleagues at the far end of one of the Whitehall corridors.

But he knew he wouldn't.

He was more suspicious of George. He was so obviously a fellow member of Trubshawe's Costa Nostra, besides which Bognor had swiftly conceived a visceral dislike of the man.

But he didn't really see how or why it stacked up. His attitude towards the deceased seemed respectably neutral, rather like an old-fashioned pre-Massingberd obituary in the *Telegraph*. You wouldn't catch George speaking ill of the dead. Not particularly well, either, so that it wouldn't be easy to work out exactly what George thought of the dead man, if indeed he thought anything at all. This was the impression George intended to convey and the one that Bognor, in a similar situation would have tried to convey himself. George was either a highly skilled professional, or an irregular Essex boy with a convincing patter on second-hand cars and an eye for fur coat and no knickers. Dislike him though he did, Bognor inclined to the latter view.

Not that these were the only suspects. In what was a classic closed-room, body-in-the-library sort of murder mystery, everyone, including the detective, was a potential criminal. There should, ideally, be at least one other crime, preferably inferior, running alongside the main one and occasionally sharing tracks, thus ensuring maximum confusion.

He fell to pondering Arizona Brown and Felipe Lee, their plausible manners, their access to everything from files on participants to recipes for lunch. Of all those in the Pueblo, they were the ones with most information and the most excuse for being in places the guests could not reach. For them nothing and nowhere was out of bounds. On the other hand, they had no motive for doing in Trubshawe, and although they had sussed Bognor being an implausible Anglo, they had not been able to finger him in the same way as Camilla and her banana-loving flamenco-playing sidekick.

And then there was the slinky Dolores Calderon, who was at the same time a part of the operation and yet not. He wasn't too sure where she fitted into the scheme of things. She was obviously grand and rich, able to come and go much as she pleased, yet not like Arizona and Felipe. She seemed to be part dogsbody and errand girl, and part grand-dame. She didn't strike Bognor as a murderess but she could pass as a high-class moll. Too high class, he reckoned for either George or Jimmy Trubshawe, and no one else in the place was old enough to run to a girl like Dolores, whether as a moll or something more conventional. Not that conventional was a word you would associate with Dolores.

He swallowed the last of the aguardiente and decided against a refill. There was a wood-burning stove with a pile of logs in the alcove behind it. The stove and the fuel implied a knowledge of rocket science, or at least of DIY skills, that he did not possess. The aguardiente had made him feel peckish but there was no sign of food in the room – not even a packet of crisps, nachos or nuts. Maybe he should walk up to the bar. It would soon be time for brainstorming round the sausage question.

It seemed an odd way of teaching the language, and he couldn't imagine that any of the Spaniards present would find a knowledge of the relative merits of the two sorts of sausage particularly useful at international conferences, or in the breaks between negotiating deals to do with fruit or pet food. Still, he supposed, you never knew.

He wondered whether to put on a woolly sweater or an overcoat; decided against, and walked outside. On the doorstep he was immediately greeted with a seductive mixture of expensive scent and rich unfiltered loosely packed cigarette.

She was right on cue.

'Good evening,' she said, 'I thought I would escort you to your next meeting.'

He had a distinct feeling that Dolores had been waiting for him. Also, that if she had fired a gun at him, she would not have missed.

TWENTY-ONE

She not only smelt of desirable forbidden fruit but she walked in a sinuous manner, which fitted with the aroma, the tight leather trousers and the totteringly high heels she was wearing. It was a clear night, and the light of the sickle moon and the evening stars was bright enough to illuminate her wiggly walk. She had snake-like hips.

'You are a friend of the Admiral,' she said, as they set off up the path. She took his arm, balancing against him so as not to fall over on the ridiculous heels.

'Admiral Picasso?' he ventured. Picasso was the only Admiral he knew either in Spain or anywhere else. Not that he had ever regarded the title as anything more than an honorific. He had always thought of Picasso as a sort of Gilbert and Sullivan admiral, not someone who would have commanded an Armada galleon in 1588. Italians who had mastered the equivalent of the three Rs were always called '*Dottore*'. Same sort of nonsense.

'Admiral Picasso,' she said, rolling the words around her tongue so that they took on a sexy quality that they completely lacked when enunciated by an Englishman like Bognor, 'Juan. Do you know him through your work?'

'No, certainly not. I know him through our mutual love of . . . er . . . classical guitar . . . Rodrigo, Segovia, Julian Bream, John Williams.'

She laughed and Bognor sensed her disbelief.

'I always understood Juan was tone deaf. It shows only that even when you think you know someone quite well, you hardly know them at all. Juan and the guitar. I must tease him the next time I see him.'

Bognor had always regarded the Admiral as a randy old goat but had never before had anything approaching proof. Old salt or not, Picasso had always played his sexual cards close to his chest. Ahead of them a door opened and closed, and there was

a brief sound of lively conversation and what sounded like
bagpipe music rinsed through Iberian muslin – something to
do with goatherds from Asturias or lobster-potters from Galicia,
he thought, slipping easily into colour-magazine travel-writing
mode.

'You know the Admiral well?'

She flicked the glowing end of her cigarette into the darkness
and he felt a shrug.

'He is a very old friend,' she said, explaining as little as
possible, 'of the family you might say.' She laughed plangently.
'He has asked me to make sure you come to no harm. I said
there was no chance of harm. This is a very safe place.'

Bognor thought of Jimmy Trubshawe and the shot that missed.
He shivered despite himself. He wondered whose side Dolores
Calderon was on, if indeed she was ever on anyone's side except
her own.

'The death was very unexpected; very unusual. It is the first
we have had in the entire history of the Pueblo.'

'I'm very sorry to hear that.'

'Thank you.'

She stopped and turned to face him. They were about halfway
to the main building. An owl hooted. A dog barked.

'Sir Simon, I would like to be frank with you. Especially as
you are a friend of my friend the Admiral, though not, of course,
in what you British call "a professional capacity".'

'Shoot,' said Bognor, not meaning to use such an inapposite
word and regretting it as soon as it was uttered. It could not
be withdrawn though. Like an e-mail message once you had
inadvertently pressed the wrong button. It didn't matter that
you sent the wrong message and possibly to the wrong person.
The pressing of the button was irreversible, just like the
speaking of words. He remembered the old adage about not
digging further when you entered a hole and did not explain
or apologize. She did not appear to notice but Bognor was
unconvinced.

'Thank you,' she said. 'If I may be honest, Mr Trubshawe
was not a nice man. Not nice at all.'

'So I rather understand,' he said.

'He was quite rich. He had money. But it was difficult to say where the money came from. Our friend the Admiral warned me that I should be careful.'

'How so?' Curious and curiouser. Admiral Picasso had confided none of this. He would have seen the files; heard Bognor's views on Trubshawe; been under no illusions regarding his character and provenance. But he had said nothing about voicing his suspicions to Dolores Calderon and indeed said nothing at all about any relationship with her. Nor her family. Bognor felt like laughing out loud.

'I mentioned that Mr Trubshawe was joining us on the seminar. But he also had what I think you call a "hidden agenda".'

'That's a very sophisticated phrase,' said Bognor, 'and quite a sophisticated concept. Can you explain?'

They were still facing each other in the dark; not more than a few inches between them. Bognor wondered, fleetingly, if it had been Dolores who fired the shot and whether or not he might be in danger even now, when, despite his age, or even because of it, he was rather enjoying the proximity of this musky, husky foreign female.

'Mr Trubshawe and the man called George claimed to have money and they were interested in buying the business. Before they finally made an offer they said they wanted to see how it worked. Close up. For themselves. Sharing the experience.'

'So Trubshawe and the man called George knew each other?'

'They were colleagues,' she said, 'so, yes, naturally. They were business associates. Maybe friends also but that was not my impression.'

'And what was your impression?' If Bognor was not so sure that he was carrying out his duty and only doing his job he might have thought that they were flirting. Ridiculous. This seemed to have become a universal truth and a source of recurring bother. He sometimes thought he was not destined for old age and uxorious slipperdom.

She lit another cigarette, dragged on it and exhaled strong, tarry smoke through her nostrils.

'My impression is that they . . . how does one say it? That they were not friends. They acted together. They had known each other a long time. They did deals. But friends, no. Looks between them. And once I heard them arguing.'

'How did they come to be here?'

'They came to the office in Madrid. You know, of course, that I am partly the owner of the Pueblo organization?'

Bognor hadn't known this. He would kill one or two people, starting with Admiral Picasso, when he returned to civilization. Why did no one tell him things any more? Maybe they never had. But he always found out in the end. For the time being he just shrugged.

'I am just what people in my part of the world call "an ordinary Joe",' he said, 'and I'm not naturally curious. Let's just say that I knew but I did not know.'

Two lies followed by an ambivalence, but she let it pass.

'We had better go,' she said. 'At least you go on. It is better that we are not seen together. I have nothing to do with the day-to-day organization. As you would say, "I am here but I am not here". Also our friend the Admiral has made me responsible for your being safe. So I will be watching. And I think you should be careful of the man called George.'

'Are you saying that he killed Jimmy Trubshawe?'

She breathed in smoke and blew it out again, appearing to give the question thought.

'I do not know why you think anyone killed Mr Trubshawe,' she said. 'He was not a very well person. It could have happened at any moment. Accident. That is all. It was very sad, but an accident. Everyone says so.'

'But someone fed him the wrong kind of mushroom.'

'Maybe,' she said, and bent forward to kiss Bognor lightly on the cheek, turned and was gone as swiftly and completely as she had arrived.

Bognor felt both elated and apprehensive, but moved on towards the main building and the impending discussion about the relative merits of Spanish and British sausages.

He felt vulnerable. He supposed everybody except Arizona Brown and Felipe Lee shared that sense of exposure. All of them were exposed and alone; the Spaniards even more so because they were dealing in a language not their own, though the Anglos also suffered from an isolation by language, all the more menacing because it was not apparent in their unnatural little cocoon of Englishness. The reality was that this was Spain and the tiny group of Anglos were, though apparently in charge of the proceedings, actually surrounded by a world of Hispanic otherness. At any moment this could intrude and break in on the artificial Anglocentric world of make-believe that was the Pueblo.

He supposed he had not known quite what he was letting himself in for when he took on this assignment. Maybe no man was an island. He had forgotten what it was like to be alone among potential enemies with the smell of death always in his nostrils. Security and status were insulating, and there was no question that as one progressed up the rungs of the career ladder one lost touch with life below. Whether life at the bottom was any more 'real' than life at the top was a moot point and a matter for conjecture and debate, but there was a widespread popular notion that 'reality' was 'synonymous' with deprivation and lack of success, whereas the further up the tree you climbed the more out of touch you became.

He personally believed that he was astonishingly adroit at keeping in touch; that he enjoyed a special rapport with young-sters such as Contractor who came from a different generation, as did his much-loved and appreciated nephews, nieces and godchildren. He did his utmost to tune into their tastes, to appreciate the same music and clothing, and even food and drink. From time to time he even took public transport, thus risking the disdain of Thatcherites who believed that any man who takes a bus or train when he has passed the age of thirty is one of life's failures. (He half-believed this himself and only used public transport in the interests of research and 'keeping in touch'.)

And now sausages.

He smiled at the manifest absurdity of the impending charade. Who would have thought that Sir Simon Bognor, Permanent Secretary at Special Investigations, Board of Trade, would have found himself in isolated Spain discussing the merits of the British banger with a bunch of complete strangers. Or that he would be there to investigate the sudden death of a known British villain who had been holed up in Spain, without apparent fear of extradition, ever since escaping in broad daylight from the care and custody of Her Majesty's Prison Service. Or that the aforementioned Sir Simon Bognor would have been shot at by a person or persons unknown, warned off by others, confided in – up to a point – by yet others, and generally been reduced to the ranks. All this of his own volition, without instruction from elsewhere, and to the definite disapproval of other parts of Her Majesty's Government, thus putting him yet further at risk, if not of physical harm, at least of verbal disgrace, opprobrium and so on.

He rubbed his hands, rather relishing the predicament in which he found himself. It was dark; it was cold; it was foreign; it was threatening. He was no longer as grand as he thought he was; he was far from home; there were precious few comforts close at hand.

Yet he was in his element.

He quickened his pace, still rubbing his hands together, and allowing himself the softest of self-congratulatory chuckles.

Sausages, eh?!

TWENTY-TWO

He was the last to arrive.

Arizona Brown looked ostentatiously at her wristwatch – an expensive Tag Heuer of the sort used by deep-sea divers many fathoms down. She did not speak but the look spoke volumes.

'Sorry I'm late,' he said. 'Got a bit tied up.'

'"Tied up",' explained Arizona to her charges, 'does not mean 'tied up' in a literal manner. Simon did not get in a muddle with his shoelaces. He has just produced an old-fashioned English euphemism for being late. It is not a reason. It is an excuse.'

'Being late is pretty rich for the country which patented the word "*mañana*",' said Bognor irritably.

'No Spanish, please, Simon.' She sounded at least as irritable. The log fire spat.

'English I may be,' he said, 'old-fashioned I am not.'

One or two people tittered. He couldn't see who they were. Didn't care. Told himself he didn't care. Not necessarily the same thing. Odd how he suddenly found himself communicating inwards in staccato-speak. Must mean that I'm rattled, he thought.

Arizona spoke. 'You're a banger,' she said, 'so you're down the far end of the room near the fire with George, Lola and Belen. Leonel, Tracey, Camilla and Eduardo are chorizos. I shall float between the two camps assisting where needed. Felipe will do the same.'

Felipe smiled and nodded, and Bognor joined his group trying to appear nonchalant and as if he did this sort of thing all the time. He could imagine himself and Monica sitting up of an evening playing chorizos and bangers like a Darby and Joan couple settling down to a mug of cocoa and a round or two of whist.

Everyone had a writing implement and a clipboard or

notebook. Each group sat round a low table with a cafetière of coffee, a bowl of sugar and a milk jug in the middle, along with a bottle of sparkling mineral water. In front of every participant was a mug and a glass. It was almost like a real conference.

Bognor sat at the spare chair at the Bangers table, smiled and nodded at his three team mates, wondered if one of them had murdered Jimmy Trubshawe and pulled out a pencil and notebook. A moment or so later, Arizona Brown clapped her hands and smiled glacially.

'Now that we're all assembled,' she said, looking pointedly at Simon, 'I'd like to run over the ground rules once more just to be certain you understand.' She said once again more or less the same as she had said after lunch. Bognor felt his attention wandering.

There were two quantities unknown to Bognor, one in each group: Banger Belen on his own side and Chorizo Tracey on the other. Belen was, if his memory served him right, in her late thirties, lived in a suburban apartment and was the export manager of a small chain of Madrid-based boutique hotels. She did a lot of business in Scandinavia and sounded rather a dull stick. There was a live-in partner. She worked out.

'You do a lot of business in Scandinavia?' he ventured, 'Dull people the Scandinavians. Not much into sausages. Cold fish.'

She smiled back at him, discomfited.

'Cold fish?' she repeated, obviously taking the remark literally and trying to equate Finns with ceviche, Danes with gravadlax. Not that difficult. 'Fish in Scandinavia I like very much,' she said.

Bognor shook his head.

'Forget it,' he said.

'Cold fish is a person with no feelings,' said Lola, the nun, unexpectedly. 'Not Latin. No hot blood. No passion. The cold fish is a person who is never impulsive. They decide everything according to ratiocination and for reasons that they have considered very carefully. Perhaps Aquarius is a cold fish because of the water. The water in Aquarius is to do with purifying and cleaning, so perhaps it is a cold water. Or more likely it is Pisces. The Pisces is the Latin word for the fish, but I do not know if the Pisces is a cold fish. Maybe hot. I think Pisces are governed by emotion and intuition, so perhaps not cold fish. I don't know. I believe in God, not the stars, but maybe you are different, Belen. Maybe you are not as holy as your name and perhaps you believe in the horoscope.'

She blushed, surprised perhaps by her verbosity, which bordered on the articulate. Bognor felt moved to clap but did not. George neither, though he too seemed impressed.

'Lola's pretty right,' said Bognor. 'The important point being that "cold fish" is a figure of speech. Not literal. That's the problem with the English language. So much metaphor and simile that it sometimes hides the truth.'

'Like life,' said Lola, who seemed to be entering into the swing of things. 'Life is full of metaphors and similes, and nothing is as obvious as it might seem.'

'Like murder,' said George. 'It isn't always the obvious suspect wot dunnit.'

The pause that followed this reversion to the nagging Banquo's ghost of the late Trubshawe and his unexpected death could only be described as 'awkward'. Even George seemed to regret that he had said it.

'So who,' asked Bognor, innocently, 'is the obvious suspect when it comes to killing Trubshawe?'

'Are you saying Jimmy was murdered?' Bognor noted the familiar 'Jimmy', but raised the palms of his hand in a gesture of ignorance and perplexity.

'I wasn't here, remember. I'm only here as Trubshawe's last minute stand-in.'

'My view is that it was an accident,' said George. 'Jimmy was an accident waiting to happen.'

'And the mushrooms . . . ?' Bognor wanted to know.

'Were the trigger. Unfortunate. But if it hadn't been the mushrooms it would have been something else. He was a sick man. He was going to die anyway.'

'What makes you so sure?' asked Bognor.

It was George's turn to shrug. He also changed the subject. 'We're supposed to be devising a marketing strategy for bangers.'

'Quite,' said Bognor. 'I think we should begin by nominating a team leader. That's the way they do it on TV. I think it should be Belen or Lola, and I think we should have a secret ballot. Quite simple. We just write down our nomination on a piece of paper, fold it up so it's secret and then do a count.'

This was easy and no one demurred. Bognor opened them up and found all four for Lola. Interesting, he thought to himself. It meant that Lola had voted for Lola. That surely said something about her self-confidence. Did it also say something about the lack of same in Belen. Belen wasn't as obviously attractive, which was odd, given that Lola was a nun and Belen worked in boutique hotels. Temperamentally, Bognor was absolutely not in favour of this sort of exercise, which reeked of the kind of team-building mumbo-jumbo practised by modern management consultants who ripped off large businesses by trading on corporate greed and indolence. In his opinion, anyway.

'A majority for Lola,' he said. Strange that he had emerged as, in a sense, a kind of *de facto*, team leader. It was he who had made the suggestion; he who had had it accepted and now he who had organized the mini-election and the votes. Perhaps he exuded natural authority after all. Perhaps there was more to these charades than he thought. 'Oh, OK, Lola, take it away. Let it rip.'

'Rip?' she enquired tentatively, causing Bognor to curse his overuse of meaningless colloquialism.

'Don't worry about it,' he said. 'It's just a lazy way of saying that you're in charge. We are putty in your hands.'

She frowned again but did not, this time, take him up on the evidently strange expression.

'We have to sell the idea of the sausage you call the banger,' she said, obviously. 'I should like to know why it is called "banger", please.'

'The British banger,' said George, 'like fish and chips or bacon and egg, is British. It's an institution back home. People like Trubshawe and me have been trying to introduce it into Spain, and I think we have a thing or two we could tell you.'

Trubshawe and *I*, thought Bognor pedantically. He was not usually a severe grammarian but everything about George irritated him, and he found his slipshod linguistics as offensive as his mindless jingoism. He tried, however, to control the urge to take irritable issue with either. No Lynne Truss, he.

'Surely something we should be doing is to universalize the banger?' he said, 'I mean, the Spanish aren't going to switch from their own distinctively Iberian sausage to a completely different sort of animal just because it's British. It would put them off, surely? And, by the way, why "banger"? I know it's slang for a particularly British form of sausage, but why? All yours, Lola.'

The improbable poor Claire dimpled nunnishly and smiled round the table. She already looked like a leader.

'Mr Bognor is correct,' she said. 'To sell something as British would, in Spain, be an invitation to a disaster. The only successful British export to Spain is criminal.'

'Football hooligans,' said Belen, nodding. 'Train robbers.'

It was a truism that only kith and kin could slag off kith and kin. It didn't matter how correct an analysis might be, the only people entitled to express it were the accused's nearest and dearest. If an outsider dared to venture a criticism the insiders retaliated as one, even if they had been tearing each other apart moments earlier. This was a truth universally acknowledged.

George and Bognor exchanged glances, recognized their mutual antipathy but acknowledged the truth of the truth. They could be as rude as they liked about each other, but if any outsider should presume to attack them then they would go to each other's assistance. There was no logic in this but it was a fact of life. Neither of them liked the other and they were not particularly proud of their Britishness, or Englishness. But no bloody foreigner could echo such sentiments with impunity.

'I hardly think—' began Bognor.

'Effing rubbish,' said George.

'Having said which,' said Bognor, emolliently, 'I don't think that a successful sales pitch is going to be able to rely on a narrow nationalist focus. It doesn't matter whether the country concerned is popular or not, you can't base these things on provenance.'

Too many long words and abstruse concepts, he acknowledged to himself.

It would be much better to stick to basics. 'The point about the banger,' he said, 'is not that it's British, but that it's basic.' 'Comes to the same thing,' said George. 'What you see is what you get. That's what being British is about. Basic. Basic British. Basic banger.'

'Maybe,' said Bognor, 'that should be the leitmotif, as it were, of our campaign. "Back to the basics with the banger"; "Back to the basic banger"; "Bangers – the basic". Or something like that.'

Belen had barely spoken. Now she said, 'Would you have said that Mr Trubshawe was a banger person? Or would he have preferred the chorizo? He came to Spain. You have a saying in England, do you not . . . ? "When in Spain . . . "?'

'It's the garlic wot does it,' said George. 'Back home we don't do garlic. We let the ingredients speak for themselves. On the continong,' that was how he pronounced the word, 'you use garlic in everything to disguise the fact that the meat's either off or it's horse.'

This, reflected Bognor, wasn't going anywhere.

'With respect,' he said, 'we're supposed to be coming up with a strategy to get people to buy bangers, not indulging in an exercise of national chauvinism. I for one simply don't believe in national stereotyping. Just because you're British or Spanish doesn't mean to say you have to be a particular sort of person.'

'Jimmy Trubshawe was British to his fingertips,' said George. 'Never come across a more British person.'

'You think that has anything to do with his being done in?' asked Bognor, slipping easily into a vernacular that he was not truly at home with.

'You mean that Mr Trubshawe was killed because he was British. A particular sort of British person.' Lola smiled. 'It's possible,' she said.

'Killed for being British!' said George. 'There are precedents for that. But if I wanted to do Jimmy Trubshawe, being British is a bloody feeble pretext.'

TWENTY-THREE

They were dangerously close to a racial meltdown, though Bognor could see that, as far as motivation went, it was not as silly as it might appear. Being killed for being British was not that absurd. You could argue that it happened all the time. The British, or even more so the English, were phenomenally unpopular throughout a world which had once been predominantly their own pink-coloured fiefdom.

'You think Trubshawe could have been killed because he was British?' asked Simon, overeagerly.

'It's possible,' said Lola. 'But we can't market a product on the basis that it's British or English. Not in Spain. Not anywhere. It doesn't make sense. If people even start to believe that it's English or British, then they won't buy it. I'm sorry, but that's a fact. Language maybe, but nothing else.'

'The point surely is,' said Bognor, 'that we're selling something completely simple, uncomplicated, unadulterated. Whether it's British, English or anything else is frankly irrelevant. We're basing our case on simplicity.'

'That's Trubshawe,' said George. 'What you saw was what you got.'

He was, thought Bognor, a master of cliché.

'It seems,' said Belen, 'that we have to say that the point about the banger is that it contains only the very best ingredients and no other messing about. Maybe pepper and salt but that is all. Let us say ninety-eight or ninety-nine per cent meat from wonderful free-range rare breed pigs, such as your Gloucester Old Spot, and just pepper and salt and the case. So it is incredibly simple. Very good for you.'

He had forgotten, momentarily, that Belen had a passing acquaintance, being in boutique hotels, with food and beverage. And fashionable F & B was about clever sourcing and not messing around with prime ingredients. Anyone worth their culinary stripes was into rare breeds and kindness to meat. As

far as he could see, Belen had absolutely no reason for wishing
Trubshawe dead. On the other hand, she would have known her
mushrooms.

'I rather agree,' said Bognor.

'So the selling point is back to basics,' said Lola. 'But, please,
why is the basic British sausage called "banger"?'

Bognor and George looked at each other. Bognor didn't know.

'If they're not properly made they explode when they're being
cooked. They go off with a big bang. Can be too much water.
Can be too much rusk or crust. Your really top-whack banger
doesn't bang because it's nearly all meat, which doesn't explode.
In the last war, the Royal Navy had a pre-cooked, tinned sausage
made by a company called Palethorpe. Submarines, mainly.
They were called "Snorkers".' He smiled, expecting congratula-
tion. 'Not many people know that.'

'What about Lincolnshire sausages? Or Cumberland? Can they
be bangers?' This was Bognor seeking to compete. 'Can you put
bangers in toad-in-the-hole'. He didn't know what any of this
had to do with solving a murder, but detection, he knew from
experience, moved in mysterious and not always logical ways.

'Let's agree,' said Lola, being firm, 'that we're going to sell
a traditional British sausage containing lots of very good pork
and some pepper and salt. Nothing more, nothing less.'

Bognor nodded.

'The key word is "bang",' he said. 'We need to keep "bang"
up front.'

'We should ask ourselves what "bang" suggests,' said George.
'To me it means explosion. Gun shot. Sudden death.' He glanced
meaningfully at Bognor. 'Not a very attractive word. Positively
dangerous, in fact. You don't want bangs around. Even little
ones. They tend to go off in the night when no one's expecting
them.'

Bognor wondered if they were getting somewhere in an
oblique fashion. Was George telling him, in code, that it was
he who had fired the gun?

He felt his mind wandering while the four of them limped
towards a coherent solution to their marketing problems. He
had never been much good at charades and age had neither
sharpened his wits or his enthusiasm. He found himself watching

for telltale clauses in his companions' body language, but had to accept that it was all lacking in conviction as far as murder was concerned, and not much more so when it came to sausages.

He had expected to go into dinner immediately after the brainstorm, but he had forgotten that this was Spain and they ate later than the Brits. It was too late and too dark for another walk, but he and Belen were sentenced to an improving chat in a quiet corner.

'Drink?' he asked her.

'Thank you, no,' she replied.

'I have something to tell you,' she said when they had settled themselves comfortably in accommodating mock-leather armchairs and been joined, unaccountably, by one of the Pueblo's mountain dogs, a shaggy monster with a bell at his neck, who answered to the name of Max. Inside was almost snug. Outside the wind was gathering and it felt unseasonably cold enough for snow. 'You are interested in Mr Trubshawe and his mushrooms?' she said, in a matter of fact sort of way.

She wore tortoiseshell spectacles and had no discernible cheek bones. Bognor liked her. She was the only Spanish woman he had ever seen wearing a cardigan.

'Not specially,' he said, silently cursing. 'I didn't know poor Mr Trubshawe and I'm sort of, er, neutral, when it comes to mushrooms. I mean, I'll eat them when offered but I wouldn't go out of my way to dig them up. Or whatever you do with them. I wonder if you could bandicoot them? Old Australian word. It means stealing vegetables, especially by cutting off the edible roots of things like carrots and parsnips, leaving the green tufty fronds still showing on the surface. So the warders don't know the veggies have gone missing. To bandicoot . . . To steal vegetables while pretending not to.' He smiled, feeling like the late Frank Muir on a good night but realizing that he had been impossibly colloquial.

'The night of Mr Trubshawe's death,' said Belen, ploughing on and paying no attention to his effusions, 'I saw two people returning from their walk with mushrooms. Wild mushrooms which they had gathered in the woods.'

Bognor was interested. Of course he was. This sounded suspiciously like a clue. On the other hand he had to remember that he was not supposed to be here in any kind of official capacity, far less as the recently knighted boss of SIDBOT.

'What makes you think I'm interested in mushrooms?'

Belen didn't reply, simply looked at him as if to say he simply couldn't be as idiotic as the remark made him seem to her. She was not a successful export manager for a hotel chain without reason.

'Tracey and Leonel had been for a walk. They came back with mushrooms. Many mushrooms. I passed them outside the main building after I had finished my own walk with Trubshawe himself.'

'You were out walking with Trubshawe the afternoon before he died?'

'Yes,' she agreed, 'but that is not important.'

'How did he seem?' Bognor wanted to know.

She wanted to tell him about Tracey and Leonel and their mushrooms. Her walk with Trubshawe did not seem relevant. Bognor himself did not agree.

'He seemed very typical. Very British. Very like George. Not nice.'

'How so?'

'Arrogant. Smug. Opinionated. Not interested in other people. Particularly if they were women. No good at listening, only in expressing his own views. He was a typical of a certain sort of English person. George is the same. I hope that you are not like that.'

'I hope not, too.' Bognor spoke with feeling. He suffered, he knew, from seeming to strangers to be a particular sort of person which he believed, emphatically, he was not. Among other things he believed was that he was the last of the Great Detectives. This, he knew, wasn't a view widely shared. At such moments of outsider doubt he reminded himself of the words of wisdom once spoken by the Emperor Marcus Aurelius. These were to the effect that there was no point in spending one's life worrying about the contrary opinions of fools and dolts; one simply had to bash on regardless, recognizing the fact that almost the whole of the rest of the world was out of step.

'Tell me though,' he asked, 'how well did you know Trubshawe?'

'I had only recently met him,' she answered.

'What, here?'

'Of course,' she said. 'He lived in a part of Spain to which proper Spaniards never go. It was somewhere near Malaga, I believe. Or maybe not. It was an enclave such as Gibraltar. More British than Britain, even though technically a part of Spain.'

'Like Ceuta and Melilla in North Africa,' said Bognor waspishly.

'Ceuta and Melilla are different,' she said.

Bognor said he couldn't agree, and that both Spanish enclaves were at least as much a part of Morocco, as Gibraltar was of Spain. He had rather a soft spot for Gibraltar despite its peculiarly old-fashioned British culture. The last refuge for once popular brands of tinned milk and for Conservative politicians totally unknown to a British audience but who were household names on the Rock. It was a perverse sort of place and Bognor rather enjoyed that.

'In any case,' she said, with spirit, 'Mr Trubshawe was, as you would say, a "nasty piece of work", but it is not right that he is dead. Also, I believe that he was killed and that it was not an accident. And I believe that your sudden arrival is somehow connected. Which is why I am telling you this thing.'

'Your English is excellent,' he said, more or less sincerely.

'Flattery, Mr Bognor, will, as I believe you say in your country, get you nowhere.'

'Well, actually,' Bognor demurred, 'it's not flattery, but I see that your personal approval of Jimmy Trubshawe is neither here nor there. As, again, we say back home.'

She nodded.

'The mushrooms,' she said, 'I believe it may be important. I have seen the woman Tracey, the hairdresser from England, returning with Leonel, who is the maker of food for dogs and cats. They had been walking according to the programme and they had returned with the mushrooms.'

'What sort of mushrooms?' he wanted to know. It seemed perfectly relevant, if not entirely reasonable, but she replied that she was no sort of expert on fungi, however, she had observed that the two conversationalists had been picking them and doing so, presumably, for a purpose. When mushrooms turned up on that evening's menu she assumed, not unreasonably, that there was a connection between what she had seen in the afternoon and what appeared on the dinner table a few hours later. Then, when Trubshawe left in a hurry and never came back, she had made another and more sinister connection.

'But you know nothing about mushrooms,' said Bognor, 'and, come to that, nothing about Tracey and Leonel.'

She thought for a moment.

'That is true,' she said.

'Why should I believe you?' he asked.

'Why should I not tell you the truth?' she replied.

Bognor considered this. Eventually, he said, 'If, for some reason, you wanted to suggest that Tracey and Leonel were in some way responsible for the death of Mr Trubshawe, and if, for some improbable reason, you assumed that I was in some way connected with solving the puzzle, then it would be logical for you to seek to sow suspicion. And this would be an effective and plausible way of doing so.'

It was her turn to think.

'I agree,' she said, after considering the matter.

'I suppose it would make sense for me to ask Tracey and Leonel for their side of the story. Establish whether or not they picked mushrooms together when they were out for their walk. See if they had any fungal expertise and knew what they were picking. Ascertain all that kind of thing.'

She smiled at him.

'You would only do that sort of thing if you were in some way involved with the mystery of Mr Trubshawe's death, and in some way supposed that it was not as accidental as we are being told by Arizona and Felipe.'

This was perfectly true and they both recognized it.

'That's perfectly true,' he agreed. 'So maybe I won't ask them after all. Just keep the information under my hat.'

'Hat?' she enquired, and they returned, without conviction, to a conversation more in keeping with the purpose of their presence.

The main course at dinner was either bangers and mash or a *cocido* of chorizos and chick peas with loads of garlic, tomatoes and red wine. The one quintessentially English and the other as exuberantly Spanish. They echoed the current exercise in an appropriate manner and were preceded by a prawn cocktail with a Sauce Marie Rose in the style of the Imperial Hotel, Torquay c.1957, and *gambas al ajillo* in the fashion of any tapas bar anywhere.

Bognor sat at the same table with Tracey, the only one of the group he had not previously met. Their Spaniards were Belen, who had stayed at his elbow, and Eduardo, the banana king who knew that he was the man from SIDBOT.

All four of them pursued the Spanish option – even Tracey – who said she was feeling adventurous, and was intending to sleep on her own and was therefore not bothered about eating garlic. The other three laughed nervously when she said this. They presumed it was intended as a joke. It probably was.

Bognor prodded his prawns with a fork and reflected on the situation morosely. What, in God's name was going on? He was sitting at dinner in an obscure part of Spain eating dinner with a group of complete strangers, one or other of whom might or might have not murdered another complete stranger who was a well-known villain. He, Bognor, was investigating the death on behalf of his government department, not least because the Spanish authorities seemed reluctant to do themselves. He was supposed to be here incommunicado but his cover appeared to be blown. Indeed, the signs were that his government department was at loggerheads with other government departments, if not with government itself.

He passed the pepper absent-mindedly and realized that he was being asked a question. It was from Tracey. She wanted to know where he lived. This was a perfectly reasonable opening gambit. He knew little about Tracey beyond the fact that she sometimes dressed hair in Clacton-on-Sea.

'London,' he said, without thinking.

'Oh!' said Tracey, 'whereabouts in London?'

Bognor said, 'South-west', which was a tad economical with the truth – he and Monica lived in an apartment with a view of the River Thames that was famous throughout the pictorial world and the building was on Richmond Hill, almost abutting the famous deer park.

If Tracey knew, she wasn't saying. Instead, she said, 'I'm

just an Essex girl. I can do the East End and some of the centre. Don't know the North or West or even the South, much. Been to Greenwich. Had an aunt who lived in Blackheath. Ran a salon there.'

'Oh,' said Bognor ungraciously. He speared a prawn and chewed it morosely. He wasn't concentrating on anything; was losing his grip. He looked around the room and wondered if, as he rather thought, everybody was looking at him. He felt, more especially after the gunshot that missed, like the next one in the firing line. It reminded him of the memorial service for Parkinson, his former boss, at St Martin-in-the-Fields. He himself had read a lesson – 'Let us now praise famous men' – which he had thought intensely inappropriate for the head of a supposedly secret branch of a secret service. There in the front row were all the dead man's contemporaries, paying their respects to the deceased, but looking for all the world like the team waiting with their pads on in the dressing room before being called out to bat. You could almost feel them looking around as if to ask apprehensively, 'Who's next in?'

It was the same here. Everyone knew that Trubshawe had been cut down by the Grim Reaper not long before and they were all, very politely, wondering who might be the next on the death list. Actually, correction, he thought with only a slight frisson of concern, they were not wondering who would be the next, they were assuming as a matter of certainty that he, Bognor, would be the next corpse. He would be the next one to partake of a fatal mushroom and be carried out feet first.

Funny thing, death. Here today, gone tomorrow. He hated that piece which everyone read at memorial services these days: a pathetic piece of sentimental whimsy by some Canon Worral-Thompson or Scott-Moncrieff, or some such double-barrelled moniker, about cheer-up, chaps, I'm not really dead at all but gone into the next room; all a bit of a jolly jape, don't you know. We'll all wake up in a moment and realize that death has no sting and grave no victory.

Having been around death most of his professional life, he took a tougher more robust view of the matter. Death was death. It was nasty and brutal, but, above all, final, decisive and terrible. It had few redeeming features and it was what the

advertisers said. He did not believe in reincarnation, redemption
or anything other than a ceasing to live. Absolutely. Trubshawe
was gone for ever and he would not be coming back, now or
ever. The Second Coming of Jimmy Trubshawe. Sounded like
a film by Richard Curtis. Hugh Grant as Trubshawe.

He shook himself, aware, once again, that he was being
addressed.

'Are you all right, sweetie?' It was Tracey doing the asking.
The others were just looking on with concern. 'You've hardly
touched your *gambas*.'

'Sorry,' said Bognor, giving outer evidence of pulling himself
together which was not reciprocated by his inner self, 'I was
miles away. Good *gambas*. And, incidentally, Tracey, if you don't
mind too much, I'd prefer it if you didn't call me "Sweetie".'

She gave the impression of being someone who was entitled
to take offence but was too well brought up to actually do so.

Instead, she said, 'Back home we'd call these Dublin Bay
prawns. Bet you it's the same fellers in the prawn cocktail, only
a different name. And what's more,' she jabbed her fork at
Bognor, 'I bet you George is having the prawn cocktail. Even
if he's the only one. Just like Mr Trubshawe would of.'

Bognor's insides were in turmoil but he hoped that his exterior
was as calm and non-committal as he intended.

'I suppose,' he essayed, 'we aren't allowed to talk shop, so
we can't discuss the relative marketing strategies of bangers
and chorizos. Notwithstanding the fact that at this table the
bangers have it by a majority of three to one.'

Eduardo smiled. 'I am the one,' he said. 'I am the chorizo.'

They all grinned. It was difficult to see where the conversation should go after this. It was the verbal equivalent of a
dead-end street, a chatterer's cul-de-sac. Not so long ago,
thought Bognor, Trubshawe must have been part of a conversation such as this. He would have seemed perfectly alive and
well. Well, perhaps imperfectly alive and well, but there would
have been no sense of impending doom, no apprehension, no
idea that within a few hours he would be dead and gone and
as if he had never been. Death was a strange, final event which
almost always took one by surprise. It was seldom predicted.
It was not shuffling off to the next room and waiting to come

back and take a curtain call. There was a tendency to reduce death to a non-event, to trivialize it, to pretend it didn't matter. Here they were eating sausages and discussing ways of marketing them. Yet a man had died. He felt like banging his fist on the table and reminding everyone of the terrible event that had taken place.

Instead, he said, 'One Spanish sausage and three British bangers. Not really a fair contest. On the other hand at the next table it's three to one in favour of Spanish sausages.'

They all grinned inanely again. Bognor decided to wrench the conversation around to the subject that was actually on everyone's mind.

'Poor old Trubshawe,' he said. 'Bad luck, very. What sort of man was he? Did he have time to make any sort of impression?'

'We have a saying in, er, Spanish,' said Belen, perhaps a shade too quickly, 'that it is not good to speak bad things about dead people.'

'We too,' said Bognor. 'In fact it comes from Latin so we've probably both inherited it from the same source.'

Another pause. Dinner conversation was, he thought, like a Pinter play. More pause than speech. And they were skirting the main issue.

'Even so,' said Belen, 'I did not think Mr Trubshawe seemed a very nice man.'

The other two looked as if they agreed, though they said nothing. Bognor didn't think it worth pushing. Personal dislike was surely not a strong enough motive for murder. Not, at least, on the basis of the sort of fleeting acquaintance offered by the Pueblo. None of them who had known nothing of Trubshawe before meeting him at the Pueblo could possibly have built up enough hatred to kill him. He wondered whether, in any case, hatred was a strong enough motive. In his experience, killing someone was the result of something more complex. It usually involved money in some shape or form. This could partly be explained by the fact that he was employed at the Board of Trade. Financial motives were implicit; they went with the job. On the other hand, it was possible that in this instance he was barking up the wrong tree. He was assuming that Trubshawe's

death was linked with his criminal past. If the Camilla woman
was the murderess, aided by Eduardo, then the motive was
politico-financial.

Eduardo had lapsed into the discretion from which he had
emerged. He might be the only non-banger on the block, but
he wasn't going to blow a public whistle on Bognor. It was a
secret between the three of them. Or presumably so. If his
cover were blown he would have to leave as suddenly as he
had arrived. Wouldn't he? He sighed. Half of him was beginning to think that Trubshawe's death was the accident so many
wanted it to be. Not that an accident would claim Eduardo's
knowledge nor Camilla's claim. He smiled at Eduardo and was
rewarded with a smile back. Was it one of complicity? He
supposed it was.

The prawn plates were removed and the main course replaced
them. It looked as if George was the only one having the bangers.

'Not like doing hair in Essex,' he said brightly. 'How did
you find out about the Pueblo plan?'

Tracey said she had read an article in some trade magazine.
'*Hair and Hair Cutting*, or something like it. Another hairdresser
had volunteered a year or so ago and had written up his experiences, encouraging other hairdressers to follow suit. It was one
way of getting a free holiday in Spain, though it was less of a
holiday than it might have appeared. Even without the sudden
death of Jimmy Trubshawe.'

'Enjoying it?' he asked.

Tracey nodded and said something more or less banal about
meeting the sort of people one would not normally meet under
the dryer.

Bognor said he supposed not. They all chewed on their
chorizos and sipped their wine. He wondered if the others felt
as desperate as he did. He would not normally meet hairdressers,
pet food executives or export managers of boutique hotels.
Doing so, he realized that there were reasons for this. He had
nothing to say to them; nor they to him. This was a statement
of inadequacy but true nonetheless.

Their faltering conversation was saved by Arizona. It was,
again, a logistical intervention to remind them that they were
performing in their two teams after the meal was finished and

she hoped that everyone was properly prepared, but that there would be a few minutes after the meal during which questions could be asked if people felt the need to do so. She hoped everyone was enjoying their meal. Blah, blah. She gave the impression of saying much the same thing on a regular basis. Which was probably true.

She and Felipe Lee had both worked out that he was not just any old punter who had come in off the street; Dolores Calderon had been tipped off by the Admiral with whom she was . . . well, who knew what her relationship with the old goat Picasso actually consisted of . . . Camilla and Eduardo were privy to some inside information which presumably emanated from London, depending on whether their relationship with the Security Services was all that they cracked it up to be. That left George and Tracey, Lola and Belen as the only ones who took him at face value. Five out of ten. Fifty per cent. It would be amazing if none of the apparently innocent half really didn't suspect that he was more than he wanted to appear to be. But Lola. Lola was supposed to be an undercover agent. So far, however, she was so undercover, that she was, as far as he was concerned, invisible. She was either useless or, conceivably, dangerous. He couldn't fathom the sexy nun and he was worried. Actually, he was worried about the whole business. He simply couldn't get a handle on it.

He sighed as Arizona blathered on and the chorizo and beans gave way to two different sorts of cheese – either cheddar and mango chutney, or a *queso* from the Picos with a liberal dollop of quince paste. Difficult to envisage bolder statements of the two country's national cuisines, or indeed national character.

Queso and a corpse; quince and questions. Maybe he was past it; perhaps there were natural causes after all.

TWENTY-FOUR

T hey began with a bang.
       The bang was a sharp report from what was alleged
       to be a 'starting pistol' and it was fired into thin air by
George. The 'starting pistol' looked suspiciously like a 'terminating
pistol', perfectly capable of wounding or even killing anyone
at whom it was aimed, so it was probably as well that the air
that George fired it into was indeed thin. More importantly, he
did not point the weapon at anyone but instead aimed it at the
ceiling before pulling the trigger. There was a flash, a crack
and a puff of smoke. The opposing team jumped with surprise,
as did Arizona and Felipe. They had not been expecting a bang.
The sausage squad were ready for the explosion. The chorizos
were not.

Apart from the opening bang, Bognor identified a double
mystery: whether or not the gun was a starting pistol, or something more lethal, and where George had found it. Pistols did
not, in Bognor's experience, grow on trees.

Apart from the pistol, starting or ending, the presentation
was well-oiled and constructed in an old-fashioned pre-war
manner which Bognor found oddly consoling. For the first time
he found himself almost warming to George, who was surprisingly diffident and seemed to understand the point of allowing
the Spanish women, Lola and Belen, to call the shots, while he
and Bognor pulled the strings. It was reminiscent of days when
'Made in England' was a guarantee of quality rather than a
signal for mirth.

Ultimately the message was that the British banger was best
because it represented certain standards of excellence and reli-
ability. Belen and Lola entered into this conceit with verve and
a surprising conviction. George, definitely, and Bognor, possibly,
believed in the product but there was no reason for the women
to do so. Rather the reverse.

Acting, pretence and deception were crucial to the operation's success and also inseparable from the reason for Bognor being there. To be a successful crook of any kind one had to be good at concealing one's true character, one's real motivation and, above all, of course, one's actual actions. Same with detectives.

The whole event reminded Bognor of amateur dramatics even, though he hadn't been to an Am-Dram production of any kind since being forced to do so as a child. He had never participated in such a thing, not being a natural joiner and preferring to leave any thespian pretensions for the office.

The banger presentation ended with a jingle which combined, more or less, Elgar's *Pomp and Circumstance March No. 1*, aka, 'Land of Hope and Glory', and the words: 'Sausage and mashed potato, bangers and mash to most / Go with a fried tomato, better than beans on toast.' Which didn't mean a lot, but sounded passable when sung by the two Englishmen, and the Spanish women particularly, and was followed by a prosaically shouted admonition from all four to 'Go to work on a banger', which might have been a crib from the egg marketing board but had, they all thought, more pizzazz than the egg advice. Bognor thought privately that it was just as well Monica couldn't see him. Nor Harvey Contractor. This was emphatically how he wished to appear when at home being, in a manner of speaking, 'himself'. Nevertheless, he rather enjoyed himself. It was like doing karaoke on a business trip.

Being at the Pueblo to investigate a sudden death, he found himself trying to fit the episode into the context of a murder mystery. Time was when such a conundrum would have been solved by patient detection, the asking of questions, the establishing of alibis, the flaws in character, the plausibility of motive and much else that went into the pot of plot of what was frequently referred to as the Golden Age. Modern science, DNA, technology, forensics and a preoccupation with murder rather than mystery had changed all that. It had, in some eyes, made people like him redundant. This was not a conceit into which he bought. Fashion had changed but not reality.

The other four, the chorizos, seemed tolerably impressed by the bangers' bang and then it was their turn. Bognor and the others settled back to enjoy and to criticize. Tracey and Camilla were Anglos, Eduardo and Leonel the Hispanics. The sexual divide was neat; two Anglo males on one side, two Anglo females on the other. Precisely the reverse true of the Spanish, making a perfect fifty per cent male–female split on each team. Try as he might Bognor could find no significance in this beyond a certain symmetry.

There were no bangs from the chorizos. Indeed, they were almost depressingly pedestrian. The two Spaniards delivered mildly solemn lectures on fermentation, curing, smoking; on the difference between *picante* and *dulce* as well as the relative proportions of chopped pork fat, chilli and paprika, plus *chile guindillas secas*. They also waxed knowledgeable on the degree of heat used in hanging the finished sausage, the fine mincing around Pamplona, the importance of the deep-fried egg in Extremadura and the inclusion – or not – of cheeks, salivary glands and/or lymph nodes. When frying eggs for use in Extremaduran *huevos con chorizo* the frying pan had to smoke and be filled with olive oil or pork fat to a depth of at least three centimetres. Basque chorizos were something else again. Confronted with such erudition, Bognor and his team felt positively inadequate. Their presentation might have been explosive but scholarly it wasn't. Not what one might have expected.

In terms of Trubshawe, Bognor wasn't sure it signified one way or another. He knew that Eduardo and Camilla were in cahoots in some way that he was not sure of yet. But in terms of the presentation you would never have guessed. Camilla said nothing while Eduardo droned quite boringly. He knew his chorizos but he did not wear the knowledge lightly. Leonel also sounded nasally portentous and knowledgeable, while Tracey, who Bognor suspected knew little or nothing about anything gastronomic except for amazingly speedy food, kept almost totally shtum. There was nothing to suggest that Leonel knew Tracey. Nor that they had known either of the other two in life outside the Pueblo. Yet, not seeming to know one another was obviously not the same as not actually knowing each other. This was proved conclusively by Eduardo and Camilla, who really did know each other but seemed not to.

They were really promoting Spanish chorizo but that didn't prevent them droning on about Portuguese *chourico* which was pork, fat, wine, paprika and salt stuffed into tripe and dried over smoke. *Chourico de sangue* was like black pudding. Then there was Mexican chorizo which could be deep red, unless green, which suggested a provenance from Toluca, and it was an urban slur that Mexican chorizo was made only from the lips and salivary glands. Puerto Rican chorizo was much like that from the Dominican Republic, which was much like Spanish but not to be confused with *longaniiza* nor the rather mild chorizo from Argentina sometimes served in a bread roll and described as a *choripan*. Brazil, naturally, favours a Portuguese *chourico*, whereas in Goa, although there is a Portuguese influence, they are made of pork, vinegar, chilli, garlic, ginger, cumin, turmeric and other spices. They are very hot and served plain, with potatoes, pearl onions or in a pilaf. In the Philippines they use their own spices and often base their sausages on chicken or even tuna. By the time this exposition was over Bognor's ears were bleeding.

Deafened by science, he supposed. It may have been better than being blinded but it came to much the same thing. The chorizos had bored on knowledgeably, piling one fact on another, until the audience caved in under the weight of statistics. Bognor's bangers had done it in a particular and very different way. They could have gone on at length about the difference in components between the Oxford and Cambridge sausages; whether or not the vegetarian Glamorgan number was a banger within the meaning of the act; the importance of linkage in the Cumberland sausage or whether the Lincolnshire was a poacher's source of sustenance and therefore a working-class edible, in the sense that some of its urban rivals were not.

But they hadn't.

Bognor's lot had taken the spinner's route, all style and no substance, and they had sought their objective by the culinary equivalent of smoke and mirrors. Perhaps that was a false analogy since smoke was, in a manner of speaking, a culinary technique, though he wasn't entirely sure whether something that had been smoked could be said to be 'cooked', in the true sense of the word, still less of the real difference between hot-smoking and cold-smoking, the one implying a level of cooking that the other didn't. Discuss.

These and other thoughts raced through his mind in the immediate aftermath of the chorizos' learned presentation. He had to concede that at the end of this speed-thinking he was no nearer solving the mystery of Trubshawe's death. Did it matter if the murder had been disguised through facile chicanery, otherwise known as 'spin', or the piling on each other of impressive and erudite 'facts' masquerading under the guise of 'wisdom'.

Perhaps it didn't matter. What really mattered was 'who pulled the strings?'

In the case of his own team this was debatable. He and George had acted rather like divine clockmakers. They had wound up Lola and Belen, and set them in motion. Then, having to employ the old firework blurb-writer's phrase, they lit the blue touchpaper and retired to a discreet distance to await developments.

So he and George had pulled the strings. That's how it seemed to outsiders but not to those more closely involved. He guessed it was the same with the other team. The methodology, in so far as there was one, was to let the Spanish-speakers front up.

He sighed. He was investigating a murder which looked like a murder when he first became aware of it. He now realized that there was a school of thought which suggested that the death was due to natural causes. Rats! Jimmy Trubshawe was an accident waiting to happen and happen he did. Shades of Bob Woolmer the unfortunate English-born, South African domiciled Pakistan cricket coach who had keeled over in his hotel room during a World Cup in the West Indies. Murder, murder, chorused the world's press. They were echoed by each other, by the local police and by many of the cricketing fraternity. Senior officers delivered pompous speeches, but then doubts began to be expressed; pathologists appeared to backtrack; autopsies seemed less certain and the world's press and the senior policemen had second thoughts.

Thus, Bognor. It happened. Conclusions unanimously jumped at could just as summarily be repudiated. Conspiracy theory turned into cock-up overnight.

And yet. There was Camilla. There was Eduardo. They would do for a start. Between them they had as much as confessed to the killing of Trubshawe, even if it was a murder they were unlikely to admit in open court. They had as good as confessed to Bognor while warning him off. If they were to be believed, they were acting on behalf of the British Security Services. Theirs was a branch which, given conflict, would result in Bognor's fiefdom being outranked and overruled. That was the way of the world. Murder was committed by the state. But because Britain was supposedly a democracy and therefore more susceptible to public opinion and press enquiry than dictatorships, the killing would be obfuscated. It would not make it less of a murder but it would be disguised and denied until, murder or not, it would become no more than an accident. That was the way life and death worked in the upper echelons of life.

Perhaps he had been wrong to infiltrate himself into this world in an unofficial capacity. It was one thing to stride in wearing a uniform and carrying a warrant, a swagger-stick and all the apparatus of authority. Quite another to proceed incognito, especially in a foreign land.

But maybe he was just past it. He was about to do the inward groan routine but thought better of it and smiled instead.

He was investigating a murder. He was doing it his own way. He would get there in the end.

These were articles of self-belief. Being right was a mantra and in the past it had never failed.

The debrief was like most debriefs. It felt authoritative and final, yet actually achieved little or nothing. It was conducted by Arizona Brown at her most schoolmistressy with Felipe Lee in the supporting role. Inconclusive though it was in deciding whether the traditional British sausage was a better buy or bet than the more charismatic cutting-edge Iberian chorizo, it was equally useless in establishing which of the two teams had made the better fist of making their case. As a teaching exercise it was fine, but in terms of the ostensible reason for the contest it was a waste of space.

Bognor, of course, had his own unique terms of reference. As far as he was concerned everyone on display was a suspect and that included Arizona and Felipe. He was aware – painfully so, to coin a cliché – that the suspects, or at least a majority of them, were aware of his special interest. He wasn't sure, however, whether this awareness put them higher or lower on his list of suspects.

Take Arizona Brown. She was a professional. She was good at her job. She was stunning to look at and had a personality to match. She had the intelligence and the opportunity to kill Trubshawe, but there was no evidence against her and – even more important in Bognor's estimation – absolutely no known motive. She had half-sussed Bognor, but there was no way in which it could be said to have rendered her a murderer. So she was low on his list of suspects.

So too was Felipe Lee. Bognor judged that employees of the Pueblo organization made unlikely suspects when one was mainly concerned with motivation. Why should the employee of an avant-garde language school wish to murder Jimmy Trubshawe? Sure, the inside knowledge, and therefore the opportunity, would be that much greater, but it seemed inherently unlikely that Arizona or Felipe would have any reason for doing in Trubshawe. Even if they did, why wait until he enrolled on a Pueblo course. Much easier to nip down to Jimmy's home on the Costa and murder him down there with a wad of easily procured and operated plastic explosive. Then you could blame the episode on a botched ETA plot or some misadventure involving so-called 'organized crime'. Crime, in Bognor's estimation, was seldom particularly well-organized and usually positively *dis*organized, but that was probably irrelevant. He was a cock-up man not a conspiracy theorist. That was the way of his world. Though there was such a thing as a cocked-up conspiracy.

He wondered if Felipe really was descended from Laurie Lee. The Gloucestershire republican had an elegiac way with the English language, a priapic affection for the female half of the Spanish nation but a fickle regard for the truth. He was an unreliable witness and an uncertain ancestor. Whether or not Felipe had any English blood in him was of no more consequence than whether or not Arizona was part-Navajo. It might be interesting but it was not germane; it wouldn't stand up in court and a judge would throw it out as irrelevant.

No, the suspects were, as far as he was concerned, the inmates.

That meant the four Spaniards and the three Anglos. In the short time he had been at the Pueblo he had made progress, but not as much as he would have wished. He was constrained by his anonymity and the need to preserve pretence. He had assumed that the machinery of the course would dovetail with his own requirements but he was no longer convinced that this was so.

This exercise was designed to elucidate character, forge bonds and create mutual understandings, at least so much as to improve the language skills of the paying participants. It ought therefore to have been a help in solving the crime yet, if anything, it only served to increase his bafflement and his growing concern that the death of Jimmy Trubshawe was more accidental than he had originally supposed. He was reminded, once more, of the strange sad case of Bob Woolmer. The police, including a senior Scotland Yard officer on permanent secondment to the Jamaican force had been adamant. It was murder. And then with the passage of time, and the complete failure to bring charges or to finger a plausible assassin, the case began to look flimsier and flimsier. The dead man looked more and more like someone who had passed away as the result of natural causes.

So perhaps Trubshawe was just another Woolmer: an amazingly suspicious demise that turned into a sadly routine death in which, before too terribly long, all but those most intimately involved lost interest. God knows, in the case of the late Trubshawe there was motive and opportunity all over the place, coupled with the fact that the dead man was, by universal consent, a nasty piece of work. Yet accidents do happen and conceivably this was one of those occasions.

Lola and Belen had done nearly all the talking when it came to defending the banger presentation. Only right. Bognor remained as silent as could be and spent as much time watching the others for signs of criminality. Likewise George. He too said little but Bognor watched him with the same interest.

Lola was an improbable nun and an unlikely agent but then, he reflected, being a nun was inherently unlikely for anyone. Bognor could not, offhand, think of any criminal nuns in fact or fiction, but he could manage a couple of detective nuns: Sister Ursula was the creation of Anthony Boucher, the American writer who gave his name to the annual crime festival. Boucher's nun was notable for her blue eyes which were 'kind and wise and understanding'. She belonged to an order named after someone named Martha of Bethany. This, like her, was the invention of the author and although Bognor enjoyed the books he didn't believe a word of her. He was also sceptical about Sister Agnes who was the brainchild of a later writer called Alison Joseph. Sister Agnes was highly sexed, had been married to an equally highly sexed man named Bourdillon and came from a convent which had owned a string of Jaguars. Rather like a football team. He wasn't sure that he believed in Sister Lola any more than the sisters Ursula and Agnes, but he had to concede that he didn't really believe in nuns, period. Not helped by the fact that he didn't think he believed in God. If you didn't believe in the Almighty then the rest of the apparatus became a touch problematic. We only, he conceded, had Sister Lola's word for her nunnishness and, even though she made a better fist of her calling than Ursula and Agnes, Bognor remained essentially unconvinced.

Being a dubious Poor Clare did not, however, turn her into a murderer. Bognor understood this rationally but there was a visceral part of him that was not so sure. A bad nun was unlikely to be a killer in bald statistical terms but he felt uneasy with Lola's obvious other-worldliness. It suggested deception, and deception was sort of synonymous with dishonesty. A counterfeit nun could easily be a crook. Likewise a counterfeit agent. On the other hand, she had no discernible motive for murdering Trubshawe. Forced to concede reality, however, Bognor had to admit that he knew so little about Lola that he had no idea whether or not she was even likely to have a motive. Like everyone else at the Pueblo she might or might not be play-acting. She might be a flirty new-age nun. Or not. The plain fact was that he didn't know. His ignorance was virtually total.

It was the same with Belen. Her persona was less preposterous and more plausible than that of Lola, but at the end of the day he and the others only had her word for who she was. She fitted the image of export manager for a small group of upmarket boutique hotels, although Bognor had never previously encountered such an animal and was forced to concede that his images were based on information which was at best vicarious and at worst false. Belen might perfectly well have been a middle to high-ranking hotel person, but she might not have been. She gave the impression of knowing her mushrooms, as indeed did Lola, but that didn't mean that either woman would have fixed Jimmy Trubshawe's starter.

Belen did not so much play second fiddle to Lola as play demure to her raunchy. The terms were relative but the one seemed relatively flamboyant and the other coy by comparison. Arizona who took the lead when it came to interrogation seemed, to Bognor, to be noticeably soft on both. It struck him that it was a girlie conspiracy and he wondered, briefly, whether Trubshawe's death had a sexual element. He suspected not. Even if Trubshawe had once been a sexual animal, probably of a crude and voracious bent, he had almost certainly been past it by the time he came to his sticky end. He gave the impression of a man who usually paid for his pleasure.

The American seemed tougher on the chorizos and Bognor wondered whether this was because their spokespeople were blokes. Eduardo and Leonel were far from being bling and tattoo-covered football fans in the manner of George and Jimmy, at least in their younger days. They were smooth in a languid Hispanic manner that was desperately old-fashioned and incorrect in British terms. Even new Tories such as privately educated Bullingdon Club-belonging Cameron, Osborne and Johnson affected a sort of man-in-the-street, next-door-neighbour style which was designed to disguise their toffy tendency. They would recoil from being thought of as 'gentlemen' with the languid, soft charm that the word suggested. Yet that was the sort of person that Eduardo and Leonel appeared to be. In criminal terms they belonged to the amateur-sleuth golden age of Lord Peter Wimsey, Roderick Alleyne and Albert Campion. They gave the impression of being able to recite Shakespeare and deferring to their grannies. If a woman came into their room they would have opened the door to her, whereas a George or a Jimmy would have slammed it in her face. Men like Trubshawe created glass ceilings and sat on them; the Leonels and Eduardos would never have been so crude. Arizona probably sussed their ersatz feminism for the sham it almost certainly was.

Bognor took a virtual back seat along with the other Anglos. They too had got the message, and even if they hadn't Arizona and Felipe made sure that the only people who really participated in the discussion were the Spaniards. The programme was not designed for English speakers. They were part of it, but as aids not beneficiaries. On the other hand, Bognor did not regard the Hispanics as prime suspects and he therefore allowed his attention to wander.

It wandered inevitably to Camilla, the belle of Byron Bay; the puppeteer who by her own admission was running Eduardo, the smooth Paco Peña enthusiast who aspired to being Spain's Stavros Niarchos. She had, in effect, admitted her guilt, disguising it under the dodgy pretext of 'only obeying orders'.

He was glad, on the whole, that he had not been recruited into the mainstream Security Services, but had ended in the relatively arcane Special Investigations Department of the Board of Trade. Funny how life panned out. It wouldn't have been like that if he had fetched up in Five or Six. He'd be dead by now. Or 'sleeping' in Byron Bay, like Camilla.

The Board of Trade seemed, by and large, to have escaped the 'modernization' that had so marred the mainstream Security Services. They had been subjected to political interference and infiltration. They had also become the victims of 'systems'. These were designed to eliminate risk, but in reality only eliminated inspiration. Risk was, in his opinion, a necessary part of the exercise.

His outfit was also, he liked to think, informed by a moral dimension which had been lost elsewhere. Others might become 'accountable' and liable to 'scrutiny' by outside bodies who knew nothing and cared less. Not so at SIDBOT.

He was roused from this self-congratulatory reverie by noise.

It was a siren: the sound of real life interfering with ivory towers and dreaming spires.

He resented it.

He always did.

TWENTY-FIVE

Police sirens, thought Bognor, sounded remarkably similar all over the world. And the flashing blue light which indicated an angry squad car was remarkably ubiquitous, too. Nothing undercover or plain clothed about either. They evoked sound and fury, the meaning of business and the business of meaning.

It was not what he was expecting. There seemed to be dozens of them, mainly male, but all wearing the uniform of *les flics* or their underworld counterpart: trainers, blue jeans, black leather jackets over roll-neck tops. They could just as well have been criminals or even extras in a new play by Harold Pinter. They had dogs, well-fed, shiny German shepherds sniffing and snarling. The police adopted a similar attitude. Bognor recognized his friend, the *Teniente*, but the policeman was not doing recognition. This was business. They were all under arrest.

Regrets were expressed but without much conviction. It was explained tersely and bilingually that a Mr James Trubshawe had died and that the circumstances of his death were regarded as suspicious. In English this meant a probability of 'foul play', though Bognor had always had difficulty with the phrase, not seeing, in his literal-minded way, what 'play' had to do with 'murder'. He was also moved to protest that he had only arrived after Trubshawe had passed away, and that for reasons of geography and location he was the only person present who could not possibly have done it.

However, he said nothing. Nor did any of the others. They behaved with a polite acquiescence which was positively British – a feather in the behavioural side of the Pueblo operation. Nevertheless, Bognor was not fooled for an instant by the velvet glove approach. He knew that this represented a failure for the serpentine methods that he himself felt he had favoured all his professional life. This was crude, macho, modern, in-your-face, throw-the-baby-out-with-the-bath-water detection and he disliked it.

Nevertheless, he had to accept that it was effective, modern and here to stay. It used science in a forensic sense which went far beyond such primitive processes as fingerprinting and identification parades. They were as fallible in their way as nearly all early forms of detection, but the discovery of DNA and techniques associated with it made them virtually obsolete. Bognor was sceptical about deoxyribonucleic acid, chromosomes and genetic fingerprinting. Ever since the man Pitchfork was convicted in the Enderby murder case, thanks almost entirely to the forensic practices made possible by Crick, Watson and Co., detection had been transformed. Bognor belonged, historically, to a pre-DNA age which men of the *Teniente*-Contractor generation considered prehistoric.

Late at night, after having taken drink, Bognor was not beyond saying that the developments had transformed the nature of his job from an art to a science. Next morning he would regret having said this but only up to a point. Tonight's performance proved his point. It was a triumph of new technology but it was also a demonstration of crude power. Supporters would have described it as a victory for professionalism over dilettante amateurism. But Bognor was not a supporter and he regretted what he believed was happening. He even felt depressed by the polite acquiescence of the alleged suspects. Only George displayed a flicker of opposition, but even he allowed himself to be cautioned and led out to the police minibus without protest.

It was a newish bus, quite smart, the sort of thing any tour company would have been proud of. The *teniente* drove and everyone was oddly and uncharacteristically silent.

'I very much regret the inconvenience caused,' he said, as he started the vehicle and moved out down the drive, 'but there has been a suspicious death, as I believe you all know, and it is necessary to ask you all to accompany me to the police station in Salamanca in order to submit to routine questioning. This is a simple process but necessary under Spanish law. When we have asked sufficient questions and obtained suitable answers, I will arrange for you to be driven back here and you will be able to resume your work.'

'All of us?' George wanted to know. There was an edge to his voice which Bognor sensed was a possible harbinger of difficulty.

'Alas, only time, as you say in your country, will tell.'

He slowed to a standstill, put the gears into neutral, checked the road for oncoming light, pulled out of the drive and turned left down the road to Salamanca.

'Routine questioning,' thought Bognor, ruefully. He had been fighting 'routine questioning' all his life and believed it to be little more than a pseudo-sophisticated version of the Inquisition. Thumbscrews and the rack were now eliminated. In fact, all forms of torture were technically forbidden, but that didn't mean that the deployment of a 'Mr Nice' and a 'Mr Nasty' was not effective, as were threats, cigarettes, cups of tea, bright lights, sleep deprivation and promises of leniency in return for self-incriminating 'honesty'. Bognor believed that 'routine questioning' was a euphemism designed to obtain convictions. He did not believe in the idea any more than he believed in the adversarial principle underlying the British legal system. This, he thought, meant that someone who was lucky or rich enough to obtain the services of the more effective lawyer nearly always won the case, whether they deserved to or not. He knew that there were built in safeguards involving judges and juries.

It was the same with 'questioning'. There were all kinds of safeguards involving admitted testimony, witnesses, lawyers and the illegality of inflicting actual bodily harm. These were, of course, waived, even by allegedly civilized nations when circumstances so demanded. Thus Guantánamo Bay and almost anything to do with the alleged war on terrorism. In real life, blacks, homosexuals and the alleged victims of rape didn't do particularly well. Indeed, you could plausibly argue that 'fair play' only applied to white Anglo-Saxon males of a certain age. If you were being particularly liberal, in an old-fashioned knee-jerk manner associated with the *Manchester Guardian* and certain inner suburbs of north London, you would argue, with some force, that only privately educated people of that description got a fair crack of the whip from 'routine questioning'. Maybe not in Spain.

He gazed out of the window and saw trees and a fullish

moon, complete with ubiquitous man. The landscape was silvery
and half-lit, a crepuscular vision in which you could make out
shapes, but only in monochrome. It was like a black and white
movie slipping past the bus windows – remote, uncoloured, not
entirely real. Inside, the mood was different – disturbed,
Technicolor and indisputably happening to creatures of flesh
and blood, including himself. He was part of an unfolding drama
involving a cast of characters who, like Bognor, were playing
themselves.

Or were they? Part of the problem with this whole charade,
he realized, was just that. It *was* just that: a charade. No one
was playing themselves. Or, to be more accurate and even more
disconcerting, they might or might not be playing themselves.
Sister Lola, for example, might be a nun or she might just as
well be an air stewardess or a truck driver. The only person
who alleged that Camilla ran a bed and breakfast in Byron Bay
was Camilla herself. And so it went on. Every potted biography
of every character was a self-invention. It was like those entries
in *Who's Who* where the participants listed their recreations
without censorship or even rudimentary editing, encouraging
each other to make jokes out of their extramural activities. Such
deceits might or might not extend to the main text, so that
university degrees, parentage, whole careers and personalities
could become mere figments, tawdry exercises in self-deception
masquerading as serious and impartial works of reference. They
said the camera did not lie, which, in an age of ever-increasing
digital hocus-pocus, was an ever more economical way of
dealing with the truth. But if the camera was more and more
of an impostor, how much more true it was of words. One of
the first rules of public speaking, Bognor had always been told,
was there is always someone in the audience who knows more
about the subject than the speaker, even if the subject was the
speaker. Here, he suddenly felt that he was that person where
every speaker was concerned. They were all telling lies about
themselves and he was the only one who realized.

The silver night sped by in the silence. He wondered if
'routine interrogation' would determine truth or merely confirm
prejudice. He presumed that checks would have been carried
out. He knew that in his own case Monica, Lady Bognor as she

now was, he remembered with a smirk of self-congratulation, was carrying out her own checks, phoning chums, calling in favours and applying her formidable but well-disguised forensic abilities to the matters in hand.

He smirked some more. Even Monica, he told himself, was an exercise in propaganda. Take the new Monica moniker: 'Lady' Bognor. That was no 'lady' that was his wife, and he knew her better than anyone. On the other hand, he had to admit that the Monica he knew so intimately was not necessarily the Monica that appeared to the butcher or the *maitre d'* at the restaurant. The Monica he saw without make-up, or even clothing, was not necessarily the 'real' Monica. Perhaps people were like books or plays and the observer was as important as the reader. Was this a post-structural view of mankind? Maybe the individual had no more right to their own personality than anyone else. Perhaps there was no such thing as a 'correct' view of a personality, any more than there could be an 'objective' version of truth. One man's 'fact' was another's opinion.

This was becoming horribly metaphysical, he thought, but notwithstanding such abstract concepts the question remained begged. Who, after all, dunnit? One of the passengers on the bus killed Jimmy Trubshawe. He was sitting, as was his wont, on the back seat and he had it to himself, which was how he liked it. He surveyed the backs of the heads of those in front of him and wondered which of them was the killer. There was always the possibility, of course, that the deceased had simply ate a dodgy mushroom. Murder was a mess, and this death was no exception. The backs of the necks told him no more than their owners had done in the few hours of his investigation so far.

Perhaps this was the story of life. Not just *his* life, but life in general – life, period. Perhaps life was nothing but a series of questions to which, ultimately, there were no answers. On this particular occasion there was one overriding question, namely the puzzle surrounding the demise of Jimmy Trubshawe; but the more one immersed oneself in the Pueblo the more questions arose and the more elusive the answers became. Perhaps this was true of everything: the more you knew, the less you knew. Every time you thought you had solved a problem another one

rose up to take its place, and as often as not the problems multi-
plied like some dreadful hydra.

So life began with the pure simplicity of infancy and became
more and more complicated as one got older, until in the prelude
to death there were no answers any more. At the beginning
everything seemed to have an answer and all was optimism and
progress. By the time one had finished, disillusion and disappointment were pre-eminent and there were no answers to
anything. Death might come as a full stop but it didn't answer
any questions. Well, maybe it did, but Bognor had become a
disciple of the Big Sleep, not a frankly incredible resurrection
in any shape or form.

These musings were punctuated only by the sound of the
engine and the passing of the occasional car or truck. Gradually
the wooded hillsides gave way to Salamancan suburbia. After
a while street lights appeared and the moon seemed to dim.
They were now back in what passed for civilization, although
the modern excrescences on the outskirts of the city were
hideous and unsightly compared with the historic beauty of the
ancient city.

Bognor was depressed. Everything, it seemed, ended in failure.
Even success.

TWENTY-SIX

Monica Bognor had been upgraded. This had become the story of her life. Not only had she acquired a title, she had also been moved up into a suite. The suite was old-fashioned, draped, velvetine, chandeliered; tall windows offered a view of Spanish antiquity with a hint of incense. It was just about the best the Hotel Fray Luis could offer. The hostelry was a refurbished palace named after the university lecturer who had been taken away and tortured by the Inquisition, only to return and blithely resume his lecture with the words – in Latin – 'As we were saying yesterday'. Style.

Lady B. had procured wine which was chilling in a bucket. Also smoked salmon with quarters of lemon. She had always possessed style. The new title suited her.

'Darling!' she said, opening the door to her new knight, who was not exactly in shining armour but was looking a tad dishevelled and exhausted in regulation dark suiting. 'Thank heaven you're safe. I was really worried. We all were.'

They embraced fondly, kissed, withdrew, gazed at each other, sighed and sat down.

'What happened?' he asked. He felt out of things, which was a not altogether unusual sensation.

'The key thing was the autopsy,' she said. '*Teniente* Azuela suspected some hanky-panky, so he got someone else in to have a second look. He was right.'

'In what way?' Bognor opened the cava and poured.

'The mushrooms were a red herring,' she said. 'If you don't mind me mixing my culinary metaphors.'

Bognor said he couldn't care less. He rather approved of mixed metaphors. Nevertheless, he wanted to know how and why.

'It wasn't the mushrooms themselves,' she said. 'It was what had been put in them. On them. Not just pepper and salt. Glass.

Powdered. Our boys became suspicious of the autopsy. It didn't stack up. They became more and more convinced that mushrooms could be seriously upsetting, but almost certainly not fatal. And after what I found out from Celia they started to get neurotic about interference from their own side.'

'You spoke to Celia?'

Monica and Celia had been at Art School together. The Slade. Celia was married to a friend in a high place. It was an ideological mismatch. Not altogether happy in other ways either. Yet Monica and Celia remained close. There were favours. From time to time they got called in. It was sometimes alleged that women were second-class citizens, that there was something called a 'glass ceiling' through which no female ever passed and, perhaps most insidiously of all, that there was an Old Boys' Network that girls couldn't join.

That was not Bognor's experience.

Nor that of his wife.

'Celia confirmed what the woman from Byron Bay told you. All incredibly unorthodox and nobody in Downing Street or even Whitehall will own up to it. And unless secret papers get left on a train from Teddington to Waterloo no one will ever know.'

'So Six killed Trubshawe?'

'Maybe,' said Monica, 'maybe not.'

'Don't be enigmatic,' said Bognor, 'it doesn't suit you.'

'You know, I suppose, that George was Jimmy Trubshawe's brother. And that Lola was alleged to have been his mistress.'

'You believe that?'

'My sources are immaculate but I'm not revealing them.'

Bognor believed her. It wouldn't be the first time.

'Did the Admiral sanction the raid?'

'Yes,' she said, 'Picasso seems to have his own sources of information and I'm not here to question them. He called the *teniente* and they agreed that, coming at it from completely different angles and points of view, you were in danger. That's why we went in and pulled you out.'

'Not exactly flattering.'

'Not much point in being buttered up if you're dead. The second autopsy showed beyond reasonable doubt that Trubshawe was murdered. You yourself said that a person unknown had taken a shot at you, or at least in your direction. You'd already got a confession from the person purporting to be Camilla, with an acknowledgement of Eduardo's role as some sort of accessory. Job done, we reckoned. Besides which, we thought you were at risk. So we pulled you out.'

'That should have been my decision,' said Bognor huffily. Huffy was how he felt. It showed. His wife noticed.

'Darling,' she said tenderly, although she wasn't feeling as tender as she seemed, and was almost as huffy, *au fond*, as her husband, 'we were worried about your safety and you'd solved the crime. It was Camilla who did it, cloaked in the security of working for the Secret Intelligence Agency. There was no purpose in your staying in and facing lots of hazard.'

'It should have been my decision.'

'For a start you were out in the field and therefore not in the ideal position for playing at captaincy. And we're in Spain. When in Spain . . . or to put it another way, our writ doesn't really run here, so if we disagree over procedures we don't do what seems appropriate to us, we do what the local authorities tell us. It would be the same in reverse if the *Teniente* or the Admiral were on our turf. Now drink your cava.'

The words 'shut up little man' hung in the air but remained unexpressed. The cava was cold and fizzy. He drank deep and gazed round the room, which was opulent, and at his wife, who seemed concerned and disconcertingly self-assured.

'Tell me about Camilla,' he said.

She shrugged. 'Not a lot to tell,' she said. 'Standard Six story. They used her too much and too obviously. She was on Diana's staff; gained her confidence; was crucial in the plot to have her bumped off. Then after the so-called accident in the tunnel the press and others started to get too close for comfort, so they sent her as far away as they could and told her to go to sleep until the coast was clear. When it was, she was told she'd have a serious front-line role. The sort of operation for which she was originally trained. Meanwhile they paid her what amounted to a very generous subsidy for her B. and B.'

'So she was part of the plot to kill Diana?'

'Looks like it.'

'Mmm.' The extent of the plot had never been properly established, and although it was almost universally accepted that the Princess's final demise was an accident, it was also commonly agreed that there was a genuine conspiracy in the Security Services. The details were less well known and Bognor preferred not to know them. It was enough that there was a plot, and its existence was proof to Bognor that parts of the so-called intelligence community were not to be trusted. He conducted most of his professional life on that basis. Intelligence work involved a visceral distrust of everyone else, especially those also engaged in intelligence, and most of all those allegedly on your own side. Enemies were bad, friends doubly so. At least with enemies there was a reasonable likelihood of knowing what was going on.

'Celia say anything else?' he asked, more or less innocently, hoping for an answer but not really expecting one.

'Sent her love,' she said, to which he replied, naturally, that this was not what he meant even though he was glad to hear it.

'Government is in terrible trouble,' she said, 'and profoundly unamused by our unilateral decision to solve the Trubshawe murder.'

Bognor laughed. 'Well,' he said, 'if they're the guilty party that's hardly surprising.'

She laughed back.

'I never cease to be amazed by what governments get up to behind the scenes,' she said. 'It's been true ever since you started in SIDBOT. Nobody outside the corridors of power seems to know anything. Nothing in the papers; nothing on TV. Just bromides and spin. It's the same with this. No one in the world at large will know or care about Jimmy Trubshawe's death; let alone Jimmy Trubshawe's brother or Jimmy Trubshawe's mistress. The public believe what people like Alastair Campbell tells them. If you went public on what you knew you'd make an absolute fortune in newspaper serials.'

'Except that no one would believe a word of it.'

'True,' said Lady Bognor. 'So we live in a fantasy world while our lords and masters get up to God knows what, protected by laziness and incompetence in the fourth estate, and assisted

by deceit and guile on the part of those who are conniving with
the government to dupe the rest of us.'

'That's a very cynical view of the world we live in,' he said.

'True once more,' she agreed, 'but don't tell me you think
differently.'

Bognor regarded the bubbles in his glass. They were a
wonderful example of life's mystery and frustrated optimism.
He had no idea how the bubbles got there in the beginning,
hadn't a clue why they continued to surge upwards and, finally,
why they evaporated inexorably as they reached the surface.
But he and Monica were just like the bubbles. They were effer-
vescent and optimistic, and they surged ever upwards until,
phut, they exploded into thin air. They were not the only ones.
In the end everyone was just a bubble floating in champagne,
but doomed to perish at the end of their voyage.

This was ludicrous. Life was not a glass of cava. He shook
himself like a Sealyham after being caught in the rain.

'You all right, darling?' asked his wife.

'Me?' he replied, surprised. 'Me. Never felt better.'

This was not entirely correct. Fatigue, wine and anticlimax
were combining to make him light-headed. A tad depressed as
well. For once he had to concede that his individual, intuitive
approach seemed to have let him down. Enemies would have
considered it quirky and old-fashioned, but it had served him well
enough in the past. This time, however, he had fallen foul of
rigorous modern interrogation, rival branches of the secret intelligence services and, though it pained him to admit it, his wife.

'So,' he asked, seemingly innocent, 'who do you think killed
him?'

She appeared to muse. 'He was murdered,' she said at last,
'the second autopsy proves that. The first one – the fake one
– was ambiguous. It could have been a simple mistake and he
ate the wrong mushroom, which, as he had cardiac problems
associated with the high blood pressure, high cholesterol and
elevated enzymes all of which are well-documented, could have
killed him. But you can't argue with ground glass.'

'So it wasn't an accident?'

The cava was slowing down, but he wanted to be sure.

'It certainly wasn't an accident,' she said, 'and Camilla's

admission of guilt, coupled with Eduardo's obvious complicity, makes it an open-and-shut case.'

'I suppose so.' He shrugged.

'Only I don't believe in "open-and-shut" any more than you do.'

'No,' he agreed.

In the street below people were singing. The music sounded like a student drinking song: rambunctious but with a plangent touch of melancholy. An anthem for youth on the verge of loss.

'The trouble is,' she said, 'the way of the world being far from straight and narrow, Camilla's so-called confession is too tidy to be quite plausible.'

'Meaning?'

'Meaning I don't think she did it,' she said. 'It's too convenient. Almost neater than an accident. Camilla will be whisked back to Byron Bay; nobody will breathe a word about Eduardo. No one need know about George and Lola or anyone else. Nobody is particularly interested in Trubshawe. He was a nasty piece of work with no visible next of kin, no nearest and dearest. No one to care what happened to him.'

Bognor demurred quietly.

'Except me,' he said.

She snorted. 'You're perverse, Simon Bognor,' she said, 'and you always have been, as you well know. If you weren't we wouldn't be married, as you also well know.'

'That's as may be,' he replied, 'but just because Trubshawe was a shit doesn't make him an appropriate candidate for being murdered. I don't think anyone should be bumped off in this world. That's partly why I've been in the line of work I have. And, incidentally, who do you think tried to bump me off and will we ever know?'

'And, in any case, does it really matter?' she asked. 'They missed.'

'Yes, well,' said Bognor, seeming hurt.

'Personally,' said Monica, 'I think it was George warning you off. I don't think he meant to harm you. Rather the reverse. He was being protective.'

'Funny way of being protective,' said Bognor, 'shooting someone . . .'

'Yes, well,' she said, regarding him fondly, 'people have funny ways of showing all sorts of thing. Why don't you just shut up, take off your clothes and come to bed.'

Bognor did as he was told.

TWENTY-SEVEN

Bognor wished to hear this from the horse's mouth with his own ears.

'I'm told that you were the deceased's brother?'

George was a key witness and so, in her silent way was Monica. There were just the three of them present.

'All men are brothers. You're my brother. I'm yours. That's what the Good Book says.'

'Fiddle the Good Book.' Bognor was the nearest to anger that he allowed his professional self to be. 'We don't give a stuff about the Good Book. We're here to establish something much more mundane. We don't deal in eternal verities, only truth, the whole truth and nothing but the truth.'

'So help me God,' said George unexpectedly.

'Absolutely,' replied Bognor, quick as the proverbial flash.

'So, were your parents Percy and Edna? Or was that what they were known as? And were you brought up in Essex?'

'In a manner of speaking,' said George. 'Though I always thought Jimmy and I were adopted. We were so alike and yet so unalike; different but the same.'

'I see,' said Bognor, not having the foggiest idea what the man who claimed to be George was actually saying.

'So you may or may not have been Jimmy's blood brother, but you were brought up as if you were.'

'Got it in one, squire,' said George. He seemed impressed.

'But, on balance, you don't think you were brothers.'

George thought a long time about this and Bognor was on the point of rephrasing the question. George cut him short, however. He understood perfectly, he said, but he was cogitating.

'It's not a difficult question,' said Bognor, trying to be helpful.

'With respect, it is actually,' said George. 'I'm naturally sceptical. Unlike James who believed everything he was told. He thought we were brothers. I was never so sure. And I wasn't at all sure Percy and Edna had anything to do with us. Not originally. I think that even if we were brothers we were fostered out.'

'What made you . . . I mean why?' Bognor was floored. This was not what he was used to or what he did best.

'We grew up like twins. We wore the same clothes; went to the same schools; had the same friends. Hell, we were one another. But there was something wrong. I suppose it was too perfect. Life isn't like that. And while conceivably we were like one another, we sure as hell weren't in any way the same as Percy and Edna. No way. They were, like, dumb. Stupid. And we were smart. Smart kids. We could do all kinds of things they couldn't. And we were restless. We wanted out. Mum and Dad were, you know, conventional.'

'Mum and Dad?'

'That's what we were told to call them. That's what we called them. Every other little boy and girl in that part of the county called their protectors, providers, what you will . . . Mum and Dad. So we did the same. No point in drawing attention to yourself when there's no need.'

Bognor decided the time had come to change the subject.

'The *Heil Hitler Rotwein*,' he said, 'tell me about that.'

'Surprisingly decent drop,' George replied, 'if you like that sort of thing. A blend I'm told. Merlot, Cab Sauv, maybe a spot of Pinot who knows – Shiraz . . . Syrah . . . Don't know. I guess they use whatever comes to hand. But it's a decent drop.'

'German?'

'Made by a guy called Strauss, but he lives in Argentina. I guess he was German originally. He emerged. Been living in South America for at least a quarter of a century. Nice enough fellow, apart from the politics.'

'The politics?'

'To the right of ye man Genghis,' said George. 'Which is a pity. And after a drop or two of the hard stuff he'd rave a bit. Most of the time he was nice enough, but not after a glass or two of the local poteen. Can't be doing with that crap myself. Easy come, easy go. That's why I fell out with James. That and the torture thing. James seemed to enjoy causing pain, even if it was only insects. He always enjoyed taking things to bits. Especially if they were alive. Not my style. Not my style at all.'

'So you and James fell out over politics and sadomasochism?'

'You could say that.' George seemed to agree. 'But then again, maybe not.' He now seemed to disagree. Bognor sensed this was part of his problem. Too busy being all things to all men.

'You don't like to be disliked, George?' he ventured.

George did some more cogitating.

'Not if I can help it,' he said at last. 'Not like James. James didn't seem to mind who he upset. In fact, I'd say he enjoyed upsetting people. And he didn't seem to care who they were.

Bognor decided to change the subject again. It was almost a technique, except that he didn't believe in techniques. They implied orthodoxy and he didn't do orthodoxy. Nor to his credit, did George. And he suspected Trubshawe didn't either, whatever else he did.

'Tell me about O'Flaherty. Oliver of that ilk.'

George flashed another of his grins. Mischief. He was obviously into mischief.

'Harmless enough fellow,' said George. 'Irish.'

'But never lived in the Republic.'

'Maybe he did. Maybe he didn't.' George also obviously enjoyed mystery. Liked to be thought a man of it.

'My information is that he didn't.'

'Maybe he just didn't live in the part of the Emerald Isle that everyone assumed was his home. But just because a man says he's living in Kinsale doesn't mean he can't be living in, say, Oughterard. Dubliners live in Limerick and vice, as they say, versa. Happens. Especially there. 'Tis a magic place.'

'Yes. Well.' Bognor felt he was being sidetracked. A certain sort of man maintained that Ireland wasn't wet, just, well, misty . . . George was evidently that sort of man. Bognor had not got where he had without being able to see through that sort of blarney.

'Identity not your strong point?' he said.

Again, George thought before speaking.

'Much overrated in my view,' he said eventually.

'Identity?'

'Who I am is really no concern of yours or anyone else's,'
he said, in a come-on sort of way which suggested that this
was the usual prelude to a losing argument in which he had
been engaged a number of times over the years. 'Actions, maybe.
They are commonly said to speak louder than words; well I
happen to believe that they speak a whole lot louder than names,
at least. What's in a name after all?'

'Identity is vital.' Bognor spoke stiffly. He hadn't really given
the question a lot of thought before. Now he did.

'Why?'

It was Bognor's turn to cogitate. Eventually he said, 'It's the
whole lynch-pin of our civilization. If you and I didn't know
who we were we'd be stuffed.'

'What possible difference does it make whether we are Fred
or Bert or Smith or Brown? Who we really are matters. That's
what's important.'

This stymied Bognor. In a sense he agreed. However, form
made life run smoothly. Perhaps in the overall scheme of things
it was insignificant. Even so. He said as much.

'There are two things going on here,' he said, 'one is organi-
zational, the other fundamental. One is a matter between you
and your God, the other is a procedural challenge which involves
other humans. You can't say one is important and the other not;
they're chalk and cheese, apples and oranges.'

'One is fundamental, the other isn't. It's as simple as that.
Identity is in the eye of the beholder. I can choose what to call
myself. That's my business. Nothing to do with anyone else.'

'If everyone adopted your attitude my job would become
impossible. I need people to be who they say they are.'

'That's your problem, not mine.'

This was true. On the other hand, it was a real problem, and
if everyone went around pretending to be someone else, or had
two or three aliases, life would become chaotic. It was why countries did not encourage dual nationality, why authority discouraged
married women from sticking to their original surname . . .

'What you are saying,' said Monica, who had remained
uncharacteristically silent, 'is that what you are matters and
who you are is irrelevant.'

George or Oliver, or whoever he was, seemed disconcerted, as well he might.

'Maybe I am,' he ventured nervously.

'I think Sir Simon has been a little too ready to concede the difference between two sorts of self,' she said. 'My view is that you cannot separate identity from behaviour. We are all responsible for our actions whoever we are. We are all one whole whatever we may proclaim. If we were able to assume a new personality by claiming simply to be someone else we could escape the consequences of our actions. So you could kill someone as George, but then become Oliver and disclaim all responsibility for the murder. But you would have committed the crime no matter what you chose to call yourself. By the same token, either you are the brother of James Trubshawe or you're not. Whether you choose to call yourself Oliver O'Flaherty or A.N. Other is irrelevant. Completely. And you still haven't told us whether or not you and James were brothers. Nor have we yet considered Lola.'

'Ah, Lola,' said George, seeking to change the subject.

'I said,' said Monica, 'that we haven't yet got on to her. There is a reason for that. And the reason is that we haven't yet finished with you – whoever you may be.'

'Quite,' said Bognor, not wishing to be left out. More important, he did not wish to be seen to be omitted, whatever the reality. 'Who are you anyway? And were you Trubshawe's brother?'

'I've told you,' said George, affecting weariness. 'It doesn't matter who I am. Which makes a mockery of your second question.'

'On the contrary.' Monica spoke crisply. 'It doesn't matter to us what you choose to call yourself, but your relationship with the deceased matters a lot. A lot. In fact we'd say it was crucial!'

George sighed.

'Very well,' he said. 'Whoever I am I was brought up with James. Whether or not we were really brothers, I simply don't know. But we were brought up in Essex by Percy and Edna and they treated us as if we were brothers. Does that answer your question?'

'And you spent time in Essex together as adults? You were in business together.'

'We did cars,' said George. 'Trubshawe's of Braintree.'

'Trubshawe Bros,' said Monica. She had been briefed. She wished him to know it.

'I see,' said her husband. He would have words with Contractor when he returned to the office. Meanwhile, he saw and was keen that the other two were aware of this.

'So,' he said, 'there was a period when you admitted a level of consanguinity.'

'Someone called George did,' said George. 'But he was not Oliver O'Flaherty, or anyone else come to that. So he may have had something to do with me. Or not.'

'Oh come on,' said Monica, 'we've had quite enough of that conceit.'

George grinned, in the manner of an old-fashioned villain admitting that his capture was 'a fair cop'.

'Jimmy always had a different way of doing business. Not crooked, exactly – he was too fly for that, but he was always out for himself. Always close to the edge.'

'Bit of a spiv,' suggested Monica.

'I didn't say that,' said George. 'Only that we had a different way of carrying on. I was always on the side of the little man. If he couldn't pay the bills I turned the other way. Money was of secondary importance. I don't say it didn't matter but it wasn't the main reason for dealing in cars.'

'What was the main reason?' This was from Bognor.

George grinned. 'What's the meaning of life?' he asked. 'In the long run we're all dead. Death may be the prelude to a wonderful new life, but I tend to think there is a finality about it. It's an end, not a beginning. And before it comes we have to find something to occupy ourselves. In the interim, so to speak. Wouldn't you agree?'

And there they left it.

Lola was not just any old nun. She was not nun in an accepted sense. Bognor said as much at the beginning of the interview, which was conducted immediately after the one with George and in similar circumstances. He phrased the statement as a question, not by changing the words but by the inflexion of his voice. It was not a question expecting the answer 'yes' or 'no'; it was a question that required no answer, and therefore Sister Lola gave none, but simply smirked. She looked pert.

'So,' he asked 'What are you?'

'I am from a Franciscan order. I am a believer.'

'But not in a conventional sense?'

'Not in an old-fashioned way,' said Sister Lola. 'But that doesn't make my beliefs any less sincere or my philosophy less profound. I concede, though, that I am not what many expect. My argument is that just because I acknowledge the existence of the next world doesn't make me less aware of the importance of this world. I see no reason, however, for argument.' She shrugged.

'Quite,' said Bognor, smitten.

In her shadowy corner Monica, unsmitten, coughed disapproval. She knew instinctively when her husband was being influenced by considerations that were not rational. This was one such. Bognor heard the expectoration and made a mental note.

'And not to put it . . . er . . . which is to say not to beat about the bush, you have been having an affair with George.'

Sister Lola was not fazed.

'You could put it like that,' she said.

'How would you put it then?'

'I'd say that George and I were friends and that we have carnal relations. That is we share a bed and exchange bodily . . .'

Bognor did go a little pink and silenced her. He was not used to such sexual straightforwardness especially from one in evident holy orders.

'I don't find George attractive,' said Monica. 'Do you?'

'Obviously,' said the nun, 'otherwise . . .'

'Quite,' said Monica, who also seemed unexpectedly embarrassed. Age thing, no doubt.

'You're unconventional through and through,' said Monica, sounding exasperated. She gave the impression of someone who expected her nuns to be more nunnish.

'If you mean that George . . .' Lola then thought for a moment and corrected herself. 'I don't think I am here to justify my choice of sexual partner,' she said.

'But maybe you should explain having a sexual partner at all. I mean, nuns are supposed to be married to our Lord, aren't they?'

She smiled. Condescendingly. 'That is almost the subject of my Doctorate from the University of Cracow,' she said. 'It touches on the masculinity of our Lord, the sexuality of ecclesiastical behaviour in a postmodern world . . . a number of related topics. The treatise exists in English. I can find you a copy. It deals with your beliefs.' The subtext of her response was 'such as they are' or 'call that a belief', but the derisory scepticism was implied, not stated.

'Sorry,' said Bognor, 'I didn't mean to impute your academic qualifications, nor criticize your choice of boyfriend. It's just that having a boyfriend at all is slightly unusual for one in your position.'

'Guilty.' Lola raised her hands in mock surrender. She was unusual for a nun in that she not only flaunted her sexuality, deployed it in a way that suited her, but also used it shamelessly. It worked with Bognor, if not with his other, arguably better, half. 'I grant you that I am not usual, but someone has to be the first in their field and if God's choice is for me to move in a mysterious way, so be it. Ours not to question. Don't you agree?' And she smiled a smile, which if she were a lay person would have led to her immediate arrest.

'It seems to me that we have to ask if you were having relations with George for reasons other than emotional. That is to say it could be a matter of self-interest. George is not attractive in a conventional way, but he may have secrets to impart and attributes that could lead to sex being merely a pretext for something else.'

'"Pillow talk",' said Monica, 'we call it "pillow talk". It means saying things to a sexual partner that you almost certainly would not say to any Tom, Dick or Harry.'

'Or George,' said Lola, flashing another of her unholy smiles. 'I admit that I am unconventional, and you have a job to do which allows you to ask questions that might otherwise seem impertinent. I am sorry. I deplore the fact that you feel it appropriate to ask certain questions and to make certain assumptions, but I recognize your right to behave in an unconventional way.

You could say that we are both allowed to be slightly unconventional. *N'est ce pas?* We have a licence to shock. Perhaps
even a licence to thrill!'

'I put it to you that your habit is no more than a disguise,
that you are simply masquerading as a nun, and that you are
no more and no less than a *femme fatale*, a *grande horizontelle*,
a secret agent and a dangerous woman in nun's clothing. Yours
is an unbecoming habit.'

'You could say so,' agreed Lola, 'but you have nothing in
the way of proof. And I maintain only that I am dangerously
progressive. Dangerous, that is, for people of orthodox beliefs,
such as yourself.'

'All right,' Bognor was slightly cross, 'I put it to you that
you and George are both working for British Intelligence, as
was Jimmy Trubshawe, and that between you, you fixed his
mushrooms in such a way that he snuffed it. You don't like the
fact that I arrived and rumbled your little plan which would
otherwise have gone completely undetected.'

'Prove it,' she said. 'You can't prove anything. If I deny it,
which I will, everyone will believe an innocent young nun's
word against that of an elderly policeman.'

'I know,' said Bognor, 'and if possible I will prove it. George
was Trubshawe's brother. You are an undercover agent working
for another branch of the secret services and between you, you
have done for poor old Trubshawe simply because he was
embarrassing to the services. No one suspects George because
he is so obviously dim and no one suspects you because you
are so apparently holy.'

'Maybe, maybe not,' she said, 'to coin one of George's
more effective phrases. He is not nearly as stupid as he may
seem. You may think that I am not so holy. But things, as you
say, are seldom what they seem. It is perfectly possible that
a jury would think – for want of a better word or concept –
along the same patterns as you yourself. However, the case
will never come before a jury. Nor will it ever come into a
court. The verdict of the Spanish authority is that Trubshawe's
death came about because of a terrible accident. He should
never have consumed those mushrooms. George knew that he
had a weakness. He liked the fatal fungi more than the fatal

fungi liked him. So. Dreadful, dreadful, pish, tush, accident, accident, accident.'

'But you and I know that it was not an accident.'

Lola looked both naughty and conspiratorial. 'I say again, maybe, maybe not. But even if we do know, then that is not the same as proving. In any case, there will be no opportunity. It has already been decided.'

'Well, to borrow your boyfriend's immortal but useful little phrase "Maybe, maybe not". I myself am not without influence. I shall take it up with the highest possible authority. I am not in the least bit happy.'

'Happiness has nothing to do with the matter. Nor content-ment. Nor justice.' For once she was being, almost, serious. 'It is expedient. Much that happens, happens because it seems sensible at the time it is planned. It is a good idea. One says that the best laid plans always go astray and maybe that is so. Life is a mess. Life is full of what you may call a grey area. But life is always like that.'

'There is such a thing as natural justice.'

'Not on this earth. It is no more than an illusion. You know that. You have spent all your life helping to prove the illusion. If something must happen then there are those who will make it happen, and as you and yours will always say "then bugger the consequences". I am a real nun, oh yes, because I believe that in the end, when we are dead, that is when some kind of justice happens. Until that moment everything is a half-truth, a deceit, a tissue of lies. Why a tissue? It is more than a tissue. A tissue is fragile, it disintegrates at a single blow of the nose. We deal with something much stronger. We deal with lies, deception, intrigue and, above all, the triumph of the strong and the failure of the weak. That is what this life is about. You should know this. You, of all people should know this. You are useless, futile, a waste of time and of space if you believe anything else. Maybe when we are dead there is some law, some justice. Until that time, the race is won by the person who cheats, who lies, who needs to have enjoyment. Before that, all is grey.'

'That's quite a speech,' said Monica from her dark corner. 'So what you are saying is that we should enjoy ourselves now and possibly answer for that enjoyment when we're dead. Perhaps. Surely, though, how we behave affects God's judgement later. He will want to know how we behaved. How else does he decide?'

'Maybe,' she laughed, 'maybe not.'

'Well, I am not at all happy about it,' said Sir Simon, aware that he was sounding pompous and that he was probably out of his depth. 'I'm not having it. And I am not without influence. I will take it up with the highest possible authority.'

She shrugged. 'You must do what you have to do, but you would be unwise. It would be much neater and much more satisfactory for all of us if you accepted that the matter is finished, and that you are only making a big interference and a foolishness where one is not needed. Go away. Eat a good meal, have a nice drink, maybe even sex . . . But do not interfere.'

Not for the first time it occurred to Bognor that he was past his sell-by date and had been only a small cog in a big wheel at best. He was approaching retirement, he had a nice wife, there were titles for both. Why not just exit left gracefully and walk off into the sunset? But he still had an old-fashioned belief in right and wrong and a possibly ludicrous idea that he might make a difference. This could have been no more than a conceit, but it was, nevertheless, what he believed, and led him therefore to say, 'You do whatever you like Sister, but I have to tell you that I am not without influence, that I still have friends in high places and I shall take this up in the very topmost circles. You haven't heard the last of this. Nor George. Trubshawe may have been expendable in your world but not in mine. He was a human being and human beings count.'

He knew he sounded pompous but truth did sound pompous. Sad but true. He may not have been able to contribute as much as he would have wished; there may have been something Pooterish about his aspirations, but he believed in justice and his whole career was based on the concept of seeing it done. If he occasionally sounded pompous that was a small price to pay.

'Rats,' he exclaimed, 'rats and double rats. You may win. You and your kind. But some of us have to be awkward and some of us believe in the right things. This may be an unpopular view but there are times when a chap just has to stand up and be counted.'

Sister Lola smiled. 'You're not altogether unlike George,' she said, 'and I respect your ideals. I really do. Not your fault, I suppose, that they are misplaced. Nor that you will always lose. Still, you'll go down fighting. Go down, you most certainly will. But I guess fighting is a good way to go.'

TWENTY-EIGHT

The Admiral and the *Teniente* escorted Monica and Simon to the airport. Superficially, this seemed like a courtesy, but both Bognor and his wife sensed that it was as much a matter of seeing them safely off the premises than any gesture of Iberian friendship.

The questioning was barely mentioned. Bognor was secretly terrified that some form of torture had been invoked, but was too scared of the answer to ask the question. This was a sensitivity that had dogged his career.

The Admiral, in particular, seemed worried about Bognor's well-being.

'I should never have countenanced such a risk,' he said, 'and someone took what you would no doubt describe as a "pot shot" at you. It is indescribable.'

'Do we know who that was?' asked Bognor, as the big black SEAT smoothed along the highway towards Barajas. A bomb had exploded at the new terminal four which was designed by one of those fashionable British airport architects whose name Bognor could never remember. The bomb hadn't achieved a great deal, except to make travellers jittery. Airports were vulnerable no matter how many people were asked to remove their shoes. Spanish airports were more at risk than many other airports because the country itself was both at risk and generally considered a soft target. The States and Britain were, if anything, a more desirable option, but neither presented as soft an underbelly. At least that was the perception.

The *teniente* smiled. 'We have found the bullet. It was embedded in the window frame of your accommodation. Therefore, I think it is only a matter of time. Unless, as I fear, your bird has flown.'

'The bird being . . . ?' asked Bognor.

His two hosts shrugged.

'The Camilla person,' said the Admiral, 'it is all most

unfortunate. My foreign minister has summoned your ambassador to issue a rebuke and demand an explanation but . . .' and here he spread his hands in an expression of inglorious impotence, 'I ask myself, what is the use? Albion seems to have been perfidious but we are, as you would put it, in bed together, and since this person insists that she was only obeying orders, and since the orders seem to have been issued by the authorities themselves, it is . . .' His voice trailed away until he said once again, lamely, 'It is unfortunate but there is very little to be done.'

'You and I have our hands tied, as we say.'

'I am familiar with the expression,' said Admiral Picasso, 'and I regret to say that you are correct. If it were my own decision I would not have let the woman go but . . . There was a Qantas flight that seemed appropriate and she will be many hundreds of miles away by now. No one will ever know. Not even the hotel guests in the bay.'

Bognor nodded. It was a *fait accompli*. The limo had reached the airport perimeter, but the status of the Admiral and the *Teniente* meant that normal procedure was abandoned and they were accorded seriously VIP treatment, being chauffeured straight on to the tarmac and deposited at the steps of the waiting aircraft, just like visiting royalty or maybe even a British Prime Minister, although their status was not like it was. The other passengers would be cross and this was gratifying. Sometimes Bognor believed that, in a quiet way, his whole life was dedicated to making the other passengers cross.

'So no one will ever know what really happened to Jimmy Trubshawe, whoever he was.'

The Admiral and the policeman glanced at each other.

'No one will ever care,' said *Teniente* Azuela. 'He is as if he had never been.'

Bognor looked out of the window and said nothing.

He cared, he thought. Even about Jimmy Trubshawe.

And, if only for that funny little reason, he would be back.

He smiled at Monica and she smiled back.

At least she, sort of, understood.

TWENTY-NINE

Bognor was bidden to the audience with the Prime Minister that he had requested on Thursday at eleven a.m. This was not a time of his choosing, nor was Downing Street his preferred venue. He knew his own office was out of the question but he would have liked a semblance of neutrality. A Whitehall club and a pink gin was ideal but, well, needs must.

At five past the hour the Balliol knight who played Sir Humphrey to the PM's Jim Hacker came into the waiting room to tell Simon that he was afraid the PM was running late, was fantastically busy, and had just had the President on the line from the White House to discuss the suicide bomb in Kabul (in other words, thought Bognor, cynically, to give him his instructions, tell him what to think, say, and not to attempt to walk and chew gum at the same time). Bognor was an Apocrypha man and not therefore impressed by Balliol, nor by the frankly even dimmer college attended by the Prime Minister, let alone Harvard, which was the President's *alma mater*.

Very little impressed Bognor, besides which he was extremely cross about Trubshawe and the mushrooms. Not for the first time the Security Services had gone way beyond their brief and bungled things into the bargain. The PM and the Balliol knight were to apologize on their behalf because this was where the buck stopped. Apology, on the other hand, came neither naturally nor easily to either man. Apology was not what government was about; self-justification was the name of the game.

Sir Simon did not care for the PM, had little or no respect for him, and regarded him as a jumped-up ninny. Just because he was Prime Minister he thought he was, well, Prime Minster. Worse still, he behaved like it. And he had strange blubbery lips, a limp handshake and, worst of all, facial hair. Bognor hated whiskers.

'Must be incredibly busy being Prime Minister,' said Bognor, not meaning it, 'Luckily, I have nothing much better to do, so I'll wait.'

The Balliol knight, whose name was Edward, was privately crestfallen but smiled all the same. 'Good,' he said. 'Yes. Good. Well, he shouldn't keep us long. Got everything you need? Tea? Coffee? Sticky bun?'

Bognor said he was fine, actually, and settled down to read *The Oldie*, which was on the coffee table. He wasn't fine, any more than Sir Edward was perky, but he was damned if he would let it show.

'Great,' said Sir Edward. 'Well this won't butter any parsnips. I'll be back p.d.q. as soon as my Master calls.'

'Good,' said Bognor, not looking up.

He was going to tell the PM where to get off. He was going to say that it was all very well to think one could ride roughshod over convention and to play fast and loose with democracy, but there were still men such as Bognor who were fundamentally decent citizens and who, not to put too fine a point on it, felt that in the last analysis there were certain things that a chap simply didn't do. And poisoning a fellow citizen with mushrooms was one of those things.

The Prime Minister was half an hour late. Sir Edward came for him, led the way briskly down corridors and into the presence.

'Very kind of you to come,' said the PM, standing up behind his desk and leading the way towards a battery of more or less easy chairs. He was wearing a dark suit, a newly ironed white shirt and an electric-blue tie. This was uniform kit for a sound-bite. Bognor, who was not into sound-bites or uniform, felt uncomfortably scruffy – like Michael Foot, the one-time Labour leader, caught out in a duffel coat at the cenotaph on Remembrance Sunday. Foot was the last party leader to dress according to his own lack of fashionable instinct and he had lost the general election by a street. There were those who thought this was a matter of substance, but many more saw it as a question of style, and since then leaders had dressed accordingly. This prime minister did as he was told, and in appearance matters his stylist ruled. He knew that in a televisual age nobody listened to what you said but they noticed your appearance.

The Prime Minister managed to convey the impression that Bognor had come down from his mountain top and that it was he, not the PM, who was making a sacrifice. This was a conceit bordering on a falsehood but it had its effect, which was to wrong-foot Sir Simon even though he knew that he was right. The Prime Minister poured coffee for his visitor and for the Balliol knight. This too was a calculated touch. He reminded Bognor of the sort of school prefect that he had once hated: teacher's pet, too smooth by half, and, despite protestations to the contrary, one of life's toadies.

'So,' said the PM, taking a sip of his black coffee and then rubbing his hands together, in what he intended to seem an ingratiating manner. Bognor was reminded of an undertaker in a bad movie. Like Uriah Heap, the Prime Minister was so very 'umble. Only, like the Dickensian character, he wasn't really. 'So . . . what can I do for you?'

Ask not, thought Bognor, and then thought better of it. The PM was PM because he had learned to say the reverse of what he meant, to appear oleaginous to all men, and to turn the tables even when this was not strictly speaking necessary. Bognor, however, had an old-fashioned belief that spades were spades and best described as such. This was why he was just another civil servant. He had not learnt diplomacy, bluff, or tact and simply rampaged about like a headless chicken whose heart was in the right place.

'It's about Trubshawe.'

'Ah,' said the Prime Minister.

'And the mushrooms.'

'And the mushrooms,' repeated the Prime Minister, sounding more and more like royalty on a good day.

'The fatal fungi,' said Bognor. 'The mushrooms that killed him. That were infiltrated on to his plate by the intelligence services.'

'Alas, poor Trubshawe!' said the Prime Minister.

'I think what the Prime Minister is saying; what he means to say, is . . . er, well . . . What the Prime Minister is really saying is . . . oh, well . . . nothing. Sorry I spoke.'

'Not at all,' said Bognor. 'Nothing to apologize for. And many a true word. The PM wants to say nothing in the nicest possible way. It's what he does naturally. It's why he is at the top of the greasy pole and I'm not.'

'Come, come,' said the Prime Minister, no longer rubbing his hands but wringing them rather, thought Bognor, in the manner of Pontius Pilate. He was washing his hands of Trubshawe and the mushrooms, and would much rather they had not been mentioned. 'The intelligence services are not secret for nothing. Nor are they described as intelligent for no reason. For both reasons I prefer to leave them alone to do their own thing in their own way. It allows me to have what the previous administration called "an ethical foreign policy".'

'I see,' said Bognor, who, not for the first time, didn't.

'I'm really sorry about Trubshawe. Really sorry. But there's absolutely nothing I can do.'

'Nothing,' said Edward, nodding with what he obviously thought was sagacity. 'Absolutely nothing. Nothing at all. To be absolutely honest, and I wouldn't want this to go beyond these four walls, we knew nothing at all about Trubshawe until it was, er, too late.'

'Nothing,' said the PM. 'Absolutely nothing.'

'But,' said the head of Special Investigations, Board of Trade, remembering who he was and not wishing to be seen to roll over, 'but, I mean . . .'

'We've set up an enquiry,' said Edward. 'Least we could do. It will take time. These things always do. Heads may roll, but it won't bring poor Trubshawe back.'

'Bloody mushrooms,' said the PM, 'bloody Spaniards. Absolute bloody shambles if you ask me, but even if heads do roll, and I sincerely hope they will, nothing is going to bring back the deceased.' He rubbed his hands and replenished cups. 'Alas, poor Trubshawe,' he repeated, echoing His Master's Voice like a well-oiled record, which, in a sense, was what he was. Never had an original thought in his life, thought Bognor, malevolently, but a past master at voicing other people's. What's more, he possessed the old politician's trademark of making the most banal utterance sound original and pertinent. He was an old ham, but then so were most successful politicians.

'And how,' asked the PM, as if a tiny local unpleasantness

had been voiced and cleared, so that they could now get down to real business, 'is the dear old Board of Trade?'

He had never been near the Board in his life. Bognor knew this for a fact. On the other hand, he had been briefed. At length. Obviously.

'The Board of Trade is in good shape,' he replied. 'Very. Which is more than can be said for Trubshawe. He's dead. Extremely. What's more I have reason to believe that he was killed by what is euphemistically described as "friendly fire". By our own people, in other words.'

'I wouldn't say Trubshawe was "one of us",' said the PM.

'Mushrooms,' said the Balliol knight, 'unfriendly mushrooms. Unfriendly to the late deceased. Which is why we have set up this enquiry. Where there is doubt, we need to ask questions. They must have taught you that at Apocrypha?'

The Master and His Voice spoke simultaneously. The effect was not productive. They drowned each other out and were, in so far as one was able to decipher the message, talking at cross-purposes.

Bognor was floundering, which was part of the intention.

'And Lady Bognor?' The Prime Minister put an undue amount of stress on the word 'lady', thus drawing attention to it, and managing to imply that Monica's social elevation was down to him and intentional. Neither of which, as they all knew, was true.

'She's fine too. But Trubshawe isn't. He's dead. And my view is that it's our fault.'

'I do wish you wouldn't keep going on about Trubshawe,' said the Prime Minister. 'We've instigated an investigation into the whole sorry business, and I have to say that until he passed away I simply wasn't aware of him. What more do you expect?'

'I think,' said Edward, 'that what the Prime Minister means is that the late Trubshawe did not loom large on his horizon. The Prime Minister is a very busy man. He can not concern himself with minutiae. If you like, he is dealing with the broad sweep of history. Oils, not watercolours. Big brushes, not fiddly nonsense.'

'With respect,' said Simon, dropping into the code, which meant more or less the opposite of what was exactly said,

'Trubshawe was not any sort of minutiae. He was a human being, a subject of Her Majesty and as such he did not deserve to be brushed under a carpet. Much less murdered.'

'But,' said Edward, 'he is not being brushed under a carpet. An investigation has been launched. In the highest possible circles. No stone will be left unturned in the search for the culprit, if culprit there was.'

'Quite,' echoed the notional boss. 'Bloody lucky to get an enquiry. Not many people get a full-blown enquiry.'

'And certainly not if they're still alive. Unlike poor Trubshawe.' Bognor spoke with feeling. 'He's dead.'

'I understand he was a pretty nasty piece of work,' said Edward, fastidiously.

'That makes absolutely no difference,' said Bognor. 'He was a human being.'

'Only up to a point,' said Edward.

'Not human in the accepted sense,' said the Prime Minister, as if he were discussing a menu or an agenda. In other words, in a bloodless, polite small talk sort of way. It would have played well at an embassy party.

'The trouble with you people,' said Bognor, regretting his words as soon as he uttered them, 'is that you have no respect for life.'

'On the contrary,' said Edward, 'it is only by having an apparent disregard for the small, that one is able to devote one's attention to the larger picture. Trubshawes are expendable. In fact, you could say that if we are to progress then we have to lose a few Trubshawes along the way. His is an essential sacrifice.'

'Absolutely,' said the PM. 'Couldn't have put it better myself.'

But Bognor had had enough. 'That's what Hitler said,' he exploded. And then, gathering his up thoughts and his carefully arranged trouser legs, he said, 'I'll see myself out.'

Which he did, with protestations about meaningful enquiries ringing meaninglessly in his ears.

THIRTY

'How did it go?' asked Monica breathlessly. She was always breathless when genuinely interested. Despite being of a certain age this made her seem sexy and husky. 'With the Prime Minister.' Despite everything she was still impressed with the title and the office, if not with the holder.

Bognor, still seething, poured them both a stiffish Bells and said only, 'I thought we might eat out this evening. There's a new bistro which got goodish reviews the other day. I could do with an absolutely straightforward steak and frites and some decent Côtes du Rhône.'

Monica, who had already spent a small fortune on rump for two, did not demur. She knew her spouse too well. All had, obviously, not gone well.

'So . . .' she said at length, sipping amber liquid thoughtfully, 'tell me about it.'

'He's a shit,' said Bognor, 'and so is that gorilla who keeps him in check. Edward something or other. Even more of a shit. Supershits the pair of them.'

'Ah,' said Monica. She was more thoughtful than ever. 'We knew that already.'

'Even so,' said Bognor, 'it's one thing to know something in theory. Quite another to be confronted with the reality.'

Monica knew better than to argue. Instead, she said. 'Should we book?'

Bognor nodded and she did so, then said, gently, 'Tell me what happened.'

'Nothing, nothing at all. I blew it. Let them run rings round me.'

Monica doubted this, but then she always did. That was one of the reasons Bognor found her so satisfactory. She backed him up, both in public, which was to be expected, and in private, which was not.

'The PM is a prat,' she said, 'so is his minder, though not

in quite the same way. You may be many things, but a prat you
are not.'

'I was this afternoon.'

'Tell me.'

And so he did. He embellished a little but not much. Made
the PM seem even more of an arrogant bastard than he actually
was. Made himself seem even more of an also-ran than he was,
too. He exaggerated. She knew this, and he knew this also. It
was the way in which he always behaved. He had not, after all,
liked Trubshawe, or the idea of Trubshawe any more than the
Prime Minister or his alleged lackey. Possibly less. That wasn't
important. He, Bognor, did not think anyone was expendable.
Be he ever so insignificant or downright unpleasant, Bognor
believed they were innocent until proved guilty, and entitled to
care and thought and consideration. The PM and his lackey
thought otherwise. Such, in his jaundiced view, was life. It
sucked. Always did. Always would.

He refuelled their drinks.

'So you see,' he said, 'I was useless.'

'I see nothing of the sort,' she said loyally.

'Well, you wouldn't,' he said. 'That's why I love you.'

Both were, in a manner of speaking, true. Theirs was a strange
kind of affection, nurtured over the years, oddly endorsed by
their lack of children, and solidified, in the end, by a grudging
mutual respect. Bognor sometimes said that his wife was the
only person he could imagine making a long car journey with
and not feeling compelled to say anything for several hours.
They were both surprisingly good in a crisis, less so, most of
the rest of the time. This was tantamount to a crisis.

'I hate power,' he said. 'Give me influence any day.'

'I know,' she said.

'Why do the wrong people always have power?' he wanted
to know, though he had his answer ready and really only wanted
reassurance.

'The wrong people wield power because achieving a powerful
position requires the wrong strategy. In other words, the means
by which one gets into a powerful position are precisely the
opposite necessary to wield power with precision and fairness.'

'So random selection is more efficient than competition.'

'I didn't say that, but, yes, possibly.'

'Which is an argument for heredity.'

'If you believe heredity is random,' she agreed. 'But most breeders would disagree. Primogeniture has its roots in logic. Bloodlines count. Look at Hitler and the Nazis.'

'You said it.'

'Touché,' she said. 'Bad example. But the Prime Minister got where he is by methods which are ghastly when wielded by someone in his position. In other words, the travelling is essential but the accoutrements are worse than useless when one has actually arrived.'

'You could put it like that.'

She smiled. 'I just have,' she said. 'Now drink up. I'm starving. I could murder a steak.'

She could too, and almost did. They both had bavette and chips, and a tolerable Béarnaise in the new bistro, which had red and white check table clothes, accordion music and generally resembled the set of 'Allo 'Allo!. They split a bottle of Beaujolais Villages (Simon thought the Cotes du Rhône overpriced) and ended with coffee and Calva. Monica had the crème caramel and he, wishing to maintain the alliteration, had a wedge of Camembert. It was all very French in an English sort of way and reasonably priced.

'The Prime Minister would hate this,' said Bognor, as the squeezebox gave them a Piaf number, ill-disguised but reeking of pastiche.

'He never pays for himself,' said Monica, 'and the Azerbaijanis and Kazakhs and the other third division football magnates, with whom he and the Duke of York consort, would only go to the sort of place where they like expense accounts. Big hotels, Gordon Ramsay, Michelin stars, all ponce and no taste.'

'Always struck me as a shepherd's pie and Bollinger person.'

'Shepherd's pie is cheap and the champagne would have fallen off the back of a lorry, or be the gift of some third division Kazakh football club owner. Like I said, he has what it takes to get to the top, but when he arrives he doesn't know what to do, so he takes his cue from other newly arrivistes – preferably foreign.'

'He obviously knew exactly who Jimmy Trubshawe was and who cooked his mushrooms. Just wouldn't admit it.'

'What do you expect?'

Monica, had, in a manner of speaking, been here before. Most of the other customers looked as if they might be paying their own bills. The proprietor called himself Gaston and had pointy moustaches, which almost certainly meant that he came from the East End of London.

'I think Trubshawe is worth something,' said Bognor. He was tipsy but not drunk. His wife also.

'Was,' she corrected. 'James Trubshawe is no more. Let's face it, we wouldn't have liked him. He probably supported Brentford or Yeovil Town; liked pickled onions; shepherd's pie, maybe, but give him a pint of ale and not some frog fizz. Know what I mean?'

'You're being snobbish. And Man U, not Brentford or Yeovil.'

'Why Man U?' she wanted to know.

'Because,' he said.

'Now,' she said, 'you're the one who's being snobbish. Mind you, I still don't really understand about Trubshawe and the PM.'

'What's to understand?' asked Bognor. 'The Prime Minister despises men such as Trubshawe but he needs them. It's all part of the same game that you mentioned when you talked about the difference between arriving and travelling.'

'Climbing is a better word than travelling. Greasy pole and all that. Many a slip. Social ditto. The point is that men like the PM believe that men like Trubshawe are expendable. Necessary, but you dump them when you have to, and if people like you protest, you set up a formal enquiry.'

'Here's to James Trubshawe, whoever he was,' said Bognor. And he and his wife drank silently and thoughtfully to the man they never knew but whose corner they were posthumously fighting.

'I wonder what Trubshawe would say if he were here,' said Monica after a while.

'Give me a pint and a pie and no foreign muck, I should think,' said her husband, grinning.

'Don't be silly,' she said. 'All right. He was a small-time

crook and not very good at what he did. And he was in exile on some Costa or other, surrounded by a lot of similar spivs and con men. Do you imagine he was happy? Or fulfilled?'

'I shouldn't think so,' said Bognor, 'but who is? Happy and fulfilled. I'm certainly not. I think I've probably done my best. When St Peter stands with his clipboard at the Pearly Gates, I think I'll be able to say that I made the most of my talents.'

'You'll be lucky to make the Pearly Gates,' said Monica. She laughed. 'You'll be way below, boiling in oil with James Trubshawe, the PM and the saintly Edward.'

'And I'm not drinking to Edward,' she said. 'Do you imagine you're introduced? Do you think some Hieronymus Bosch crea-ture takes a moment off stoking with his trident and says words to the effect of "I don't think you've met your former Prime Minister. Prime Minister, I don't believe you've met James Trubshawe."'

'And the blessed Edward will tell everyone what they really mean,' said Simon. 'I suppose that's his role in life. Translator max. Always putting his own words into more important mouths.'

'Do you imagine Trubshawe was middle class?' asked Monica.

'He would have said so because everyone now calls them-selves middle class, even if they are really upper or lower. Very few people admit to belonging to any other class except middle. Fact of life. Distressing but true. Shall we call a cab?'

They called a cab. Gaston said it would take five minutes.

'Cabbies are working class. By definition,' said Bognor. 'And members of the Marylebone Cricket Club are middle class. Yet most cabbies are members of MCC and many members of MCC are cabbies. So what class do you belong to if you are a cabbie and a member of MCC?'

'Now who's being silly!' she said. 'Trubshawe wasn't a member of MCC and he never drove a cab.'

'Prove it,' said Bognor with an air of triumph. 'Prove it! All right the Club will have records and they should be able to prove membership one way or another. But driving a cab is something else. And the only person who really knows about the cab is Trubshawe, and he's dead.'

'You could be right.' Monica spoke grudgingly. 'I always maintain that death is doubly deceitful. It's not just that it destroys evidence and witnesses, but that it gives credence to the last one left standing. Last one alive gets the final word. So if Trubshawe hadn't succumbed to the mushrooms, but had outlived the rest of us, he could have invented whatever he wanted and no one would have been able to contradict him.'

'Which is why letters and diaries and written evidence is so historically important.'

'Up to a point,' said Monica, 'but what are they worth without verbal corroboration. Not a lot in my view. Just because it's written down doesn't make it accurate. Trubshawe could have written "I am middle class" a million times but that wouldn't make it accurate. We believe he was originally working for "us", whoever we may be, and that he was murdered by "us" as well. The PM and others are doing their darnedest to prove otherwise and, who knows, they may even believe it. I doubt that, but I am a cynical old biddy. Bears out what I say, though. "Death, he taketh all away".'

'But them he cannot take,' said Bognor, completing the quote. 'I accept what you say but only up to a point.'

Their cab arrived. They got up. Bognor paid by credit card. Monica left a tip in cash. It was ever thus. Outside, the minicab was Japanese, small and the driver came originally from Beirut. He was a university professor fallen on hard times. Maybe that made him middle class going on working. Maybe it didn't matter.

'That's part of your problem,' said Monica. She sounded censorious but, actually, she was fond. 'You only ever believe things up to a point.'

'Well,' he said, 'up to a point.'

They laughed and squeezed hands.

In the driver's seat their cabbie tried to remember his Euclid.